KAMCHATKA

Kamchatka

Marcelo Figueras

Translated from the Spanish
by Frank Wynne

Black Cat
NewYork

First published in Spanish in 2003 by Santillana Ediciones Generales, SL.

First published in English in 2010 by Atlantic Books,
an imprint of Grove Atlantic Ltd.

This novel is entirely a work of fiction. The names, characters, and incidents portrayed in it are the work of the author's imagination. Any resemblance to actual persons, living or dead, events, or localities is entirely coincidental.

ISBN: 978-0-8021-7087-3

Printed in the United States of America

Black Cat
a paperback original imprint of Grove/Atlantic, Inc.
841 Broadway
New York, NY 10003

Distributed by Publishers Group West

www.groveatlantic.com

11 12 13 14 15   10 9 8 7 6 5 4 3 2 1

It is not down on any map; true places never are.
Herman Melville, *Moby-Dick*

KAMCHATKA

First Period: Biology

Noun: the study of living organisms.

1

THE LAST WORD

The last thing papá said to me, the last word from his lips, was 'Kamchatka'.

He kissed me, his stubble scratching my cheek, then climbed into the Citroën. The car moved off along the undulating ribbon of road, a green bubble bobbing into view with every hill, getting smaller and smaller until I couldn't see it any more. I stood there for a long while, my game of Risk tucked under my arm, until my *abuelo*, my grandpa, put his hand on my shoulder and said, 'Let's go home'.

And that's all there is.

If you want, I can give you more details. Grandpa used to say God is in the details. He used to say a lot of things, like 'What Piazzolla plays isn't tango' and 'It's just as important to wash your hands before you pee as afterwards – you never know what you've been touching', but I don't think those things are relevant.

We said our goodbyes on the forecourt of a petrol station on Route 3, a few kilometres outside Dorrego in the south of Buenos Aires province. The three of us had had breakfast in the station café, croissants and *café con leche* in bowls as big as saucepans, with the petrol company logo on them. Mamá was there too, but she spent the whole time in the toilet. She'd eaten something that had upset her stomach and she couldn't even hold down liquids. And the Midget, my kid brother, was asleep, sprawled on the back seat of the Citroën. He wriggled his arms, his legs, all the time while he was asleep, as though staking his claim, a king of infinite space.

At this moment, I am ten years old. I look normal enough apart from an unruly tuft of hair that sticks up like an exclamation mark.

It is spring. In the southern hemisphere, October days shimmer with golden light and today is no exception; the morning is a palace. The air is filled with fluttering *panaderos* – dandelion seeds, those daytime stars that in Argentina we call *panaderos* – or little bakers. I catch them in my cupped palms and, with a puff of breath, set them free again, urging them on to fertile ground.

(The Midget would crack up if he heard me say: 'The air is filled with fluttering *panaderos*'. He'd roll on the ground, clutching his belly, laughing like a lunatic as he imagined tiny men, their brown and white aprons covered in flour, floating like bubbles.)

I can even remember the other people at the petrol station. The petrol pump attendant, a chubby man with a moustache and dark armpits. The driver of the IKA truck, counting a fat wad of banknotes as big as bed sheets on his way to the toilet. (I guess grandpa's maxim about washing your hands before you pee *is* relevant after all.) The backpacker with the messianic beard, crossing the forecourt as he heads for the open road, his billycans clanking, like tolling bells calling to repentance.

The little girl sets down her skipping rope to go and wet her hair under the tap. She wrings it dry as she walks back, water dripping onto the dusty forecourt. The drops that just a moment earlier spelled out Morse code in the dust vanish as the seconds pass. Obedient to the call of gravity, they trickle down into the mineral particles, snaking through the spaces that exist where there seemed to be none, leaving behind some part of their moisture to give life to these particles even as they lose themselves on their journey towards the molten heart of the planet, the fire where the Earth still looks as it did when it was first formed. (In the end, we always are what we once were.)

Gracefully, the girl in front of me bends down and, for a minute, I think she is bowing. But in fact she's picking up her skipping rope. She starts to skip again, a perfect rhythm, the rope whipping through the air, whup, whup, creating the bubble in which she hovers.

Papá opens the door to the station café and lets me go in; grandpa is already inside, waiting for us. His teaspoon creating a whirlpool in his *café con leche*.

Sometimes there are variations in what I remember. Sometimes mamá doesn't get out of the Citroën until we leave the café because she's busy scribbling something on her pack of Jockey Club cigarettes. Sometimes the numbers on the petrol pump run backwards instead of forwards. Sometimes the backpacker gets there before us and by the time we arrive he's already hitchhiking, as though in a hurry to discover a world he's never seen, the clank of his billycans pealing out the good news. These variations don't worry me. I'm used to them. They mean I'm remembering something I hadn't noticed before; they mean that I'm not exactly the same person I was when last I remembered.

Time is weird. That much is obvious. Sometimes I think everything happens at once, which is anything but obvious and even weirder. I feel sorry for people who brag about 'living in the moment'; they're like people who come into the cinema after the film has started or people who drink Diet Coke – they're missing out on the best part. I think time is like the dial on a radio. Most people like to settle on a station with a clear signal and no interference. But that doesn't mean you can't listen to two or even three stations at the same time; it doesn't mean synchrony is impossible. Until quite recently, people believed it was impossible for a universe to fit inside two atoms, but it fits. Why dismiss the idea that on time's radio you can listen to the entire history of humanity simultaneously?

Every day, life gives us an intimation of this. We sense that, inside us, every 'we' we once were (and will be?) coexists: the innocent self-absorbed child, the sensual young man generous to a fault, the adult, feet planted firmly on the ground yet still clinging to his illusions, and finally we are the old man who knows that gold is just another metal; as his eyesight fails he has acquired vision. Sometimes, as I remember, my voice is that of the ten-year-old boy I was then; sometimes the voice of the seventy-year-old man I am yet to be; sometimes it is my voice, at the age I am now . . . or the age I think I am. Who I have been, who I am, who I will be are all in continual conversation, each influencing the other. That my past and my present together determine my future sounds like a fundamental truth, but I suspect that my future joins forces with the present to do the same thing to my past. Every time I remember, the person I was speaks his lines, performs his actions with increasing confidence, as though with each performance he grows more comfortable with the role, and understands it better.

The numbers on my petrol pump will start to go backwards. I can't stop them.

Grandpa is back in his truck, one foot on the running board, softly singing his favourite tango: '*decí por Dios qué me has dao, que estoy tan cambiao, no sé más quien soy*'.

Papá leans down and whispers a last word into my ear. I can feel the warmth of his cheek as I could feel it then. He kisses me, his stubble rasping against my cheek.

'Kamchatka.'

Kamchatka is not my name, but as he says it, I know he is thinking of me.

2

ALL THINGS REMOTE

'Kamchatka' is a strange word. My Spanish friends find it unpronounceable. Whenever I say it, they look at me condescendingly, as though they were dealing with some sort of savage. They look at me and they see Queequeg, the tattooed man from Melville's novel, worshipping his little idol of some misshapen god. How interesting *Moby-Dick* would have been narrated by Queequeg. But history is written by the survivors.

I can't remember a time when I did not know about Kamchatka. At first, it was simply one of the territories waiting to be conquered in Risk, my favourite board game, and the epic sweep of the game rubbed off on the place-name, but to my ears, I swear, the name itself sounds like greatness. Is it me, or does the word 'Kamchatka' sound like the clash of swords?

I am one of those people who always hunger for things remote, like Ishmael in *Moby-Dick*. The magnitude of the adventure is measured by distance: the more distant the peak, the greater the courage needed. In Risk, Argentina – the country where I was born – is on the bottom left of the board, just below the pink lines of the trade winds. In this two-dimensional universe, Kamchatka was the most distant place you could imagine.

At the start of our games, nobody ever fought for Kamchatka. The patriotic coveted South America, the ambitious looked to North America, the cultivated set their sights on Europe and the pragmatic set up camp in Africa and Oceania – easy to conquer and even easier to defend. Kamchatka was in Asia, which was too vast and consequently almost impossible to defend. And as if that wasn't enough, Kamchatka isn't even a real country: it exists as an independent nation only in the curious planisphere of Risk, and who wants to conquer a country that isn't even real?

Kamchatka was left to me; I always had a soft spot for the underdog. To me, Kamchatka boomed like the drums of some secret savage kingdom, calling to make me their king.

At the time I knew nothing about the real Kamchatka, that frozen tongue Russia pokes into the Pacific Ocean, mocking its neighbours. I knew nothing about its eternal snows, its hundred volcanoes; I had never heard of the Mutnovsky glacier or the lakes of acid. I knew nothing of the wild bears, the fumaroles, the gas that bubbles up on the muddy surface of the thermal springs like pustules on a thousand toads. It was enough for me that Kamchatka was shaped like a scimitar and was utterly inaccessible.

Papá would be surprised if he knew how like the real Kamchatka is to the landscape of my dreams: a frozen peninsula, which is also the most active volcanic region on Earth. A horizon ringed by towering, inaccessible peaks shrouded in sulphurous vapours. Kamchatka is a paradox, a kingdom of extremes, a contradiction in terms.

3

I AM LEFT WITH NO UNCLES

On the Risk board, the apparent distance between Argentina and Kamchatka is misleading. When these flat dimensions are mapped onto a globe, this journey, which had seemed impossible, suddenly seems simple. There is no need to traverse the known world to get from one to the other. Kamchatka and the Americas are so close, they all but touch.

Similarly, the goodbyes we said on the forecourt of the petrol station and the beginnings of my story are superposed extremes, each nested inside the other. October sun melds with April sun, this morning blends with that one. It is easy for me to forget that one sun is the promise of summer and the other its farewell.

In the southern hemisphere, April is a month of extremes. Autumn begins and with it comes the cold. But the flurries of wind do not last and the sun always returns in triumph. The days are still long, some seem to have been stolen from summer. Ceiling fans begin their last shifts and people escape to the beach for the weekends as they try to outrun winter.

April 1976, in all its glory, was just like any other. I had just started sixth grade. I was trying to make sense of timetables, to decipher the lists of books I had to get hold of. I still packed more into my schoolbag than I needed and complained that I had to sit too close to Señorita Barbeito's desk in class.

But some things were different. The military coup, for a start. Although papá and mamá didn't talk about it much (they didn't seem angry or upset, simply uncertain), it was obviously something serious. Meanwhile all my uncles were disappearing as if by magic.

Up until 1975, in our house in Flores, people came and went at all hours, talking and laughing loudly, thumping the table when someone said something interesting, drinking *mate* and beer, singing, playing the guitar and putting their feet up on the rocking chair as though they'd lived here all their lives. Most of them were actually people I'd never seen before and would never see again. When they arrived, papá invariably introduced them as 'uncles' and 'aunts'. Tío Edward, Tío Alfredo, Tía Teresa, Tío Mario, Tío Daniel. We never remembered their names, but it didn't matter. The Midget would wait for a few minutes, then amble into the dining room and, in his most innocent voice, say, 'Tío, can I have a glass of Coke?' Five men would leap to their feet to get it for him, and they would come back with glasses filled to the brim just in time for us to watch *The Saint*.

Towards the end of 1975, these uncles gradually began to disappear. Fewer and fewer of them visited us. They didn't talk so loudly now; they didn't laugh or sing anymore. Papá didn't even bother to introduce them.

One day papá told me Tío Rodolfo had died and asked me to come with him to the wake. I said I would, because he'd asked me and not the Midget, given my superior status as older brother.

It was my first wake. Tío Rodolfo lay in the back room in an open coffin. The three or four other rooms were full of angry, single-minded people drinking sugary coffee and smoking like chimneys. I was relieved. I hate it when people cry, and I'd figured that everyone would be bawling their eyes out at a wake. I remember talking to Tío Raymundo (I'd never met him before; papá introduced us when

10

we arrived). Tío Raymundo asked me about school, about where I lived and, without even thinking, I lied. I told him I lived near La Boca. I don't know why.

Out of sheer boredom, I went over to look in the coffin and discovered that I *did* know Tío Rodolfo. His cheeks seemed a little more sunken, his moustache a little bigger, or maybe it just looked bigger because in death he appeared thinner, more formal, or maybe he just looked more formal because of the suit and the shirt with the wide collar, but it was definitely Tío Rodolfo. He was one of the few 'uncles' who had been to our house more than once and he had always made an effort to be nice to me and the Midget. The last time he visited, he'd given me a River Plate football shirt. When we got home from the wake, I looked in my wardrobe and there it was in its own coffin, second drawer from the bottom.

I didn't even touch it. I shut the drawer and tried to put it out of my mind, but that night I dreamed the shirt had somehow crawled out of the drawer by itself, slithered over to my bed like a snake, wrapped itself around my neck and tried to choke me. I had that dream several times. And every time I woke up, I felt stupid. How could a River Plate shirt strangle me when I wasn't even a River Plate supporter?

There were other signs too, but this was the most frightening. Fear had taken root in my own house, in my drawer, carefully folded, smelling of fresh laundry, nestling among the socks.

I didn't ask papá what Tío Rodolfo died of. I didn't need to. You don't die of old age when you're thirty.

4

AN INCONVENIENT
PATRIARCH

My school was called Leandro N. Alem, after the gentleman who glowered down at us from the gloomy portrait every time we were sent to the headmaster's office. The school was a nineteenth-century building on the corner of Yerbal and Fray Cayetano, opposite the Plaza Flores in the heart of one of Buenos Aires' most traditional neighbourhoods. It was a two-storey building set around a central courtyard lit by a skylight whose shabby marble staircase bore witness to the generations who had taken it in their ascent to Learning.

It was a public school: its doors were open to everyone without distinction. For a small monthly fee, anyone could come to class, get a mid-morning snack and participate in sporting activities. For this notional fee we were granted access to the engine room of our language and to mathematics, the language of the Universe; we were taught where on the globe we were situated, what lay to north, to south, to east and west; what pulsed beneath our feet in the igneous core of the Earth, and above our heads; and before our virgin eyes unfolded the history of humankind, the history of which, for better or worse, we were at that time the culmination.

It was in these high-ceilinged classrooms with their creaking floors that I first heard a story by Cortázar and first opened Mariano

Moreno's *Plan Revolucionario de Operaciones* and learned of the part it played in our independence. In these classrooms I discovered that the human body was the most perfect machine and thrilled at the elegant solution to some problem in arithmetic.

My class could have served as a model for any campaign promoting peace among the peoples of the Earth. Broitman was a Jew. Valderrey had a thick Spanish accent. Talavera was two generations removed from his black ancestors. Chinen was Chinese. Even those boys who were more typically Argentinian – a mix of Hispanic, Italian and indigenous tribes – were noticeably dark-skinned. Some of us were the sons of professionals, others of working men with no education to speak of. Some of their parents owned their houses; others rented or still lived in their grandparents' houses. Some of us spent our spare time studying languages and playing sports; others helped their fathers to fix radios and televisions in their workshops, or kicked a ball around on whatever piece of waste ground they could find.

In the classroom, none of these distinctions meant anything. Some of my best friends (Guidi, for example, who was already an electronics wizard; or Mansilla who was even blacker that Talavera and lived in Ramos Mejía, a suburb so far out of the city that it felt even more remote than Kamchatka) had little or nothing in common with me, and the life I lived. But we all got along.

We all wore a white school smock in the mornings and a grey one in the afternoons, we drank *mate* at playtime and we jostled and shoved to get our favourite pastry, which the janitor brought in a sky-blue plastic bowl. Our uniforms made us equals, as did our youthful curiosity and energy. Our childlike passions rendered our differences insignificant.

We were equal, too, in our complete ignorance on the subject of Leandro N. Alem, the school patriarch. With his beard and his intimidating scowl, he looked a lot like Melville. Maybe because he was tired of the two-dimensional confines of the painting in the headmaster's office, he seemed intent on pointing to something just outside the frame. The obvious interpretation might suggest that he was pointing to the future path we would travel. But the nervous expression the painter had given him made it seem more likely that Alem was saying that we were looking in the wrong place; that we should not be looking at him but at something else, some mystery that did not appear in the painting and, being ambiguous, could not be but ominous.

In all the time I spent in these classrooms, nobody ever taught us anything about Leandro Alem. Many years later (by which time I was living in Kamchatka) I discovered that Alem had rebelled against the conservative administration of his time in support of universal suffrage, taken up arms and wound up in prison though he lived to see his ideas finally triumph. Maybe they did not mention Alem to us because they wanted to spare us the inconvenient fact that he had committed suicide. The suicide of a successful man can only cast a pall over his ideas – as it would if St Peter had slit his wrists or Einstein had swallowed poison while living in exile in the US.

So it would be naive to imagine that it was only by chance that I attended the school that bore his name every day for six years – until the morning that I walked out and never went back.

5

A SCIENTIFIC DIGRESSION

That April morning Señorita Barbeito closed the classroom blinds and showed us an educational film. The film, in washed-out colours, with a voice-over dubbed by a Mexican narrator, discussed the mystery of life, explaining that cells came together to form tissue and tissues came together to form organs and organs came together to create organisms, though each was more than the sum of its parts.

I was sitting (to my frustration, as I've said) in the front row, my nose almost pressed against the screen. I only paid attention for the first few minutes. I registered the fact that the Earth had been formed in a ball of fire 4,500 million years ago. I remember it took 500 million years for the first rocks to form. I remember it rained for 200 million years – that's some flood – after which there were oceans. Then, in his deep voice and his thick Mexican accent, the narrator started talking about the evolution of species and I realized he had skipped the bit of the story between the Earth being barren and the first appearance of life. I thought maybe there was a section of the film missing and that this was why the Mexican kept banging on about mystery. By the time I'd finished thinking this and tried to go back to the film I'd lost the thread, so I didn't understand anything after that.

But this business of the mystery of life stuck with me. I raised some of my questions with mamá, who explained to me about Darwin and

Virchow. In 1855 Virchow had proposed that *omnis cellula e cellula* ('all cells from cells'), thereby stipulating that life was a chain whose first link, mamá had to admit, was not a trivial matter. It was also mamá who filled in some of the holes in the Mexican narrator's calendar. She explained that the first single-cell life forms appeared on Earth 3,500 million years ago in the shallow oceans, produced by the longest thunderstorm in history.

Other things I discovered later while I was living in Kamchatka among the volcanic eruptions and the sulphurous vapours. I discovered, for example, that we are made up of the same tiny atoms and molecules as rocks are. (Surely we should last longer.) I discovered that Louis Pasteur, the man who invented vaccinations, conducted experiments that proved that life could not appear spontaneously in an oxygen-rich atmosphere like that of our Earth. (The mystery was getting bigger.) Later, to my relief, I discovered that a number of scientists contend that in the beginning the Earth had no oxygen, or only trace amounts.

Sometimes I think that everything you need to know about life can be found in biology books. They discuss the way that bacteria reacted to the massive injection of oxygen into the Earth's atmosphere. Until that point (2,000 million years ago, according to my chronology), oxygen was fatal to life. Bacteria survived because oxygen was absorbed by the planet's metals. When the metals were saturated and could absorb no more, the atmosphere was filled with toxic gas and many species died out. But the bacteria regrouped, developed defence mechanisms and adapted in a way that was as effective as it was brilliant: their metabolism began to require the very substance that, until then, had been poisonous to them. Rather than die of oxygen toxicity, they used oxygen to live. What had killed them became the air that they breathed.

Perhaps this ability that life has to turn things to its advantage doesn't mean much to you. But let me tell you that, in my world, it has meant a lot.

6

FANTASTIC VOYAGE

Five minutes into the film, I wasn't thinking about cells or mysteries or molecules at all – I was playing. I discovered that if I looked at the screen and let my eyes go out of focus, the images became 3-D: psychedelia for beginners. After I'd been staring at the little moving circles and bananas of cell tissue for a while, the edges of the screen began to disappear and it was like I'd fallen into magma.

At first it was fun. It was like being in *Fantastic Voyage*, that film where they shrink a submarine down to microscopic size and inject it into the bloodstream of a human guinea pig. But after a while, I felt dizzy. If I didn't stop, I was going to throw up my breakfast.

I turned around in my seat, looking for somewhere to rest my tired eyes. In the half-light of the classroom, Mazzocone was eating the sandwich that was supposed to be his lunch, Guidi had fallen asleep and Broitman was playing *Six Million Dollar Man* with a toy soldier. (Making it run in slow motion and jump like a cricket.) Bertuccio had his back turned to me. True to form, he had leapt to his feet and was telling Señorita Barbeito that he was not about to swallow the idea that once upon a time there was just a single cell in the ocean, then time passed and – boom! – that cell turned into us.

7

ENTER BERTUCCIO

Bertuccio was my best friend. It might sound like bull, but I swear that by the age of ten Bertuccio was reading Anouilh's *Becket* and claiming he wanted to be a playwright. I had read *Hamlet*, because I didn't want to be outdone, and because we had a copy of it at home (we didn't have a copy of *Becket*) and even though I didn't understand a word of *Hamlet*, I wrote an adaptation that I planned to perform with my friends in the alcove between the kitchen and the patio, which would make a fantastic stage if mamá moved the washing machine.

But I was only trying to seem grown up; Bertuccio actually wanted to be an artist. He had read somewhere that an artist questions society and ever since he had been questioning everything, from the cost of school fees and the point of wearing a white smock in the morning and a grey one in the afternoons to the veracity of the story about French and Beruti handing out blue and white ribbons to the rebels of the revolution of 1841. (How could they have known that Belgrano would make the Argentine flag blue and white? What were they, psychic?)

Bertuccio was forever embarrassing me. One time we went to the cinema to see *Gold*, which was over-fourteens only and the guy on the ticket desk asked us for ID. Bertuccio admitted that he was underage but said that he had read the book and hadn't found anything liable to deprave or corrupt in it and informed the guy that no one had the right to presume that he was too immature to see a movie. When the ticket seller tried to interrupt him, Bertuccio solemnly announced that he, my dear sir, had already read *Becket*, *The Exorcist* and *Lady Chatterley's Lover* (or parts of it, at least) 'which is more than many adults can say, or are you calling me a liar?'

Whenever he got me into this kind of mess, I was the one who came up with the solutions. When Bertuccio got tired of talking and the guy on the ticket desk couldn't stand it any more, we went up the marble staircase to the first floor of the Rivera Indarte Cinema and hid in the toilets, waited until the usher had punched all the tickets for the Pullman seats, then, when he went into the cinema to show a latecomer to his seat, we snuck in behind him and hid behind the curtains. We'd missed the first fifteen minutes, but at least we got to see the film.

Gold was shit. There weren't even any naked women in it.

8

THE PRINCIPLE OF NECESSITY

On this particular morning, while Bertuccio was challenging Señorita Barbeito over the very foundations of the temple of science, I was looking for a pencil and some paper to play Hangman.

Señorita Barbeito sighed and told Bertuccio that of course there was a principle that explained everything: cell division, cells combining so as to develop complex functions, creatures leaving their aquatic environment, developing colours and fur, seeking new sources of energy, evolving paws, moving about and standing erect. Mazzocone was getting upset now because he realized he would have nothing to eat at lunchtime; a thread of drool was trickling down Guidi's chin; Broitman was explaining to me that his Action Man cost $6 million and I was thinking how cool it would be to actually throw up and splatter the screen while Señorita Barbeito was explaining to Bertuccio that this principle that explained how an organism develops and adapts to changing circumstances is the principle of necessity.

Bertuccio wanted to stand his ground; he was determined not to let Señorita Barbeito twist his arm on this, so I twisted his arm, literally. He asked what I wanted and I said would he like to play Hangman. He looked as though he was considering the possibility; his philosophical debate could always be resumed later. (I had come up with a word with lots of Ks that I knew would baffle him.) Bertuccio agreed but only if he could have the first go. He marked out an eleven-letter word while I was drawing the gallows. I said 'A' and he started filling in the blanks. There were five As in Bertuccio's word.

'You're crazy', I said.

'Just wait,' he said, 'you'll see,' theatrical as ever.

I said 'E' and he drew the head.

I said 'I' and he drew the neck.

I said 'O' and he drew one arm.

I said 'U' and he drew the other arm.

This is hard, I thought. An ill-fated 'S' earned me the body and after a suicidal 'T', I was hanging by a thread.

Then there was a knock at the door and mamá came in.

The only thing I learned from the whole cell business: people change because they have no alternative.

9

THE ROCK

We used to call mamá the Rock. In the *Fantastic Four*, a Stan Lee comic, one of the Four is this guy made of rocks called 'The Thing'. That was where we got the idea. Mamá wasn't exactly thrilled about being compared to some bald, knock-kneed guy, but she was flattered that the name acknowledged her authority. She was happy as long as it was only me and the Midget that used the nickname. When papá called her the Rock – and papá did it more than we did – it was like everything was happening in Sensurround, the effect they use in disaster movies where all the seats shake.

To us, mamá had always been blonde, but from old photos we could see that she had become blonder over time. She was slim and full of life, the complete opposite of the Thing. When I was little, she liked movies and doing crosswords. There was a photo of Montgomery Clift on her bedside table from back when he was still handsome, before the car crash smashed his face up. She was a Liza Minnelli fan too. Every morning she would wake us with the soundtrack from *Cabaret*. Mamá had a good voice and she knew all the words by heart from 'Willkommen, Bienvenue, Welcome!' at the beginning to 'Auf wiedersehen, à bientôt' just before the cymbal crash at the end. Given the stars she idolized, it seems obvious I was supposed to grow up to be gay, but that's just one of the things that didn't pan out.

I thought mamá was beautiful. All boys think their mothers are beautiful, but in my defence I have to say that mine had the Searing Smile, a superpower Stan Lee would have paid good money for. Whenever she knew she was in the wrong – like the time I asked her to give me back the birthday money she'd asked me to lend her – she would use the Searing Smile and something inside me would melt and I would suddenly feel too weak to insist. (Actually, she never did give me that money back.) Papá said we were the lucky ones; he said that in the bedroom she used the Searing Smile for sinister purposes but refused to say anything more, leaving the details to our feverish imaginations.

But her other powers, the powers that earned her the nickname the Rock even the Thing would have envied. Mamá could wield the Glacial Stare, the Petrifying Scream and, in exceptional circumstances, the Paralysing Pinch. Worse still, if mamá had an Achilles heel, we never discovered what it was. No kryptonite worked on mamá. This, however, did not stop us from trying her patience every day, exposing ourselves to the Stare, the Scream and the Pinch. Weaklings that we were, we always succumbed. There was something atavistic about our confrontations. They were like battles between man and wolf, between Superman and Lex Luthor, a larger-than-life struggle that we played out over and over, aware that it was a drama written to delight some deity with Elizabethan tastes. We fought because fighting defined us, one as much as the other. Because, in conflict, we *were*.

Mamá had a doctorate in Physics and worked as a professor at the university. She always claimed that she had actually wanted to study biology and that the blame for her changing courses and studying the laws of the universe lay with her equally intractable mother, grandma Matilde. You'd have to know grandma Matilde to realize how ridiculous that was. I don't think my grandmother was much concerned with mamá's future beyond her ability to ensnare a man of good pedigree. (Another expression that tickled the Midget: was this the same Pedigree you feed to dogs?). This was a dream grandma Matilde had to give up once my father appeared on the scene – papá had a pedigree all right: mongrel. But I don't think grandma Matilde cared a hoot whether mamá studied biology, physics or acupuncture. Besides, I couldn't imagine mamá falling in with grandma Matilde's master plan anyway. I don't know where this primal family legend came from, but what I do know is that my love of science, what the Mexican narrator referred to as the mystery of life, I owe to mamá.

That, and my passion for Liza with a Z. Got a problem with that?

10

A SHORT FAMILY PARENTHESIS

When mamá met papá, she was already engaged to some other guy. Breaking off the engagement caused a huge scandal in the family. But mamá, who was not yet the Rock but the stone in David's slingshot, was not one to give up easily.

Not long after, she organized a dinner to introduce papá to the clan. Legend has it that mamá's family had adored her previous fiancé. But papá went one better. He arrived, all serious, set on playing the part of the lawyer with a promising future (which is, incidentally, exactly what he was). Papá carefully dropped references to his 'cases' into the conversation and mentioned the offices he had just opened in Tribunales. By the time dessert was served, everyone had relaxed and mamá and her cousin Ana got up to dance a *cueca* or a *samba*, some dance that involved them flicking handkerchiefs. Papá shouted, 'Watch where you're flicking that snot!' It was this comment that finally tipped the scales. Mamá's family breathed a sigh of relief. Papá was one of them.

They married the same year. I showed up a year later. If the stories are to be believed, I was born after a ten-month pregnancy. Mamá's due date was 1 January. The 10th (her birthday) came and went and still nothing. The 20th: still nothing. Regular check-ups revealed that I was perfectly healthy: I was still breathing, still growing normally. Nevertheless, by the end of January, the doctors decided to induce labour.

Papá claimed that the whole thing was just a mix-up, that the obstetrician had simply got the dates wrong – a logical explanation – but whenever mamá disputed this, papá would get nervous as somehow he sensed that all that separated him from the unthinkable was a piece of card and a doctor's illegible scrawl.

As for me, the story of my birth gave me a taste for stories of other extraordinary births. According to tradition, unusual births are noteworthy. Julius Caesar, for example, was 'born by the knife' (cut from his mother's belly, hence the term *caesarean*), and died by the knife on the Ides of March. Pallas Athena was – literally – the product of the worst headache Zeus ever had. I suppose I could have tried to come up with some reason for my refusal to be born, but something always stopped me. Midwives say that no one ever knows anything until the time is right and that is the tradition I respect above all others.

Five years later, the Midget showed up. According to papá, the Midget was the result of a wild night celebrating a win on the horses at the Hipódromo de Palermo. According to family legend, it was papá's first time at the races – he'd been dragged there by colleagues from the law office in Tribunales and rapidly developed a taste for gambling. Having picked two winners on his first night, he suddenly thought he was an expert. I don't remember him ever winning again. This was probably why the Midget was the only brother I had.

For a long time, I thought there was some kind of connection between fate, fortune and children (I liked to imagine I was the son of a professional poker player and consequently of royal birth) and, more specifically, a fateful connection between my little brother and racehorses. I stoically endured him breaking my Matchbox cars, tearing my comics, breaking my Airfix models, because I believed his actions were dictated by fate. His bestial behaviour was something that was written in the stars, a theory supported by the fact that he was born on 29 April, World Animal Day. My brother was born under the sign of the beast.

It was about then that mamá began working as a professor and started some group at the university, something to do with trade unions, and ended up winning elections. It was because of mamá that papá devoted his career to defending political prisoners: mamá found new cases for him every week. A lot of the 'uncles' were mamá's political friends or from the union; some had been in jail. Tío Rodolfo, for example.

At first papá wasn't too keen on all this politics. He used to tease mamá, saying he was happier when she was reading trashy novels by Guy des Cars rather than political pamphlets by Hernández Arregui and *El Descamisado* and huge tomes with titles like *Instability and Chaos in Nonlinear Dynamical Systems*, but he didn't mean it. Whenever they talked about politics, I could tell he was just as passionate as she was. Papá was the sort of man who screamed at the news on TV as though the newscasters and politicians could hear him. People say Shakespeare's soliloquies are contrived but what's the difference between Hamlet talking to a skull and papá talking to the TV?

For a while, during the time of the 'uncles', they used to drag the Midget and me along to any protests and demonstrations they went to. We loved this, because there was always an 'uncle' who'd sit us on his shoulders or give us a piggyback. People would buy us drinks or sweets, and we'd learn songs with words like '*policía federal la vergüenza nacional!*' ('federal police, a national disgrace!'), which made us popular in school the day after. Besides, everyone seemed to know everyone else at these demonstrations, so everyone was happy and it's well known that happiness is contagious.

In the beginning, papá was none too happy about mamá's open-door policy but, in the end, he gave in. It was partly because mamá kept nagging him, calling him a 'reactionary shyster' and a 'pencil-pusher'; but at least he was true to his pretentious, little-rich-boy roots, she used to say, a *niño bien* just like in the tango. But actually papá gave in because he believed in what she was doing and because he genuinely liked the uncles. They'd drink beer and he'd talk about the races, about his 'sure things'. He'd get angry if one of them was having trouble with the police or the Triple A (in books it says it stands for the Argentine Anti-communist Alliance, but papá always called it the Argentine Assassins Alliance) when they were thrown in jail or beaten up.

One day he told me that Tío Rodolfo was dead. He asked me to go to the wake with him. And when Tío Raymundo asked me where I lived, I lied. I told him I lived near La Boca.

11

LET'S GO

Mamá put her head around the classroom door and asked if she could come in. She was wearing the navy blue tailored suit that I always liked because it gave her a wasp waist. She had a lit cigarette between her fingers, as she always did. I think this is the only trait of the mad scientist I ever associated with mamá, that and her obsession with explaining everything in terms of physics – her inability to see a game of football as anything other than a complex system of masses, resistances, vectors and forces. If mamá needed to remember anything, whether it was a phone number or a formula, she jotted it down on the back of her pack of red Jockey Club cigarettes; then she'd forget she'd written something important on it and throw the packet in the bin. This was a law as unchanging as the law of gravity.

Señorita Barbeito turned the projector off, went to the door and had a whispered conversation with mamá. I took advantage of her well-timed interruption to stop playing Hangman so I could regroup (one more mistake and I was hanged), pretending to be interested in what was happening. What was mamá doing here? Shouldn't she be in the lab? Maybe she had come to pay the bursar and stopped by to say hello?

'Get your things, you've got to go,' said Señorita Barbeito.

I made a covert triumphant gesture and started stuffing my things into my schoolbag. Bertuccio looked annoyed. Mamá had robbed him of his victory.

He filled in the missing letters and asked what we were doing that afternoon.

'Same as always,' I told him. 'I'll come by your house right after my English class.'

'My mother is making *milanesas*,' Bertuccio said to tempt me. And boy did it work. To extrapolate my grandpa's expression: 'God is in the details – and in Bertuccio's mother's *milanesas*.'

Then Bertuccio gave me the piece of paper we'd been playing Hangman on. Now, it didn't read A _ _ A _ A _ A _ _ A. The solution was simple and elegant. In fact, it was magic.

Bertuccio's word was 'ABRACADABRA'.

12

THE CITROËN

At this point it's essential to dwell for a moment on the merits of the car in which we made our getaway. Mention the name Citroën and the average man pictures an elegant car driving around Paris with the Arc de Triomphe permanently in the background. But while it's true that our car had the same name and could trace its ancestry back to France, Citroëns in Argentina in 1976 were as different from that stereotype as Rocinante is from Bucephalus.

First: the shape. Seen in profile, our car might be described as having the classic curves of a Volkswagen Beetle, a large semicircle comprising the boot and the interior with a smaller semicircle containing the engine sticking out in front – but you'd be wrong. Whereas the Volkswagen has the reassuring sturdiness of German engineering, our Citroën was so flimsy it was like a Matchbox car.

The chassis was the problem. If a Volkswagen Beetle crashed into a common or garden wall, it would simply plough through it, whereas our Citroën would crumple like an accordion playing 'La Vie en Rose'. The roof was just as flimsy. It was a canvas roof, but don't confuse this with the folding roof of a European convertible. When I say it was made of canvas, I mean it could be unhooked and rolled up.

The flimsiness of the chassis was obvious as soon as the car was in motion. On sharp bends, it listed to port or starboard – it felt like sitting in a bowl of custard. Fortunately, the engine was incapable of reaching any great speeds, only of making a great deal of noise.

Two details about the interior should be enough. The design of the gearstick was unique, utterly unlike the popular floor-mounted gear stick (sports cars), or those tucked behind the steering wheel (Dodge, Chevrolet). Our gearstick, a metal lever embedded in the dashboard, looked as though it should have been on the control panel of the flying saucer in *Plan 9 from Outer Space* rather than a car. And the seats were designed around a metal frame that dug into your flesh when you sat down. The only practical solution was to sit with the metal rod carefully aligned with the cleft of your arse, unless you wanted another crack in your buttocks or a bad case of scoliosis. Sleeping stretched out on the back seat felt like what Indian fakirs must feel lying on a bed of nails. Maybe it was during his frequent naps in the back of the Citroën that the Midget developed his taste for the ascetic.

Lastly, and most glaringly, our Citroën was a lime green colour which, on a cloudless day, when the sun hit it just right, could blind even the most experienced driver.

But please don't read any contempt into this description of our steel (aluminium? who knows?) stallion. Our Citroën was a noble beast. It never failed us, not in the beginning, nor at the last. We loved everything about it, even bizarre features like the roll-down roof through which we liked to pop out and launch projectiles at other cars with the precision of a Panzer tank.

Every word I write about it is written with love; not the wide-eyed infatuation that makes virtues out of flaws, but genuine love, a precise sense of the importance it had – and still has – in my life.

I would like to think that if I've learned anything during my odyssey, it is to be true to those who have been true to me.

13

ENTER THE MIDGET

The Midget was waiting for us in the car. He was sitting in his usual place, curls falling into his eyes, wearing his check pre-school smock. He didn't react when we climbed into the car, as if we hadn't yet arrived, as if he operated on a time-frame different from ours, similar but not identical.

I didn't want to disturb him. He was still absorbed in his thoughts. Two minutes later he split my head open with his lunchbox.

According to scientists, a black hole is a dark region of space whose gravity traps all matter and radiation that comes within its field. Sort of like an intergalactic Hoover. Though they have not yet been able to prove it exists, there is irrefutable evidence to corroborate the phenomenon: the Midget is one indicator – he is a singularity of negative energy.

The Midget destroyed everything that came within his field. He did not seem physically violent, things simply disintegrated the moment he touched them. Though he turned them with infinite care, the pages of the books I lent him tore in his hands. Though he did nothing but twirl it around, pieces dropped off my Airfix model Spitfire as though it was suddenly struck with metal fatigue, as though the glue had turned to water. Though my medieval soldiers never left my side, the accessories that came with them – helmets, pikes, swords, shields – gradually disappeared. I never found them again, even after an intensive search and repeatedly pleading with mamá and papá to buy me a gold panning sieve and a Geiger counter.

It was impossible to ignore the phenomenon. Even mamá, who always tried to downplay it to mitigate the impact of my various losses, must have had a hard time trying to come up with a rational scientific explanation. Yet the Midget, this Lord of Chaos, was deeply attached to certain objects and certain rituals. He liked *these* sheets and *these* pyjamas, which had to be washed while he was at school so they would be ready for him the same night. He loved drinking chocolate, but it had to be made using a brand of milk called Las Tres Niñas and a brown powder called Nesquik, and it had to be mixed according to a precise formula: pouring the milk from a specific height, stirring four times – no more, no less – and obviously it had to be made in *that* cup.

In spite of this combustible combination of elements, the chemistry of our relationship had always been stable. For example, before we got our own record player, I used to phone Ana, my mother's cousin, and ask her to put on a Beatles record for us. She would crank up her Rasner and put on a single with two songs on each side ('I Saw Her Standing There', 'Chains', 'Anna' and 'Misery') and the Midget and I would sit in silence, sharing the phone as the music came through the receiver all the way from the Avenida Santa Fé.

When the record ended, the Midget was always the first to shout 'Again, again!'

14

BLIND IN THE FACE
OF DANGER

Mamá lit another cigarette and twisted the gearstick of the Citroën. We were between potholes, our heads bobbing like the little tigers taxi drivers always have in their rear windscreens.

Everything was fine until I mentioned Bertuccio's mother's *milanesas*.

My mother's failings as a housewife were an essential weapon in our regular battles, and I often used Bertuccio's mother's *milanesas* as a battering ram. As a cook, mamá had never moved beyond the grill – grilled steak, grilled sausages, grilled hamburgers. Her rare attempts to fry meat turned out *milanesas* so tough it felt like chewing a Pompeii dog charred in lava.

I had planned to steal one of Bertuccio's mother's *milanesas* that night, hide it in my school bag and smuggle it into our house where I could subject it to a battery of experiments destined to reverse-engineer the phenomenon: degree of cooking, composition of oil, chemical composition of the butter. Blabbermouth that I was, I informed mamá of my intentions in advance.

'You're not going to Bertuccio's tonight,' she said.

'But it's Thursday today!' I pointed out.

Going to Bertuccio's house was an ineluctable weekly ritual. On Thursdays I went to English lessons at the Institute and Bertuccio lived only one block away. When I got out of English class, I would ring his doorbell, we'd have our afternoon milk, watch *The Invaders* and then act out scenes from a play. (Bertuccio played Polonius – hilariously – in the voice of the pompous radio presenter Jorge Cacho Fontana.) I'd have my dinner there, and then they would drop me home. When Bertuccio's mother made *milanesas*, I'd arrive home in a state of rapture much like Pepé Le Pew's when he gets a whiff of a *petite femme skunk*.

'I know today is Thursday, but you're not going to Bertuccio's,' said mamá.

His curiosity aroused by the unfamiliar landscape, the Midget asked where we were going.

'To a friend's house,' mamá said, smoking furiously.

I asked why I couldn't go to Bertuccio's.

'Because we're going to visit a friend and then we're going on a trip,' mamá said.

'On a trip? In the middle of term? How long for?'

'Your papá can tell you that,' said mamá, kicking the ball wide for a corner.

'Are we leaving as soon as we get to your friend's house or are we staying there for a while?'

'We're staying until papá gets there.'

'Then why can't you just drop me off at Bertuccio's and pick me up later?'

'Because I say so.'

'That's not fair!'

I only said this to cause trouble. Nothing annoyed mamá more than when I resorted to this pet phrase, especially if she knew or suspected I was right. My obsession with justice infuriated her, even more so when I raised the stakes and threatened to ask papá to get me a good lawyer.

At this stage of our game of mother–son ping-pong, we both knew what came next. When I said 'That's not fair', mamá would get angry, then she would snap back with her standard line ('Life might be beautiful, but it's not fair') and that would be the end of the argument. Mamá would have won a Pyrrhic victory, elevating the specific to the universal and thereby diluting it.

The Midget interrupted to ask where his things were. Although she knew the answer, mamá chose to ask him what he meant.

'My pyjamas,' said the Midget. 'My cup, my Goofy!'

Mamá glanced over her shoulder, silently pleading with me for help. She was hoping I might limit the devastation caused by the Midget's inevitable explosion. He couldn't get to sleep without his toy Goofy.

I ignored her look and glared at her. 'Who is this friend we're visiting anyway? What about school? How I am supposed to catch up? Why do we have to go right now?' And then my $64,000 question, the question with which I deliberately betrayed her, since I knew it would send the Midget off the deep end, 'And why can't we stop by our house, even just to get his Goofy?'

At some point in the silence that followed, I realized the Citroën had stopped. We were stranded in a huge traffic jam, cars in front, cars behind, cars to either side. But the traffic jam was not the result of a red light or a double-parked car blocking the road. Thirty feet ahead, two police cars were parked across the avenue, creating a funnel though which only one car could pass at a time.

Mamá lit another cigarette and brought it to her lips, her hands were shaking. In any other circumstances, this intimation that she was on the brink would have made me wary, but I had nothing to lose – or that, at least, is what I thought. What could I possibly have left to lose,

I wasn't allowed to go to Bertuccio's and I'd been temporarily deprived of my precious possessions, all of which were back at our house?

I kept on nagging her, the Midget's voice providing counterpoint. Mamá endured our litany of complaints in suspicious silence as the Citroën inched at walking pace towards the police roadblock, like a grain of sand flowing towards the neck of an hourglass.

'Why can't we go an' pick up my Goofy?'

'It's not fair!'

'I want my Goofy!'

'How can we go on holiday with just the clothes we've got on?'

'I want my *pyjamas*!'

'And I want my game of Risk!'

Mamá stared straight ahead, her knuckles white on the steering wheel of the Citroën. Out of the corner of my eye, I registered the police at the neck of the funnel. Though I was scared of them, and I instinctively hated them ('federal police, a national disgrace'), right at that moment the person I most hated in the world was mamá.

It was my thoughtlessness that saved us.

I imagine that when it came to our turn and the police peered into the car, they saw an olive-skinned woman, her face contorted in pain as she listened to her screaming kids, and thought 'Poor woman', and waved us on.

When the roadblock finally disappeared in the rear-view mirror, mamá reached back to pat us, but I pushed her hand away and the Midget followed my example. I thought this was her pathetic way of trying to ingratiate herself – since she could hardly use the Searing Smile while she was driving – and I didn't want to give her the satisfaction of giving in. The only thing I could think about was Bertuccio and his mother's *milanesas* and Risk and school and the episode of *The Invaders* I was going to miss and the fact that I was being forced to go on a holiday I didn't want to go on, wearing my school shoes.

She must have felt terribly alone.

15

WHAT I KNEW

When you're a kid, the world can be bounded in a nutshell. In geographical terms, a child's universe is a space that comprises home, school and – possibly – the neighbourhood where your cousins or your grandparents live. In my case, the universe sat comfortably within a small area of Flores that ran from the junction of Boyacá and Avellaneda (my house), to the Plaza Flores (my school). My only forays beyond this area were when we went on holiday (to Córdoba or Bariloche or to the beach) or occasional, increasingly rare visits to my grandparents' farm in Dorrego, in the province of Buenos Aires.

We get our first glimpses of the big wide world from those we love unconditionally. If we see our elders suffer because they cannot get a job, or see them demoted, or working for a pittance, our compassion translates these observations and we conclude that the world outside is cruel and brutal. (This is politics.) If we hear our parents bad-mouthing certain politicians and agreeing with their opponents, our compassion translates these observations and we conclude that the former are bad guys and the latter are good guys. (This is politics.) If we observe palpable fear in our parents at the very sight of soldiers and policemen, our compassion translates our observations and we conclude that, though all children have bogeymen, ours wear uniforms. (This is politics.)

Given my circumstances, I had a much greater formal experience of politics than children my age in other times and places. My parents had grown up under other dictatorships, and the name of General Onganía came up in stories throughout my childhood. Would I have been capable of identifying this bogeyman? My parents called him *La Morsa* (The Walrus) so I associated him with that crazy song by the Beatles. I had gleaned all the essential details from a quick glance at a photograph: he had a peaked cap, a huge moustache; you could tell from his face that he was a bad guy.

I remember that, at first, I loved Perón because my parents loved Perón. Every time they mentioned *El Viejo* (The Old Man) there was music in their voices. Even mamá's mother, my *abuela* Matilde, who was a snooty reactionary, gave Perón the benefit of the doubt because, as she put it, why would the Old Man return from exile in Spain at the age of seventy-something unless he was motivated by a desire to put things right? But something must have happened, because the music changed, became more hesitant and then more melancholy. Then Perón died. The rest was silence.

(Around about this time, grandpa and grandma went to Europe for the first time and brought us back many souvenirs, including a catalogue of the Prado collection. I used to look through it all the time, but after my first time, I was careful to skip the page depicting Goya's *Saturn Devouring His Children*, because it terrified me. Saturn was a hideous old giant; in his hand he held the body of a little boy whose head he'd already bitten off. I remember thinking that Saturn and Perón were the two oldest people I'd ever seen. For a while, Saturn alternated in my nightmares with the River Plate shirt I got from Tío Rodolfo.)

After that point, things get confused. There were kidnappings, shootings and bombings. The Old Man's supporters were among the victims and the victimizers. But there were some people about whom there could be no doubts. 'Isabelita', Perón's widow, spoke in the same high-pitched voice that ventriloquists use for their puppets. López Rega, her right-hand man, looked suspiciously like Ming the Merciless (the bad guy from *Flash Gordon*) but with shorter fingernails and no beard. Everything else seemed pretty grey to me. When I found out that some trade-union leader called Rucci had been murdered, I was confused. Was I supposed to feel happy or sad? I never worked it out. What was significant was that he had been murdered a few blocks from our house, in the middle of Flores, on a corner near to where I lived. If I hadn't taken my normal route to school that day, I might easily have walked past it, heard the shots and seen the blood.

The murder of Rucci hadn't happened in the big wide world beyond my universe, the world I only got to see when we went on holiday, when I went to the cinema downtown or when I watched television: he had been gunned down in 'my' world, the area that stretched from my house to my school. One way or another, I must have realized that evil is no respecter of borders and makes no exceptions for individuals.

This is politics.

When the *coup d'état* came, in 1976, a few days before school term started, I knew straight off that things were going to get ugly. The new president had a peaked cap and a huge moustache; you could tell from his face that he was a bad guy.

16

ENTER DAVID VINCENT

We got to mamá's friend's house just in time to watch *The Invaders*. Her friend sat us in front of the TV and mamá went off to buy milk and Nesquik to appease the Midget.

The Invaders was our favourite TV show. The hero, an architect named David Vincent, is the only person who knows that aliens have secretly invaded the planet and taken on human form. Obviously no one believes him. How could anyone believe that that fat man over there, or that blonde girl, are aliens when they seem so nice, so ordinary, and when they speak such perfect Spanish? (Like Señorita Barbeito's documentary, *The Invaders* was dubbed.) But David Vincent has an ace up his sleeve: he knows that as a result of some design flaw or something, when the aliens take on human form they can't bend their little fingers, they're completely rigid. And when you kill one of them, they fall to pieces and disintegrate, leaving nothing but a dark stain on the ground.

In the 1950s, in the context of the Cold War, paranoid fantasies like *Invasion of the Body Snatchers* made some sort of sense. Behind the face of every ordinary American, a communist might be lurking, plotting to destroy the very fabric of democracy and replace it with a multitude of automata. But by the 1970s, *The Invaders* was just a mediocre genre piece with terrible production values and a cast led by the sort of po-faced actor Hollywood usually hired to play Nazis. And yet the theme of *The Invaders* resonated with the younger section of its audience. Any kid stepping out into the world for the first time could identify with the story of David Vincent, this man who had to study every stranger's face to work out whether he was friend or foe, his ally or his nemesis.

Like all the best TV series, *The Invaders* had implications far beyond the small screen and it leached into our games. The Midget and I were constantly staring at every stranger's little finger, on the lookout for aliens in disguise. Restaurants proved particularly rewarding hunting grounds, since back then holding your glass or your cup with your little finger sticking out was still considered to be good manners.

We never imagined that our game might one day turn serious, that one day we really would have to study every face, every little finger on every hand, looking for some sign that might tell us whether we were in the presence of the enemy.

17

NIGHT FALLS

Mamá's friend was a woman who didn't much like kids, at least that was how it seemed to me. From the moment she opened the door and peered at us over the security chain, her face bore an expression I interpreted as irritation at our presence. The fact that she was a friend of mamá's clearly did not mean she had to extend the same courtesy to us; after all, it's possible to love someone and hate their relatives, like I hated my friend Román's cousin even though he had the same name as me (my *Doppelgänger*). As soon as she saw kids, this woman obviously thought about screaming and finger marks all over her white walls, scratches on her floors and sticky marks on every surface. That, at least, was what I thought until night fell and they ordered pizza. Then, given that papá still hadn't shown up, the friend said, 'Why don't you stay the night?' and showed us into a bedroom that obviously belonged to her own kids, who for some reason weren't around.

So this woman obviously didn't hate kids; she had simply been terrified. But even so, she had invited us into her home. I don't remember her name and I wouldn't be able to work out where she lived; I don't even remember if it was in Buenos Aires or out in the suburbs. All I remember is that it was an apartment, that we had to go up in a lift, and that there was a globe on a shelf in the kids' bedroom with a bulb inside. Sometimes I think I'd like to see her again, or meet her children and tell them about the night that they harboured fugitives in their bedroom. But then I think that things are better as they are, because the people who proved to be heroes back then had no names, and that's how we should remember them.

Luckily for mamá, the Midget fell asleep watching TV. They put us in the same bed; the other bed was meant for mamá and papá. I couldn't imagine how both of them could fit in it, given that me and the Midget barely managed to fit onto the narrow mattress. What was worse, the Midget kept tossing and turning in his sleep, hitting and kicking me.

I tried to concentrate on the globe. From where I lay, the section of the world I could see seemed strange. I could make out parts of China, Japan and Kamchatka, of course; the Philippines, Indonesia, Micronesia and Oceania and the far side of the Pacific; all of North America and the Pacific coast of South America, where I could make out Chile and the west of Argentina. Since maps always showed North America in the top left corner and Oceania in the bottom right, it took me a moment to recognize the face of the Earth shining down on me. I thought it was some other world, a parallel Earth.

It was at this point that papá showed up. He seemed in good form, his shirt sleeves were rolled up, his tie loose, his collar unbuttoned. Assuming that we would be asleep, he had clearly only intended to pop his head around the door. When he saw that I was still awake, he smiled but when I opened my mouth he brought a finger to his lips; the Midget's sleep was sacrosanct.

'He keeps kicking me,' I said in a whisper.

'I'll make up a bed for you on the floor if you like,' he said, whispering too.

'You're the one who's going to have to sleep on the floor. If you and mamá get into that bed it'll collapse!'

45

Papá came into the bedroom and closed the door carefully. He nodded in agreement. Our bed creaked as he sat on the edge to give me a kiss.

'Did you get to see it?' he asked, concerned.

'We got here just in time. But it was a repeat. It was the one where some girl sees the Invaders disintegrate a truck and David Vincent is trying to track down the driver because he stole some file.'

'Oh, yeah, I've seen that one about three times. So, how is your mother holding up?'

I made a fist and brought it up to my face, a gesture papá understood immediately.

'The Rock.'

'She wouldn't even let me call Bertuccio to let him know I wasn't coming over. And today is Thursday!'

Finally realizing what day it was, Papá frowned. 'That wasn't very fair, but think about it this way: by being here we're not just protecting ourselves, we're also protecting Bertuccio.'

'Why? What's going on?'

'Didn't mamá tell you?'

'She spent the whole time talking to her friend and every time I went into the kitchen, they changed the subject. But I did hear them saying something about Roberto and the office.'

Roberto was papá's partner at the law office on the Calle Talcahuano. He had a son called Ramiro who was the same age as me, but in a class below me at school. Now and then we'd go to their *quinta* – their country house – in Don Torcuato for a barbecue. It wasn't like Ramiro was my best friend or anything, but we got along OK.

'Some guys showed up at the office this morning.'

'Soldiers? Policemen?'

'I don't know. They were obnoxious arseholes. They arrested Roberto and turned the place upside down.'

'Roberto's in jail? But why? What did he do?'

'He didn't do anything.'

'Well, why then?'

Papá shrugged his shoulders helplessly.

'If he didn't do anything, they'll have to let him go!'

'I hope so. His family is trying to track him down.'

'What about Ramiro?'

'What about him?'

'How is he? Where is he?'

'He's fine, he's with Laura. I talked to them earlier, they're fine.'

'What's going to happen to him now?'

'Nothing's going to happen to him.'

'What about us?'

'We're going to go away for a few days until things calm down. We'll be staying in a house down in the country, a *quinta*.'

'The one near Dorrego?'

'No, it's near here.'

'What's it like?'

'It's a *quinta* with a swimming pool. A *quinta* with lots of land. A *quinta* with a mysterious house.'

'Did you go by our house?'

Papá shook his head. This was how bad things were.

'But we can't go with just the clothes we've got on!' I protested.

'Whatever we need, we can buy.'

'Well, then, we'll have to buy a new game of Risk.'

'You fancy losing again?'

'No way, José!'

'I think you've got a death wish.'

I tried to think of a brilliant comeback, a zinger that would hit him like a smack in the mouth, but I was the one who got smacked when the Midget rolled over in his sleep and gave me a right hook.

18

SIRENS

That night I woke up on the thin duvet, which was the only thing separating me from the hard floor, to find that papá, who had been lying next to me when I fell asleep, was not there. The room was still dark. It smelled of sweaty socks.

Papá and mamá were sitting on the cold floor in a corner of the room. Mamá had raised the blinds a few inches and was peering through the narrow slit, out at the road, barely lit by the glow of the streetlights. She was wearing a nightdress I'd never seen before and she had no shoes on. One of her feet was tap-tap-tapping on the floor. Papá was sitting beside her in T-shirt and boxer shorts, staring at nothing. Dressed like this, or rather undressed, he looked even more like the Midget. The lock of hair plastered to his forehead, the self-absorption. All he needed now was his own Goofy.

Papá and mamá were huddled together as close as their bodies would allow and yet they looked incredibly distant.

Then the noise of a siren, far away but clear, broke the silence of the early morning. I don't know if it was an ambulance or a police car. Papá and mamá reacted as one, suddenly connected again, peering through the blinds as though they could actually see anything in the street but the shadows.

'What's going on out there?'

Mamá hushed him.

A few seconds later, the siren faded as abruptly as it had begun, a calamity that was not part of our world, one that had brushed past, sparing us.

The silence was transparent and now I could hear again, the tap-tap-tap of mamá's foot and the sound of breathing, of a heart beating, that I suppose must have been my own.

In a hushed whisper, papá told mamá to try to sleep for a while, even if it was only a couple of hours, because she would need to be clear-headed in the morning. It was going to be a long day, there was a lot to do and then there was us. 'We have to try not to spook the boys.'

Mamá nodded and lit another cigarette. The harder she puffed on the cigarette, the brighter the tip glowed. I thought she'd gone crazy, because she leaned across to the blind and kissed it. Actually, she was just blowing her smoke out through the crack in the window. She didn't want the room to get full of smoke.

I felt like getting up and going over to them. Hugging them, saying something stupid, joining their vigil, peering through the blinds and, when the church bells chimed, saying 'Three o'clock and all is well,' like they used to when Buenos Aires was still a colony.

I think I wanted to protect them – for the first time. But I figured papá would probably say the same thing to me he had said to mamá. He'd give me a little lecture on the salutary effects of a good night's sleep and send me back to my thin eiderdown and my aching bones.

I closed my eyes and pretended to sleep and in the end I dozed off again.

Playtime

Can I view thee panting, lying
On thy stomach, without sighing;
Can I unmoved see thee dying
On a log
Expiring frog!

Charles Dickens, 'Ode to an expiring frog',
The Pickwick Papers

Second Period: Geography

Noun. 1. Science concerned with the
physical features of the Earth's crust
and as a habitation for man.
2. The topographical features of a
region: 'The danger extends across the
entire geography of Argentina.'

19

'OURS WAS THE MARSH COUNTRY'

For centuries, no one wanted to settle the land where Buenos Aires now stands.

The native peoples turned their backs on it, preferring the green pampas to the insalubrious air of the marshes, this zone that is neither sea nor land, nor anything. When the Conquistadores arrived by sea, the natives attacked them more out of curiosity than anything else and finally left them to their own devices, knowing well how things would turn out for them. Locked up in their fortresses, the Europeans succumbed to plague and starvation until they were finally forced to eat each other. The land on which the city stands retains the memory of these cannibals. I'm not sure whether this was an isolated incident or whether it was a sign of destiny.

When they aspired to glory, the indigenous peoples of the continent chose the other ocean, the Pacific. Lima was the golden city of the Incas while Buenos Aires was still a swamp. And when Europeans set up military outposts in South America, they too preferred the line that runs from México with the Peruvian high

Andes. Buenos Aires was a last resort, a city beyond the pale, the last bastion of civilization standing on the frontier of barbarism. Or was it beyond that frontier, capital of a savage kingdom?

All we know for certain is that no one wanted to live in Buenos Aires. Even the name was like a tasteless joke. The air was unhealthy, heavy and humid. It was like breathing water. Oxen and carts sank into the mud. This oppressive weather still reigned when, in 1947–48, Lawrence Durrell, in his letters from Buenos Aires, described the area as 'large, flat and melancholy . . . full of stale air', where the powerful fought over meagre resources and 'the weak are discarded . . . Anyone with an ounce of sensitivity is trying to get away from here – including me.' Lest there be any doubt about the malign influence the city had upon his soul, Durrell also wrote: 'One's feelings don't rise in this climate, the death-dew settles on me . . .'

To the imperial powers of the eighteenth century, Buenos Aires looked – on paper – like a marvellous opportunity. It was the last port on the Atlantic seaboard before Cape Horn and offered access to a network of rivers that connected it with the heart of the continent. Rivers meant trade and trade would bring wealth, civilization, culture. But in practice Buenos Aires was a nightmare. The River Plate offered scant depth, making it difficult for large ships to dock and though there were rivers, they presented even greater navigational problems. It was at this point that the dichotomy between the idea of Buenos Aires and the reality of Buenos Aires became apparent, a dichotomy that has never been resolved: the conflict between what we might be and what we are leaves us paralysed, a ship run aground on a muddy spit of land.

Sometimes I think that everything you need to know about life can be found in geography books. The result of centuries of research, they tell us how the Earth was formed, how the incandescent ball of energy of those first days finally cooled into its present, stable form.

They tell us about how successive geological strata of the planet were laid down, one on top of the other, creating a model which applies to everything in life. (In a sense, we too are made up of successive layers. Our current incarnation is laid down over a previous one, but sometimes it cracks and eruptions bring to the surface elements we thought long buried.)

Geography books teach us where we live in a way that makes it possible to see beyond the ends of our noses. Our city is part of a country, our country part of a continent, our continent lies on a hemisphere, that hemisphere is bounded by certain oceans and these oceans are a vital part of the whole planet: one cannot exist without the other. Contour maps reveal what political maps conceal: that all land is land, all water is water. Some lands are higher, some lower, some arid, some humid, but all land is land. There are warmer waters and cooler waters, some waters are shallow, some deep, but all water is water. In this context all artificial divisions, such as those on political maps, smack of violence.

All the people who inhabit all these lands are people. Some are blacker, some whiter, some taller, some shorter, but they are all people: the same in essence, different only in details because (as geography books teach us), that part of the Earth allotted to us is the mould from which our essence pours forth, molten and incandescent as in the first days of the planet. What form we take will be a variation moulded by that place. We grow up to be placid in the tropics, frugal in the polar regions, impulsive if we are of Mediterranean stock.

Durrell intuits something of this in his letters when he talks of flatness, of melancholy; Buenos Aires forces him to adapt or die, as bacteria were once forced to contend with oxygen, forced to convert this toxin into the air they breathed. Durrell left, but those of us who choose to stay, adapt our sensibilities. Some of the characteristics we develop as a result of this mutation are as extraordinary as those developed by bacteria. Tango, for example: music of Baltic melancholy which expresses the flatness, the humidity and the nostalgia which mark us out from the rest of the Hispanic world. On this point I disagree with grandpa: I believe what that Piazzolla plays *is* tango. But it is a conclusion I arrived at through reading geography books.

Between the primeval swamps and the Buenos Aires of today, centuries have passed, but time is the most relative of all measurements. (I believe all time occurs simultaneously.) We are still shapeless creatures, as shifting as the muddy coastline. We are still creatures of mud, God's breath still fresh in our cheeks. We are still amphibious, on land we long for the sea, and longing for land we swim through the dark waters.

20

THE SWIMMING POOL

The *quinta* papá had borrowed was on the outskirts of Buenos Aires. It had a kidney-shaped swimming pool surrounded by flagstones. The water was not exactly what you might call clean. It had a Citroën-green tinge, and the surface of the water and bottom of the pool were covered with leaves that had fallen from the trees. Getting the leaves off the surface was easy. There was a net with a long handle specially designed for the purpose. The leaves on the bottom of the pool were a different matter; they had rotted into a slimy gloop we had to walk on.

As soon as we arrived, I asked papá if I could go for a swim. Papá, obviously, glanced at mamá. She made a disgusted face. What the swimming pool contained was not water, but something like a soup of bacteria, microorganisms and decomposing vegetation. But that afternoon, the April sun was still beating down and mamá owed me one because of the whole Bertuccio thing.

I didn't have a swimsuit with me, but I dived in anyway – in my underpants. The water was cold and slightly soupy. When I tried to stand on the bottom, my feet slithered around as though the bottom was covered in cream. It was better to keep swimming, even if all I could do was doggy paddle.

I had never really been interested in style. Most boys learn the front crawl so they can race, or they learn something showy like the butterfly so that they can splash people on the side of the pool. But what I liked best was staying underwater. I'd hang on to the bottom of the ladder and exhale all the air in my lungs, bubble by bubble, until there was nothing left and then lie on the bottom with my tummy pressed against the tiles for a few seconds before shooting back to the surface for air.

The things my mother thought were disgusting about the pool were exactly the things that most fascinated me. The green tinge, the shifting rays of light, made it easy to pretend that I was at the bottom of the ocean. The leaves and the branches suspended in the water gave a sense of depth to my underwater adventure, the long-legged insects diving like me but with more grace. There were curious formations all along the waterline, countless clusters of tiny translucent eggs. And the dark slime at the bottom – a mixture of moss and decaying leaves – added to the feeling of being at the bottom of the sea.

People say that being underwater stirs memories of the place where we were conceived and spent our first nine months. Being surrounded by water rekindles sensations we first felt in our mothers' wombs: the weightlessness, the languid, muted sounds. I'm not about to argue with this reasoning, but I prefer to believe that the pleasure of being underwater has another explanation, less Freudian and more in keeping with the history of our species.

When, at the dawn of life, our ancestors left their aquatic environment, they took the water with them. The human womb replicates the water, the weightlessness, the salinity of our erstwhile ocean habitat. The concentration of salt in the blood and in bodily fluids is the same as that in the oceans. We abandoned the sea some 400 million years ago (by my chronology), but the sea has never abandoned us. It lives on in us in our blood, our sweat, our tears.

21

THE MYSTERIOUS HOUSE

When he said the house was 'mysterious', papá set my imagination racing. I had imagined a dark, dank, two-storey English manor house, walls shrouded in thick ivy, hiding thousands of long-legged spiders. I imagined looking up as we arrived and noticing a boarded-up window high up near the chimney stack – a secret room that no staircase in the house led to. I imagined a neighbour nodding sagely and confessing that the window was a mystery, then asking ominously if I had heard what had happened to the previous tenants, a strange family . . .

The actual house was very different. It was a simple, low-rise square box with a tarred roof. It looked more like a compromise with reality than with architecture. The walls had been whitewashed, though the job looked half-finished.

I wandered into the house half-naked, wrapped in a huge towel with the price tag still attached. I was wet and my whole body itched from the pine needles. Papá and mamá were coming and going, bringing in shopping bags and going out to fetch more. In an attempt to keep the Midget occupied – he was more dangerous when he tried to help with family chores than when he skived off – they had sat him in front of the TV, an ancient Philco with a rabbit-ear aerial; the knobs fell off as soon as you touched them.

The house was full of mismatched cast-offs and second-hand furniture in different styles and colours. The living room alone had a fake Louis XV sofa, two wooden chairs – one pine, one mesquite. The coffee table was made of wicker and the TV stand was orange Formica.

Papá stood, captivated before a broken grandfather clock. He slipped his hand inside the case and ding, dong, ding sounded the chimes – a little ominous, a little magical.

All houses retain something of their former residents. People shed traces of themselves everywhere they go, the way we constantly shed and renew our skin without even noticing. It doesn't matter how efficient the movers were, or how thoroughly the house was cleaned. The floors might smell of wax polish and the walls might be freshly whitewashed, but a vigilant eye will still detect the clues left by history: the floor, worn where it has been walked on, a dark groove on the windowsill where someone set down a cigarette as they gazed out at the gardens. Marks on the floor indicated where the original furniture had once stood.

We didn't know anything about the people who owned the house. All papá told us was that it had been lent to some people and they were now lending it to us. Maybe this was where the mystery lay. What was the logic behind such generosity? Were these cigarette burns made by the owner or by one of the brief tenants of the house? Why were there so many signs that the house had been recently occupied: a jar of mayonnaise in the fridge that was still within its best-before date, the March issue of a magazine? Who were the last tenants here, how long did they live here and what had forced them to leave?

Still dripping wet, I started to look for hidden clues. Mamá said I looked like a ghost in my big white towel and told me to dry myself right away before I dripped water all over the house.

First I explored the living room and dining room, opening all the cupboards and all the drawers. I didn't find any personal items. One of the drawers was lined with a piece of paper that fascinated me, it was covered with a magician's props: top hats, white rabbits, magic wands. I thought of Bertuccio's word, the game of Hangman and I wondered where I'd put the piece of paper he had scribbled the word on. I thought I remembered stuffing it into my trouser pocket and that calmed me.

There was an old radiogram with a record-player that looked even cheaper than the cabinet it was in. The bottom shelf was full of singles. There was nothing I liked, it was mostly stupid instrumental stuff by Ray Conniff and Alain Debray, along with a bunch of singers I'd never heard of like Matt Monro and some guy with a name like a tongue-twister called Engelbert Humperdinck. It was Engelbert's record that slipped out of its sleeve and fell to the floor.

I bent down to pick it up and noticed something odd underneath the radiogram. It looked like a scrap of paper that had slipped down behind the cabinet and got stuck between the skirting board and the wall.

It was a postcard of Mar del Plata: a typical photograph of the *rambla*. It was dated that summer, the summer of '76. The sentences were simple and the handwriting was terrible. '*My dear little Pedro, we hope you are having a lovely holiday. It's good to have fun once in a while. Tell your mamá you can come and stay with us for a few days if you like. If you need anything, just call. You can both come and stay. You know how much we love you. Xxx*' and it was signed Beba and China.

I wondered who Pedro was, whether he was a kid as the postcard made it sound. But the line I found most disturbing was: '*It's good to have fun once in a while*'. Was this Pedro a really serious kid, or was he 'special' (deformities, extra-sensory powers, pustules all over his body, the sort of thing that makes a family lock their son up in an attic so no one ever sees him)? Or was there some tragedy in his past? A tragedy that still loomed over him, much to the regret of Beba and China?

I took the postcard with me, a damp ghost seeking the privacy of his room.

22

I FIND TREASURE

Our room was at the back of the house. From the window you could see the washing line and the small hut that served as a tool shed. Papá was wandering around, collecting wood for a barbecue. I called out to him through the window screen and asked if the people who had lent us the house had a son called Pedro. He said no, he didn't know any kid called Pedro.

The bedroom had two mismatched beds, a bedside table and a wardrobe. Otherwise it was completely empty. The drawers weren't even lined with paper. I put the postcard on the bedside table and sat down on the bed. Under the bedspread, the mattress was bare.

It was sheer frustration that prompted me to go to the wardrobe and stand on the bedside table to check a high shelf that, from what I could see, was empty. I had the bright idea of blowing hard to clear the thick layer of dust and almost blinded myself. I rubbed my eyes until they watered, but when I opened them again, it seemed to me I could see colours on the shelf that hadn't been there before.

Pedrito had left a book behind. I used the bedspread to wipe off the dirt and opened it. The proof was right there on the first page. It read 'Pedro '75' in what was clearly a child's handwriting.

The book didn't have many pages, but it was big and had colour illustrations on the title page. It was called *Houdini, the Escape Artist*.

Inside the book were a number of colour plates printed on glossier paper than the text, and at the bottom of each photo there was a caption. The first one read: 'Harry practises his first escapes with the help of his brother Theo'. (Houdini's first name was Harry.) Another caption read: 'In the asylum' and showed Houdini in a padded cell, his arms strapped into a straitjacket. Another caption read: 'The Chinese Water Torture Cell' and the photo was of a glass box filled with water, with Houdini inside, upside down, his wrists handcuffed.

Everything I knew about Houdini, I had seen in a TV film. Houdini was Tony Curtis. He was kind of like a magician and he escaped from all kinds of places. I remember them throwing him into a freezing lake, in a big trunk, I think. Houdini escaped from the trunk but nearly died because the lake was frozen and he couldn't find a hole in the ice to get out. He had practised in his bathroom at home, filling his bath with ice cubes. ('Houdini on the rocks.')

I read the book until I felt cold; then I got dressed and went back to reading. After a while I had to turn the light on because it was getting dark.

23

HOUDINI ESCAPES . . .

This is a list of the things I found out from the book about Houdini:

Houdini was born in Budapest on 24 March 1874 – a little more than a century ago!

Houdini's name wasn't really Houdini, it was Erik Weisz. His father was Mayer Samuel Weisz, he was a rabbi (they're the ones who breathe life into the Golems) and his mother's name was Cecilia.

Houdini's family emigrated to the United States when he was four years old, and they were really poor so he had to go out to work shining shoes and selling newspapers when he was still a kid. In New York, he worked as a messenger boy and cut cloth for a tailor's called Richter & Sons. But the only job he was any good at was being a messenger boy. Not only was little Erik fast, but he had a lot of stamina for his age; he could run and run practically all day. And in the spring, when the frozen surface of the Hudson had barely melted, he was always the first to dive in: swimming was his great passion.

When Houdini began his career, he called himself Eric the Great, but later on, inspired by his famous French forerunner Robert-Houdin, he decided to call himself Harry Houdini.

When Houdini first started performing, his assistant was his little brother Theo.

Houdini met Wilhelmina Beatrice Rahner in 1894; they married two weeks later and after that she was always his assistant. (In the film, she was played by Janet Leigh, who was Tony Curtis's wife in real life.)

Houdini offered a reward to anyone who could defeat him with handcuffs, straitjackets, shackles, by locking him up in cages, in jail cells, in coffins, by throwing him into water weighed down with chains, claiming there was nothing he could not escape from. He was right; he never paid out a single reward. He often escaped from prisons to the mystification of dozens of journalists and the cheers of prisoners delighted to see that it really was possible to escape.

Houdini's most spectacular escape was the Chinese Water Torture Cell, where he spent four minutes suspended upside down underwater, escaping from his bonds before the very eyes of his enraptured audience.

Houdini's mother Cecilia Weisz died in 1913, plunging him into terrible grief.

Houdini kept on going in spite of everything and became the most famous escape artist in history, a true artist, a man no one could contain, who made freedom his vocation.

One not insignificant distinction made in the book (it opened my eyes) was the difference between what we call a magician (who is really just an illusionist, he has no magic powers, he just pretends he has) and an escape artist. Houdini belonged to the second category. He hated illusionists because they sullied the purity of his art: illusionists claim they can do things they can't actually do whereas an escape artist only claims to be able to do things he actually can do, using no tricks apart from his peak physical condition and his ability to control his body. This was not a minor distinction to Houdini, who expended enormous effort on unmasking tricksters and frauds. Magicians deal in lies. Escape artists, on the other hand, dedicate themselves to the truth.

Although at the time I didn't notice anything missing, I should mention here that the book didn't give any information about certain things that, as time went by, would come to obsess me: for example, the reason why the Weisz family decided to leave Budapest and cross the Atlantic. Or why little Erik was inspired to try his hand as an escapologist. Lastly, and most importantly, the thing I wanted to know more than anything in the world, the one thing I longed to know, the question that kept me awake at night, was how the hell did he do it?

24

FUGITIVES

In deciding on a barbecue, papá made two mistakes. First, he had forgotten to buy charcoal, and second he went ahead anyway, figuring sticks and small pieces of wood would do. The fire burned out far too fast, which not only meant eating half-raw steak for dinner, it also meant having to sit through a lecture from mamá on the different combustible properties of wood and charcoal.

In desperation, the Midget and I resorted to eating fruit. In general we only liked bananas and mandarin oranges, which could be peeled easily, or grapes – any kind of fruit we could prepare ourselves because unlike other mothers – Bertuccio's mother, for example – our mother was incapable of so much as peeling an orange for us. But that night hunger got the better of us. We would have shelled a coconut with our bare teeth if necessary. We opted for apples. The Midget started massacring his fruit. Mamá lit a cigarette and cleared her throat.

It was at this point that she told us about the new rules. We didn't know how long we would be staying here, she explained; it might be a couple of days, maybe a week, maybe longer. She told us that we wouldn't be returning to school for a while. On Monday, she said, she would have to go back to work at the laboratory, but papá would take a few days off and stay at the *quinta* with us.

Given our new circumstances, there was a set of basic ground rules we had to observe. We were not to go into the pool without telling a grown-up first. We were not to open the fridge or turn on the TV if we were barefoot or wet from swimming. And since the only water in the *quinta* was from the water tank, we were not to drink from the tap, spend more than ten minutes in the shower or leave it running for no reason. This last instruction signified an additional responsibility for me as the older brother. (Mamá promised to show me how to fill the tank if it was empty.)

But there was another set of rules too, that related to our curious status as fugitives. For example, mamá explained that on no account were we to use the telephone. We were not to answer the phone and we were certainly not allowed to ring anyone. We weren't allowed to call Ana or grandma Matilde or Dorrego, and under no circumstances (this proscription was emphasized by a serious tone and stern look) was I allowed to ring Bertuccio. The best thing we could do, she said, was to imagine we were on holiday on a desert island, that we were the only tourists and there was no post, no phones and we could not leave until the boat that had brought us here came back to pick us up.

The Midget asked if there was a television on the island. Mamá said there was and the Midget threw up his arms in triumph, one hand brandishing the knife that still bore shreds of his sacrificial apple.

I argued that nobody went on holiday without a suitcase, so the only way we could have ended up on this island was if we'd been shipwrecked. (The word 'shipwreck' made mamá and papá nervous, especially when they saw the Midget was getting upset.) I said, nobody can have fun on holidays when they have to wear the same clothes and the same shoes every day, when they have no books, no Risk, no trading cards and no Goofy (this, I admit, was a low blow), no friends and . . .

At this point papá interrupted me and said that as soon as the mists surrounding the island had cleared a little, he planned to go back to our house and pick up some things, or send someone with a list and a set of keys. But in the uncertain atmosphere of this new island, I refused to be placated by this news. Who knew how long it would be before this fog that cut us off from civilization lifted?

The grown-ups exchanged a quick glance and then papá got up from the table. For a moment I took this as an admission of defeat (and if papá was defeated, we were all doomed), but he reappeared from the bedroom carrying a bag and handed a shiny gift-wrapped package to the Midget and another to me.

My present was a new game of Risk. I was saved! It was beautiful, perfect, brand spanking new, it had everything: the board, the dice, the instructions, everything.

'Whenever you fancy losing again, just say the word,' said papá.

The Midget's present was a toy Goofy. He ripped off the paper like a wild animal and gave a squeal of excitement when he saw what was inside. Papá and mamá heaved a sigh of relief, but I immediately realized that this new Goofy was about to cause more problems than it solved.

The Midget started shaking Goofy with a worried look on his face. He looked at papá, then at mamá, but they didn't understand. He asked them what had happened to Goofy. 'This Goofy is sick,' he said.

The Midget's original Goofy was a stuffed toy. The new Goofy was made of hard plastic.

It was not just a matter of feelings (unlike games of Risk, which are interchangeable, Goofy was an anthropomorphic toy, and so the Midget's relationship with it was personal and non-transferable), but also a matter of practicalities. The Midget always slept with Goofy in his arms, and while it was one thing to snuggle up with a soft, well-worn cuddly toy, trying to hug a piece of hard, bumpy plastic was a very different matter. All boys love toy trucks, but they don't use them as pillows.

25

WE ASSUME NEW IDENTITIES

Papá had another trick up his sleeve. He made a number of concessions (promising to play a game of Risk with me as soon as the table was cleared; reassuring the Midget that the new Goofy was a distant cousin of his old Goofy and that it would get softer over time the same way people get softer when they become friends), and managed to appease us sufficiently so that we were prepared to listen to his explanation, one which, in the weeks that followed, we would come to understand.

For papá, it was not enough that we wouldn't be at home, at the office, at school. Holing up in this villa on the outskirts of Buenos Aires (the 'island' mamá claimed we had been washed up on) was a necessary precaution, but not the only one. However much we might want to be, we were not invisible. There were probably people living in the neighbouring houses, a travelling salesman might knock at the door at any minute, people who regularly walked past the house were bound to notice – from the rubbish bags, the smells, the noise – that new tenants had moved in.

Given all this, we had to be prepared in case we should run into someone. We had to be discreet and try not to attract attention, but if we were noticed, it was important that nobody would know who we really were. And what better defence could there be than pretending to be someone else?

We had to assume new identities. Like spies who pretend not to be spies so they don't fall into enemy clutches. Like Batman, hiding his secret identity beneath his mild-mannered alter ego. Like Odysseus tricking the Cyclops by telling him his name was 'No-man'. Odysseus was a born escape artist. To escape Polyphemus, the Cyclops who had vowed to eat his men, Odysseus first got him drunk on wine and then plunged a spear into his one eye, blinding him. When the other Cyclops heard Polyphemus scream in pain, they asked who had hurt him. 'No-man,' replied Polyphemus, so the other Cyclops, thinking his pain must be a plague sent by Zeus, told him to accept his fate.

Papá was counting on the fact that this part of the plan would get me excited. Becoming other people was the key element in all of our games. Cowboys or monsters, superheroes or dinosaurs, even when we played sports we pretended to be other people.

But what papá had not counted on was the fact that my mind worked faster than any set of rules, and faster than common sense. In a matter of seconds the whole universe of possibilities offered by this opportunity to become someone else lay before me, and I found myself standing before a shining, tantalizing doorway papá had not thought of, and one which clearly took him by surprise.

Suddenly hopeful, I said that if I became a different person, that meant I'd be able to phone Bertuccio. I was convinced that if he listened carefully, Bertuccio would work out it was me even if I told him my name was Otto von Bismarck, and obviously he'd work out that there was some kind of emergency, so he'd play along with these new rules. We could even invent a secret language!

At this point, mamá immediately became the Rock and dashed my hopes. The embargo, she said, still applied. 'You are not to call Bertuccio under any circumstances, even if you tell him your name is Mandrake the magician, full stop, end of story. Saints alive!' (Over time, this was to become the Midget's favourite saint; he fully expected to see St Salive riding with the four horsemen of the Apocalypse.)

I was beaten. I pushed away the plate with the apple on it and folded my arms angrily. The only reason I didn't get up and storm out was because there was nowhere to go.

'From now on, our name is Vicente,' said papá, still hopeful.

I didn't react. I didn't care. I didn't want to know.

'My name is David Vicente and I'm an architect,' said papá.

Vicente was a horrible name, but as a surname it was even worse.

'David Vicente!' papá repeated, shaking my shoulder.

Then the penny dropped. David Vicente, the architect. Papá was David Vincent!

I burst out laughing. The Midget looked at me like I was crazy and mamá looked at papá in search of an explanation.

'Don't you get it?' I said to the Midget, still laughing. 'David Vicente is like the Spanish version of David Vincent. Papá is the guy in *The Invaders*!'

'Aaaaah,' said the Midget, clapping his hands.

Mamá glared at papá, not knowing whether to kill him or hug him.

'If anyone asks, we are the Vicentes,' said papá, pleased with himself. 'If the phone rings and someone asks for the people we used to be, just tell them no one by that name lives here, tell them we're . . .'

'You won't need to tell them anything at all because you won't be answering the phone,' mamá interrupted. 'How many times do I have to say it?'

'Sorry. I meant if I answer the phone, I'll just say, sorry, wrong number. Is that clear?'

Me and the Midget nodded.

I asked papá if we would be getting false papers to match our false identities. I expected him to dismiss the idea out of hand but he looked to mamá for approval and then said yes, it was possible that we would all need new papers.

I asked if I could pick my own name.

The Midget asked if he could pick his name.

'It depends,' said mama. 'It has to be an ordinary name, you can't call yourself Fofó or Goofy or Scrooge McDuck.'

'Simón!' yelled the Midget. Like I said before, he was a big fan of *The Saint*. 'Like Simon Templar!'

Mamá and papá happily agreed, Simón Vicente sounded normal enough.

'I could call myself Flavia,' said mamá.

'Flavia Vicente. OK, but only if you tell me where you came up with the name,' said papá.

'Over my dead body.'

'In that case, I'll just call you Dora, or maybe Matilde, like your mother.'

'Just try it,' said mamá, 'and you can kiss your conjugal rights goodbye.'

'Flavia Vicente,' papá said quickly. 'Going once, going twice, sold to the lady . . .'

'What's conjugal rights?' asked the Midget.

'There's still someone here who hasn't got a name,' said mamá, changing the subject.

But I already had a name. It was clear as day. All the signs pointed to it and I congratulated myself on being able to read them.

My name would be Harry. Yes, Harry. Pleased to meet you.

26

STRATEGY AND TACTICS

Herodotus recounts that during the reign of Atys, the son of Manes, the kingdom of Lydia suffered a terrible famine. The Lydians endured these privations for a time and then realized that they needed to find something to distract them from their suffering. This is how games were invented, the sort of games that are played with dice, jacks and balls. Herodotus credits the Lydians with inventing all games apart from backgammon, which is the name English pirates gave to the Arab *tawla*, still played by old men throughout the Middle East, sitting at low tables in the streets, drinking sweet mint tea.

I always loved that story. Herodotus doesn't tell it as though it were actually true, simply as something the Lydians said about themselves, but he nevertheless recounts it with eloquence and grace. The paragraph is one of the most effective in the *Histories*. Herodotus knew that the stories people tell are important because they convey their sense of themselves in a way that documents and the (inevitably) tragic toll of battles cannot.

There was something else that appealed to me in the story of the Lydians. I liked the fact that they did not attribute the invention of games to boredom or to philosophical idleness, but to suffering. The Lydians did not play games because they had nothing better to do. They played so that they would not perish.

In a sense, Risk is a direct descendant of *tawla*. In both there is a board, a pair of dice, there is a goal (conquest), there are rules and a logic to the game (strategy) and the more cunning the player, the closer he comes to victory. The chance element of the dice is crucial, but in this battle strategy has to make chance an ally.

The West's contribution, what we add to the strategy and tactics, is the art of war. The board is no longer divided into geometric, purely abstract shapes, it is now a planisphere. The world map, more figurative than realistic, imitates the style of ancient cartographers. And the political boundaries add to the anachronistic feel of the game. The United States does not exist as a nation; instead there are a number of independent states: New York, Oregon, California. Russia refers to a large European state while its Asian territories are divided into states: Siberia, Ural, Yakutsk and, of course, Kamchatka.

Every player is represented by pieces of a single colour – I liked to play with the blue pieces – and is given control of X countries, depending on how many players there are. Up to six people can play, and every player is given a secret goal, for example: *Occupy North America, two territories in Oceania and four in Asia*, or, *Destroy the red army, or, if that proves impossible, the army of the player on your right*.

Wars between the armies are settled using dice. If I'm attacking, I have to roll a number higher than the defending army. If I win, then the defender has to withdraw his armies and I get to occupy the country he has left empty.

My favourite variation was the simplest. Me against papa: papá against me. The whole world divided in two: papá was the black army, I was the yellow army. Our goal was not remotely secret: we were trying to destroy each other, to wipe each other off the face of the Earth (the Earth as it appears in Risk).

I don't remember how it started, whether I brought the game home or whether papá bought it. (I don't remember a time when I didn't know about Kamchatka.) What I do remember is that papá always beat me. Every single game. It happened every time. He would beat me hollow, or – when it was obvious there was no way I could win – we would call the game off.

That first night in the *quinta* was no exception. After a promising start, papá set about undermining the morale of my armies and began routing them one by one. From time to time, mamá would wander past and look at the board. At one point she clapped papá on the shoulder and said, 'Why don't you let the kid win for once?' And papá gave the same answer he always gave – it was one of the scenes from our family drama which was played out every time we sat down to a game – 'Are you crazy? He can win when he's able to beat me,' and his inexorable victory march went on.

Over time, the idea that I might beat papá grew from a vague desire to a need, until finally it became a categorical imperative. The law of probability was in my favour, I figured. Sooner or later it would impose its implacable mathematical laws, raise me up and make me victorious. Now that I was Harry, luck had to turn in my favour. Harry was a name that had never known defeat!

Herodotus continues the story of the Lydians: according to his account, the famine continued and King Atys finally realized that games were not in themselves a solution but simply an endless deferral of the moment of truth. So he made a decision. He divided the Lydian people into two groups by drawing lots. (Games of chance had become an addiction.) One group was to leave the kingdom and the other to remain with him. Atys was to be king of those chosen to stay in Lydia, and placed his son Tyrrhenus at the head of those who were to leave.

Tyrrhenus and his people travelled to Smyrna where they built ships and put out to sea. In time, they were to find new homes where they would prosper. Those who stayed behind in Lydia were conquered by the Persians and enslaved.

27

WE FIND A DEAD BODY

The next day, when me and the Midget were finally allowed to go down to the swimming pool, we found someone had got there before us. Floating among the leaves, stiff as a board, was a huge toad.

'I'm not going in there anymore,' said the Midget.

I used the net to fish out the toad. It was dead, its feet splayed, ready to be put on the barbecue.

Toads are vile, horrid creatures. Consider their beady eyes, cruel and black as obsidian. Consider their cold, clammy skin covered with ridges and pustules, the webbing between their toes, the almost human agility of their back legs . . .

'Once upon a time we were just like that toad,' I said.

'Don't start . . .' said the Midget.

'No, it's true, thousands of years ago. We lived in the ocean and we crawled out to try our luck on land. First we stuck our heads out, then we crawled out and lay on the beach for a while.'

'I'm telling mamá.'

'Some species stayed in the water and they're still aquatic, some got used to both and they became amphibians, like toads, who spend half their time in the water and the other half on land. If they stay in one place for too long, they die, like this one.'

'Can a toad drown?'

'This one obviously saw the pool and jumped in thinking it was a pond or a lake and then he realized he was stuck. Ponds and lakes have a bank, so you can go in gradually and get out gradually. Swimming pools are different – either you're in or you're out. And toads don't know how to use ladders.'

'We have to bury him.'

'You're right.'

'But first we have to hold a wake for him. Grandma Matilde says the wake is the most important part.'

'She only says that because she likes parties.'

'*Abuela* says you have a wake for someone to make sure the person is dead and not just asleep.'

'That's just an old wives' tale. How could anyone sleep with all their relatives bawling in their ear?'

'What's the difference between a wake and a vigil?'

'None, I think.'

'It has to be that at a wake, they're trying to wake the dead person and at a vigil they're just . . . they just vigil. Are you sure it's dead? What if it's just asleep?'

I picked the toad up by one leg, dangling it in front of the Midget's face. He ran off howling and only stopped when he got to a safe distance.

'Actually, he looks a lot like you,' I said.

'Liar!' the Midget yelled from afar.

We picked a shady spot at the foot of a tree. I went and found a spade in the shed and started digging a hole. While I was digging, I went on explaining to the Midget all the stuff Señorita Barbeito had taught us with her illustrations and the documentary, about how after the first amphibians, species evolved who could only absorb oxygen directly from the atmosphere and live on land, and about specialized habitats and stuff like that. The Midget glared at me suspiciously because he couldn't believe that all vertebrates shared common characteristics.

'Frogs have a sense of taste just like hens, honest, I swear. If you peel the skin off a chimpanzee it looks just like a huge frog, they even smell the same. You're lucky you have a big brother to explain all this stuff to you.'

As a rule, reality and all its trappings are more improbable than any fiction. What writer would have dreamed up the Komodo dragon, or tonsils or the weird way we go about reproducing? What imagination could have thought of having coral reefs made by tiny animals excreting calcium from their bodies? Who would have the nerve to create a world like ours, ruled over by the descendants of toads and frogs and salamanders and newts?

During the digging and the burial, the Midget said nothing; he listened to what I was saying, a gleam of suspicion in his eyes. But in the end, something I said must have got through to him, because after we had levelled off the grave, he placed stones on the little mound and asked me if toads go to heaven too.

28

A PEACEABLE INTERREGNUM

The weekend slipped by peacefully. An outsider watching us would merely have witnessed the Vicente family in blissful *dolce far niente*, making the most of the sunshine, the grounds, the swimming pool and enjoying the gastronomic holy trinity of the Argentine middle class: *asados* (barbecued meat), pasta (store bought, obviously, since mamá never set foot in the kitchen) and *facturas* (pastries).

A more attentive eye would probably have noticed that mamá and papá left the *quinta* with bizarre frequency for periods of no more than fifteen minutes, sometimes in the Citroën, sometimes on foot, but never together. (When they needed to phone someone, it was safer to use a payphone rather than the phone in the *quinta*.) And if this attentive eye were accompanied by a keen ear, it might decide that the Vicente family's habit of constantly asking each other blatantly obvious questions (What's your name? When were you born? What are your parents' names? What's your brother's name?) was some private family game whose rules were incomprehensible to the general public.

Of the events that took place during those days, a few deserve to be recorded; for example, Papá started to grow a moustache. After three days he had a perceptible shadow on his upper lip which, to me and the Midget, looked like a respectable moustache, but mamá said it looked like papá had been drinking the Midget's Nesquik and forgotten to wipe his mouth. On Sunday morning, the three men of the house stood in front of the bathroom mirror. Papá David declared himself satisfied with his moustache and, taking a pair of scissors, began to shape it. Harry, his first-born, bewailed his own smooth face and declared his desire to grow a thin moustache in the style of Mandrake the magician as soon as possible. Simón, the younger son, pronounced himself perfectly content with his fresh-faced, clean-shaven appearance, in keeping with his television idol, Simon Templar, and asked why Templar was the only saint he'd ever seen who didn't have a beard or a moustache.

There had been three games of Risk, the results of which require no comment. I had time to reread the book about Houdini and to come up with some ideas about my future, which I'll talk about later.

The Vicente family's visit to the local church for midday mass was an event in itself. As far as I could remember, I had never been in a church in my life, except for baptisms and weddings. Consequently I knew nothing whatever of the peculiar rites of the Catholic mass. Worse still, what might have been an adventure became a sort of torture as soon as we started to get ready. Mamá had got it into her head that the Vicente family was very devout, so she had us repeat the words of the Our Father, the Creed and the Hail Mary both in the *quinta* and again in the car, because as soon as we got to the church we had to be able to pretend to follow the ceremony with the confidence of committed believers.

Both my parents had been raised Catholic and both, in time, had lapsed. Papá had put his faith in the laws of man while mamá devoted herself to the laws of science, thereby distancing herself from the sanctimonious superciliousness of grandma Matilde. Together they had agreed that the Midget and I should be raised in complete and utter ignorance of all things religious. I suppose they thought they were doing us a favour, but growing up differently, we had real trouble dealing with commonplace concepts like heaven and hell. Our lack of reliable information about our eligibility for membership of certain clubs caused us occasional distress. And our meagre understanding of the central articles of the Catholic faith also contributed to my sense of being a fish out of water.

I remember that one Holy Week, the magazine I got every Thursday, *Anteojito*, came with a free poster depicting the Stations of the Cross. I burned the poster and flushed the ashes down the toilet to dispose of the evidence. The idea that I was supposed to pin this graphic depiction of torture and death on my wall seemed to me as obscene as if someone had suggested decorating my room with pictures of the inner workings of Auschwitz.

But my most traumatic experience came when I watched *The Miracle of Marcelino*, an old movie I caught on Channel 9 one night. Marcelino is an orphan boy taken in by the monks of the local monastery. One day he's up in the attic, looking for something, when suddenly he hears a voice asking for water. Marcelino looks around but he can't see anyone, because there's no one in the room except him. The voice is coming from a huge crucifix on the wall, where the wooden figure of Christ is asking him for a drink.

The worst thing about the movie was that, at the end, when Marcelino dies, the fat monk cries tears of joy and the bells ring out to celebrate the fact that the boy had been 'chosen' by the wooden doll. (The film, I should point out, ignores the basic fact that wood expands when it gets wet. With all the water he was drinking, there wouldn't be a cross strong enough to hold up a fat Christ.) Everything about the film made it seem as though we were supposed to rejoice because Marcelino was a saint and had been taken up into heaven, but all I could think was that Marcelino had been murdered by a big wooden statue and nobody was doing anything about it.

From then on, whenever me and my friends told each other horror stories, they would tell stories about Frankenstein and mummies and

Dracula, but whenever I mentioned the wooden Christ (oh, I nearly forgot, the statue rips one of his hands from the Cross so he can take the cup Marcelino offers him) there was a stony silence and they all looked at me like I was weird, which I suppose I was. After a while I learned to keep my mouth shut. My friends would wake up in the middle of the night, terrified they were being hunted by werewolves and headless horsemen. I'd wake up screaming, trying to escape from murderous T-shirts, ravenous Saturns and wooden Christs who clambered down from their Crosses and lumbered after me, trying to convince me that the only good child is a dead child.

On the subject of religion, the Midget had his own issues, but they were minor by comparison. He asked mamá if he could skip the line in the Our Father where it says, 'forgive us our trespasses as we forgive those who trespass against us', because he was too little to have done any trespassing. The thing that really worried him about Catholicism was the concept of the resurrection of the flesh; I don't know exactly what he imagined the phrase meant, but I have a pretty good idea.

And so we arrived at the village church with quavering hearts, determined to play the part of the devout Vicente family to the hilt. Papá was in his Sunday best, mamá was wearing a tailored trouser suit and me and the Midget were wearing the matching shirts and ties we usually wore under our white school smocks, an outfit I loathed with every atom in my body. The church, built on a corner of the main square, was as unremarkable as the village. Clearly everyone in the village went to midday mass on Sundays, since we had to park the Citroën two blocks away.

After the first few minutes of panic, I was bored stiff. Whenever we were supposed to do something, mamá would squeeze my leg and I'd say the Creed or whatever it was I was supposed to say. The rest of the time was just spent standing up when everyone else stood up and kneeling down when everyone knelt.

I know that the Midget, for his part, was profoundly affected by his first time at mass. He had been so thoroughly instructed in the simple art of making the sign of the Cross (which he practised over and over, even though, like most kids his age, he couldn't tell his left from his right), that the sign that begins and ends the mass made a profound and lasting impression on him. Like Pavlov's dog, the Midget had been prepared to make that sign whenever he was told to, what he was not prepared for was the sight of hundreds of people all making it at once. The combination of the mysterious, cabbalistic nature of the gesture, and the sight of all these people performing it simultaneously so astonished the Midget that his eyes popped out of his head as if he'd just seen water turned into wine. I suspect that, for the first time, he felt part of something bigger than the sacred family unit, something that both transcended and included us.

When we got back to the *quinta*, there was another dead toad in the pool. I cursed my lack of foresight and resolved to do something so this wouldn't happen again, because I didn't believe that the only good toad was a dead toad – just the opposite.

The Midget asked if he could perform the last rites.

29

WE FIND OURSELVES ALONE

When we woke up on Monday at about noon, mamá wasn't there. Papá, in the dining room, had taken the old grandfather clock apart, laying the countless pieces over an old blanket, the dining-room table, even the sideboard. It looked as though Time itself had exploded, scattering tiny pieces all over the place.

The Midget made himself some Nesquik. I grabbed a banana and went out into the grounds with the book about Houdini under my arm. (The Citroën was not parked in the usual place. Obviously mamá had taken it.) At noon papá turned on the news and turned up the volume so he could listen without having to stop working on the clock. I was some way away but even so, I couldn't help hearing. There was nothing new. Presidente this, Armada that, new economic measures, the military government's tireless struggle against traitorous subversion, evil guerrillas, the province of Tucumán, the dollar, same old same old. The day stretched out languidly, we didn't even have a proper lunch. If one of us felt hungry we just went to the fridge, grabbed whatever we could find and tried to find somewhere to eat that wasn't already covered with fragments of time. Cold chicken sat next to the packet of Nesquik, which sat next to the carcass of an empty packet of biscuits.

Given its strategic position in front of the TV, the coffee table was quickly covered in rubbish and dirty dishes. (By common consent, we decided: a dirty glass is a discarded glass. Every time one of us wanted a drink, we simply took a clean glass from the kitchen.) Over the hours, the dirty glasses piled up in strata with geological precision. I went into the pool whenever I felt like it and nobody nagged me about waiting an hour after eating. There was news followed by soap operas followed by cartoons and then the news again with more stories about the economy, more deaths, more about the man with the moustache who looked like a bad guy.

By now, papá seemed to have given up on the clock, whose entrails still lay strewn where they had fallen. Having decided to watch the news, he made some space on the coffee table for his bottle of Gancia and his ulcer medicine and began to soliloquize. 'Who cares what you have to say, you reactionary lackey,' he began, talking to the newsreader, a phrase that would have been interesting coming from the mouth of Hamlet in Act I, scene IV, when he first meets the ghost. 'I know more about what's going on in this country from watching *The Invaders* than listening to you,' he grumbled, still glaring at the newsreader. 'Go ahead! Whitewash the prisoners,' papá was now offering advice to the Minister of the Interior. 'Go on, whitewash the whole situation, there are no "Disappeared", there are no prisoners . . .'

Since by now the sun had set, and it was chilly, me and the Midget gravitated towards the warm glow of the TV screen. The Midget was conducting some experiment using empty bottles, dirty glasses, water, flour, and some screws and paintbrushes he'd taken from the tool shed. Whenever his experiment seemed to come to a standstill, to some scientific crossroads, some other item on the coffee table offered him a new way forward. The coffee table was laden with potential. Coke, for example, mixed with Nesquik, increased the potential for making froth.

I was rereading the Houdini book, looking for clues about how he managed his escapes. The book talked a lot about physical preparation and mental concentration but it was silent on the details of how each escape was done: the writer was probably an escape artist himself and had the greatest respect for professional secrecy. And so I found myself looking at the frontispiece, '*Harry practises his first escapes with the help of his brother Theo*', as if the illustration might give me some answer the text refused to divulge, and glanced over at papá with his Gancia, at the disembowelled grandfather clock, at the Midget, who had now whipped his experimental gloop until it was just right, and it occurred to me that maybe the illustration had given me the answer, maybe it was just a matter of starting.

I took off my belt (my belt that, apart from the usual buckle and holes, was made of some kind of elastic material: don't ask) and asked the Midget to tie me to my chair. His face and hands covered in flour, the Midget stared at me, trying to figure out if this was some kind of trap. I showed him the illustration in the book. He understood straight off.

The lackey newsreader must have said something terrible because papá leapt to his feet and stormed out into the garden where he could say any words he liked without having to restrain himself.

The Midget tied my hands behind my back. He made a slipknot and then wound the belt around my wrists a thousand times, pulling the elastic as tight as he could. He asked me if he had done it right. I struggled a bit, just enough to make sure the belt didn't come off at the first attempt.

'Wait, I forgot something,' he said. He grabbed the bottle of gloop he'd been stirring with an old paintbrush and painted some on my face.

Since I was tied up, there was nothing I could do. I asked him if he'd gone crazy. The gloop tasted like Nesquik-flavoured pizza dough.

'I'm whitewashing the prisoner. Didn't you hear what papá said? You have to whitewash the prisoners!'

We ate dinner in silence, just the three of us. Cold leftovers from the barbecue, with lots of mayonnaise. It was getting late. We surveyed our handiwork – the living room and dining room were a disaster area, stained chairs, scattered clock parts, organic waste – silently evaluating our complicity in this chaos. There never was a more perfect demonstration of the concept of entropy and the second law of thermodynamics (which concerns the dispersal of energy), establishing the tendency of systems to gradually move from order to disorder. And yet, our efforts had fallen short. All the chaos in the world had not been enough to conjure up mamá.

When, in despair, we finally decided to wash the dishes, we discovered there was no water. We had forgotten to fill the tank.

30

A DECISION AT DAWN

The whole region was divided into *quintas* – country houses owned by middle-class families that stood empty most of the year except in summer, or at weekends. There was nothing showy about them, the plots were small, and most of the houses, like ours, were simple bungalows, some of them half-finished, waiting for some spare cash, or for a new owner willing to take a chance on them. The roads were just dirt tracks; it was a five-minute drive from our gate to the nearest proper road. The plots were bounded by fences or by young poplars, their suppleness an attempt to soften the rigid boundaries.

At dawn, in the middle of the week, the silence that pervaded the *quinta* was as piercing as a siren. Sometimes you might hear cicadas, a burst of static from a radio carried on the wind, but in general the silence was total. It devoured everything, it rang in your ears, it was impossible to ignore.

When the television shut down for the night, the Midget's energy depleted rapidly and he quickly fell asleep. TV was the sun to him: he rose with it in the morning and set with it at night. His surrender marked the beginning of peace in the house. The other noises – dishes being washed, teeth brushed, bolts shot home – were muted, bedtime conversations were conducted in a whisper so as not to disturb the Midget's sleep, but also as a mark of respect for this silence.

I wasn't asleep yet, but I was tucked up in bed with my book in my hand. It was just then that I heard the Citroën calling to me from beyond the silence. When everything else was silent, the engine of the Citroën could be heard half a mile away. It sounded like an ordinary car bogged down in sand, its wheels spinning uselessly.

I heard the gate, then mamá and papá whispering.

Five minutes later, mamá came up to see us. The Midget was fast asleep, his face deformed from being pressed against his plastic Goofy.

Mamá sat on the bed and told me she'd bought me the new issue of *Superman*, but it had been confiscated by customs (which meant that papá wanted to read it first). I kissed her, genuinely grateful. Back then I was a Superman kid. Superman fans liked superhuman powers, the brightly coloured costumes, the troubling presence of Lois Lane; we waited for each fortnightly issue of the Mexican edition with a religious fervour and despised Batman fans, who we considered behind the times.

Mamá looked over at the Midget and asked if he had given me much trouble. Actually, I said, he was behaving himself pretty well, given the circumstances. He was bearing his privations with a stoicism we never realized he was capable of. Mamá nodded. She asked how I was bearing up. I sighed. I didn't want to be more Midget-like than the Midget but the truth was I missed everything – I missed Bertuccio, I missed the girl in my English class I had a crush on. (Her name was Mara and she was prettier than a Barbie doll.) I missed my bed and my pillow, my books and my bike; I missed my Airfix planes, my fortress with the movable drawbridge and the model Stuka my grandparents had given me; I missed my drawing pads and my drawings, my sailboat and my battery-powered speedboat; I missed my remote controlled Mercedes and the few Matchbox cars that had survived my brother, my fibreglass bow and arrow, my collection of *Nippur de Lagash* comics, my Editorial Novaro magazines and the Beatles record that Ana gave me when she got tired of us calling and begging her to play it over the phone.

I told mamá I was fine.

She asked me about the book I was reading. I told her where I'd found it and showed her Pedro's signature and the postcard from Beba and China, the glue that held together my theories about the previous tenants. The truth was I felt sorry for Pedro. I assumed he was devastated at losing his book on Houdini; I was particularly sensitive to losing things. But mamá demolished my theory, suggesting that maybe Pedro had done it on purpose, maybe he had left the book and the letter as a welcome present for me, hypothesizing a chain of gifts that stretched back to the kid who had lived in the *quinta* before Pedro (what had Pedro's present been?) and forward to me, because at some point we would leave and I should think about the boy who might come here after me. Alluding to our Spartan circumstances, I pointed out that for me to leave something, I had to have something in the first place. Mamá shot me a look, the look that means she's thinking this kid is going to grow up to be a lawyer, took the book from my hands and looked at it, trying to find some way to change the subject.

Houdini was staring her in the face. 'Houdini the magician?' she asked, proffering the carrot of an easy response.

But I volleyed the ball firmly back into her court. 'Houdini wasn't a magician, he was an escape artist. It's not the same at all. That's what I'm going to be when I grow up, an escape artist!'

Since the uncertainties of the present weighed heavily on me, I had been spending a lot of time thinking about my future. The idea of becoming an escape artist struck me as clearly as a vision: once the notion was firmly planted in my brain, all my worries disappeared. Now I had a plan, something that would, in the near future, make it possible to tie up the loose ends of my circumstances. I imagined that Houdini himself had done much the same thing. Making his

95

choice made it possible for him to rearrange the jigsaw pieces of his life, giving meaning to each individual piece (leaving his native Hungary, the longing for transcendence of his father, the rabbi, the poverty, his physical prowess) and, by fitting the pieces together differently, turn it into something new.

Mamá looked at the illustration of the Chinese Water Torture Cell, then stared at me as if trying to gauge how serious I was. I had gone through phases of wanting to be a fireman and an astronaut, which mamá had ignored, knowing they were just passing whims. Later I had wanted to be a doctor, an architect, a marine biologist, choices she approved of since they meant I would go to university. Mamá had a tendency to think that any career choice was valid if you could get a doctorate in it. Given there was no such thing as a Ph.D. in escape artistry, I knew there was trouble ahead.

'It looks dangerous,' she said, looking at the illustration again.

'That's the whole point.'

'There's nothing wrong with danger, as long as you take all possible precautions.'

'Public transport is dangerous,' I said.

'And being a TV repair man,' she said.

'And living in Argentina,' I said.

'So you called yourself Harry after Houdini?' she said, sidestepping the subject.

'Where did you come up with the name Flavia?'

'I don't think I can tell you.'

'That's not fair.'

'Life isn't fair. It may be beautiful, but it's not fair. So what's with this sarcophagus?'

'Houdini used to get inside all chained up, then they'd throw the trunk in the water. He'd be in there for ages, but he never drowned.'

'Because he carefully calculated the air.'

'You don't calculate air, you breathe it.'

'What I mean is that he knew how much air he had when he was in the trunk, so he knew how long he could stay underwater. If you really want to be an escape artist, you'll need to be able to calculate too.'

'OK then, I've changed my mind. Do bus drivers have to calculate things?'

'Journeys.'

'Archaeologists?'

'Years.'

'Nurses?'

'Doses.'

'I could be an escape artist and you could be my assistant.'

'For a reasonable price. Let's talk figures.'

She kissed me, tucked me in and told me that she loved me. I must have fallen asleep in her arms. My sun was different from the Midget's.

Señora Vicente was a very good mother.

31

A FOOLPROOF PLAN

That night another toad drowned in the swimming pool. Without even waiting for breakfast, me and the Midget decided to put a stop to this.

It was tempting to create a physical barrier to stop the toads from getting into the water, a solution as drastic as it would be effective. But I didn't want to alter the course of their lives, to usurp the pre-eminent role of Destiny. Besides, the swimming pool might be of crucial importance to the toads without my knowing – it might be full of their eggs.

Consequently we opted for a middle way, which also had the benefit of being practical. Using an old wooden board we found in the shed and a length of wire, we managed to make a diving board that worked in reverse. Whereas diving boards were designed for men to launch themselves into the water, our reverse diving board would be used by toads to launch themselves onto dry land.

I used the wire to attach the board between the handrails of the ladder. This way, one end of the plank stuck out into the air. The other end dipped below the surface of the water.

Until now, if a toad fell into the pool it was bound to die. It would swim around, exhausted, searching vainly for a way out, crashing into the sides of the pool until finally it went under. The reverse diving board offered the toads the way out that they hadn't had up until then. If they swam up to it, they could clamber onto the plank and breathe and they could climb up to the other end and leap into the long grass whenever they wanted, as often as they wanted.

Some of them would still die. They wouldn't notice the plank, or they wouldn't understand its potential. But the lucky toads would use the reverse diving board to save themselves, and the cleverest toads, hearing the word 'Eureka' in their tiny brains, would save themselves a second time, and a third time. Their offspring (I was still a Lamarckian back then) would be born with an innate 'Eureka' and they would know what to do, what to look for whenever they fell into this swimming pool which had proved so lethal to their forebears.

'When you have no choice but to change, you change. That's what Señorita Barbeito told me. It's called the principle of necessity. The toads have to change so they won't die. All they need is a chance,' I explained to the Midget.

'D'you think that we're as disgusting to God as toads are to me?' asked the Midget.

'Right, that's it,' I said, giving the wire a last twist.

All that was needed now was time.

32

CYRUS AND THE RIVER

When one of his favourite horses drowned while attempting to cross it, Cyrus the Great, king of the Persians, furious with rage, vowed to humble the river Gyndes. He stopped his army, who were marching on Babylonia, and forced his soldiers to divert the course of the river, digging 360 trenches to channel the water away. Cyrus wanted the waters to dissipate onto the plain, pooling in swamps and marshes, and for the original riverbed to run dry. The extent of the humiliation he inflicted on the river was precise: at its deepest point the river Gyndes was not to come above a woman's knee.

This story is usually told to emphasize the power of Cyrus, the king who mutilated a river, who had his soldiers work like slaves to avenge a horse. The leader of the most powerful army in the world, whose hail of arrows could eclipse the sun, Cyrus would have punished the sun for its envy, or the moon, or the seas.

My response to the story of Cyrus was always different. Even as a kid I thought Cyrus was ignorant and stupid. A river can't murder someone, let alone be malicious; a river is just a river. It was stupid to jeopardize his campaign on a whim, making his men run the risk of injuring themselves as they dug the trenches, reducing their effectiveness with their bows and arrows and their swords. The story doesn't say as much, but some of the soldiers must have died during the digging, making his revenge all the more costly. No horse would ever receive a more bizarre tribute.

Over the years, my view of Cyrus ceased to be quite so black and white. At first Cyrus was an exotic prince, with braids in his beard, who spoke a barbaric language and whose decisions could be understood only in the context of the Olympian logic of great kings and warriors. Then time passed (there are rivers that even Cyrus could not stop) and when I went back and read the story of Cyrus again, he didn't feel alien or unfathomable. He seemed like a lot of people I knew, people with whom I shared a human frailty: the tendency to accumulate power without wondering why or how to use it. People who have Cyrus's power (military, political, economic) always forget that with power come responsibilities, they prefer to believe that evil exists only in other people. Diverting a river is easier than facing the truth; Cyrus did not want to acknowledge the fact that his horse would not have drowned if he had not forced it to try and cross the river.

I've known a lot of Cyruses in my life. Some of them now only appear in books nobody ever reads. Others walk the same streets, breathe the same air as we do. And though they now live in palaces and people pay them tribute, time will do to them what it did to Cyrus. Men who accumulate power and misuse it are like coins with only one face, they have no currency in any market.

I was thinking about the story of Cyrus as we worked on the reverse diving board. The fact that there was no obvious connection between the two ends of the plank did not mean no connection existed; we don't see the network of roots that keeps the tree anchored in the ground, but it's there just the same.

But I admit, I came to no conclusions. I like to think that the way in which others had forcibly diverted the course of my life back then had conferred on me a compassion beyond my years. I like to think that I was better than Cyrus, that I assumed responsibility for the death of the toads and respected the existence of the river. I like to think I was trying to act according to the wisdom of nature, doing no more than nature might have done in toppling a tree whose branches might dip into the swimming pool. At the time I thought none of these things, preoccupied as I was by *The Invaders* and Houdini, but that does not mean these things did not contribute to my actions. If I have learned anything in life, it is that we do not think only with our brains. We think with our bodies too, with our emotions; we think with our concept of time.

On the face of it, the fact that, a few pages later, Cyrus dies and has his head cut off and plunged into a bath of blood has no connection with the story of the river Gyndes. And yet something tells me that the truth is not so simple.

We see with more than our eyes; we think with more than our brain.

33

WHAT THEY KNEW

I knew we were in some kind of danger. I knew that the military *junta* was hunting down all those who opposed it, in particular self-confessed Peronists and/or those who held left-wing views – a broad category that included papá, mamá and the 'uncles'. I knew that if mamá and papá were caught, they'd be arrested, just as papá's partner had been arrested. And I knew that there was a risk of lethal force. The bullets that killed Tío Rodolfo had not come from his own gun, if in fact he had actually been carrying one when he died.

But danger was a secondary consideration. Papá had already disappeared for a couple of days once before, some time in 1974 or 1975, at the peak of the Triple A's activities, only to reappear safe and sound and convinced that things had calmed down. Life went on. Nothing serious ever happened. Political stuff. People campaign, go on marches and demonstrations, sing songs and make speeches. Sometimes they get a round of applause, sometimes a brickbat.

This time things were clearly more serious – after all, this was the first time that me and the Midget had become caught up in it – but not *really* serious. For the time being we all had to disappear for a few days. After that, we'd go back to our house, back to our lives and everything would go on as before, with or without the military.

What bothered me, my main preoccupation, was the disruption to my daily life, the fact that I had been cut off from my games with Bertuccio, from my belongings (given that I no longer had access to them whenever and wherever I wanted to); cut off from my world, the streets, the neighbours, the local grocer, the guy at the local newsstand, my club; cut off from a universe of familiar sensations: the smell of my bed linen, the feeling of the floor beneath my feet when I got up, the taste of tap water, the sound of sawing and hammering drifting in from the patio, the sight of mamá's flowerbeds, the rough feel of the knobs on *my* TV.

I could pretend our time at the *quinta* was a spur of the moment holiday – after all, that first weekend we spent more time with papá and mamá than we had in months – but it was hard to forget that it was a holiday we had been forced to take. A holiday that is planned, that you dream about, is one thing. It was a very different matter to be forced to run away, forced to live somewhere else – however wonderful the *quinta* was – until the mists cleared and we got our own lives back.

For years, when I was living in Kamchatka, keeping watch for wild bears, I thought I was the one who had been forced to go through the long tunnel that was the winter of 1976 blindfolded. In time, I came to realize that mamá and papá had been almost as blind as I was. Their political beliefs were clear and unambiguous; they would never give them up. But before 24 March 1976, when the military coup occurred, they knew exactly what to expect. Afterwards, they didn't know what to expect anymore. (The dictatorship began on 24 March, Houdini was born on 24 March. Time is strange and everything occurs simultaneously.)

The advent of the dictatorship changed the rules of the game. Everywhere my parents looked they saw shadows. They knew the military *junta* were hunting them, just as they were hunting down their political comrades, but what they didn't know was what happened to those who were caught. They simply vanished into thin air. Their families searched for them, but in the police stations, the army barracks, the courts, everyone claimed to know nothing. No arrest warrants had been issued, no charges brought. Their names did not appear on any list of prisoners. A week after papá's partner was hauled away, nobody knew anything of his whereabouts.

These first months were the months of devastation. Many people thought that all they needed to do was retire from political activism and they would be spared. But they were dragged from their homes regardless. Public places – bars, cinemas, restaurants, theatres – were dangerous because a raid could occur any place, any time. Leaving the house without papers was dangerous because being unable to prove one's identity was sufficient reason to wind up in a police station. But leaving home carrying identity papers was more dangerous still. Once identified, there was no need to take someone to the police station; they were dragged away and – *poof* – they vanished into thin air.

Those who thought that the crackdown would abide by clear rules, observe defined limits, were mistaken. In early April, papá met up with Sinigaglia, a lawyer friend of his who told him, over a cup of coffee, that he believed things were going to get back to normal. Sinigaglia explained that the military's natural deference to order and discipline would force them to enact laws to legalize the repression, outlaw paramilitary groups and publish a list of prisoners. Papá thought that Sinigaglia's view was logical, but even so he advised him not to show his face in the courts at Tribunales. Sinigaglia dismissed his advice. He had been threatened a thousand times before, he said, and he was not about to give up defending political prisoners and applying for writs of habeas corpus. I remember Sinigaglia well. He was a tall man, ramrod straight, with Brylcreemed hair; his old-fashioned taste in suits made him look much older than he was. He always called me *pibe* (kid). What are you up to, *pibe*?

How are things, *pibe*? And he'd muss my hair, I suppose because he was fascinated by the unruly shock of hair so unlike his own.

Sinigaglia was the first to fall. They took him away in an unmarked car. I can imagine him as they pushed and shoved, worrying about creasing his carefully pressed suit and saying to me, see this, *pibe*? There's no need for this insolence, it's completely unnecessary.

Roberto was the next to go, on a morning when papá was not at the solicitor's office. If papá had been there, they would have taken him too. Ligia, papá's secretary, told him that the men who arrested Roberto took him away in an unmarked car. When he asked her to describe the men, Ligia said they were rude. They dragged the poor man away like a common criminal, said Ligia, another disciple of the old school.

Mamá felt a little safer. The union she headed up at the university described itself as non-aligned. Not only was it not Peronist, it had actively campaigned against Peronism during the elections. Feeling protected by the apolitical nature of her profession, and given her tendency to analyse everything in terms of rational propositions and scientific facts, mamá thought that she would be able to weather the storm without any difficulties.

But day after day, she heard the same stories about professors and students who had disappeared off the face of the Earth. Some, people said, had been hauled away, and the modus operandi was always the same, plain clothes officers armed to the teeth, in unmarked cars. Others simply disappeared and no one ever heard from them again. Now, roll calls were suddenly filled with the silence of people marked absent.

For papá and mamá, in those first days of April, the shadows began exactly at the boundaries of the *quinta*. The image of the desert island which mamá had suggested to make our life here easier now took on a life of its own and began to torment her, just as the wooden Christ had tormented the terrified Marcelino. Beyond the *quinta* there

106

was nothing but uncertainty – dangerous waters, impenetrable fog. They tried to phone certain people only to discover that the ground had opened and swallowed them up. Sometimes their phone calls went unanswered. Sometimes they were answered, but the voices at the other end of the line denied all knowledge of anything. What information they had was vague and incomplete. The assessments of the situation they heard didn't square with reality as they saw it. In the midst of this fog, it became increasingly difficult to know what to do, what to expect.

This was why mamá had gone back to work. She wanted to keep at least one line of communication open so they would know what was going on. In her laboratory, mamá could speak, ask questions, arrange meetings and organize a modest political course of action.

After a few days, fear began to take its toll on papá, and he too decided to go back to work. The question was what to do with us.

34

THE MATILDE PERMUTATION

One Saturday we set off with mamá to fetch grandma Matilde. The official story was that she was coming to spend the weekend with us and we would drive her home on Sunday evening. We didn't know, and nor did grandma, that the whole thing was a secret mission. Papá and mamá were testing us. They wanted to find out whether grandma could survive living in the same house with us. Had we been told what they were planning, we would have pointed out that it was just as dangerous, maybe more dangerous, to leave us to the tender mercies of grandma.

Grandma Matilde was one of those people who believed that her responsibilities as a parent lapsed on the day her children left home. In all the photos from mamá's wedding, she looks radiant under her big hat, but while everyone else in the photos is looking at the camera, grandma looks as though she is at her own private party. From that day on, grandma spent her time travelling the world, playing canasta with her friends, and getting involved in whatever charity event happened to come her way.

Once I read a *Mafalda* comic where Susanita – the little girl who's obsessed with finding a good husband, getting married and having a traditional family – explains one of her dreams of the future. In the dream, she's at a tea party with other posh women with fancy pastries and things. It's a charity event to raise money to buy polenta, rice 'and all that horrible garbage poor people eat'. I remember showing the comic to mamá and saying, 'Look, it's grandma Matilde when she was little.' Mamá gave a complicit giggle, but avoided actually saying something that would compromise her, and went back to reading her newspaper. Later on, when she thought she was alone, I heard her giggle as she was chopping onions, and I heard another giggle again as she went up to her bed. I think she probably giggled herself to sleep.

Grandma Matilde hardly ever phoned. She only ever showed up for our birthdays. Her presence made us all (including papá, obviously) slightly uncomfortable, especially when it came to gifts: we never worked out how to say thank you for the pair of socks or the underpants or the handkerchiefs which represented the full range of her ideas for presents. Whenever we had to go to her house – usually for her birthday – she spent the whole time making sure we didn't open the piano or ruck the rugs or put our feet up on the Louis-the-Something chairs.

Just the idea of grandma Matilde travelling in the Citroën made the long journey to and from the *quinta* worthwhile. Grandma said she'd prefer to hire a private car, but mamá said that was impossible, that she couldn't give grandma the address of the *quinta* for security reasons. Predictably, grandma was peeved. 'You don't even trust your own mother,' she protested. Mamá told her it wasn't about trust, it was about security; by not giving her the address she was protecting her. In the face of such a demonstration of filial love, anyone else might have surrendered, but this was grandma Matilde, so the battle was only just beginning. 'You don't trust my chauffeur?' she argued stubbornly. 'I've been using the same chauffeur for years!'

Grandma always stank of face cream and hairspray. She never went anywhere without jars of gunk and a huge black can of hairspray in her handbag. (I owe this information to the Midget.)

When mamá suggested she put a headband over her eyes and wear a pair of sunglasses to hide the blindfold, grandma raised the roof. 'You expect me to ruin this perfect hairdo which, I might add, I had to have done at eight o'clock on Saturday morning since it was the only available appointment?' (Grandma is the sort of person who goes to the salon to have her hair done even if she's going out to the country.) In that case, mamá told her, she would have to keep her head between her knees for the whole journey. Grandma immediately agreed to this, thinking that at least this way her hairdo would be spared. Me and the Midget knew better.

I'm sure that when Houston is training astronauts to withstand changes in gravity, NASA uses an old Citroën. The combination of the car's bizarre suspension and the springy seats subjects the body to a series of opposing forces which, I imagine, are pretty similar to shifting from gravity to zero gravity every minute. And if the person in the driving seat of the Citroën is impulsive – like mamá for example – the effect is multiplied a thousandfold.

Grandma had to spend the entire journey – more than an hour – staring at her shoes as she was buffeted from side to side, and thrown back against the seat every time mamá braked. It was more than even a veteran sailor could take. Me and the Midget giggled every time mamá brutally twisted the steering wheel, especially if grandma happened to be talking at the time, because her voice would be choked off as if someone was bouncing on her stomach; she sounded like Foghorn Leghorn.

But we giggled to ourselves, waiting for the inevitable. It came about halfway on the journey back to the *quinta*, when a truck pulled out of the side street before his light had turned green. Mamá was forced to brake sharply and grandma's hairdo crashed into the glove compartment.

Life may not be fair, but it has its moments.

35

THE EXPERIMENT FAILS

Grandma Matilde was not born to contend with nature. Once we had arrived at the *quinta*, she did not set foot in the grounds until it was time for her to go home. She couldn't stand the flies and the ants. She couldn't stand walking on the grass in her high heels. She couldn't stand the sun because it would ruin her complexion. She couldn't stand the toads: even the sound of their croaking made her shudder. To grandma Matilde, the swimming pool might as well have been the river Ganges, dark with ashes and corpses.

She wasn't much better inside the house. Grandma announced that the living room looked like a garage sale with cast-off furniture to be sold to the highest bidder. 'It's like a gypsy caravan in here,' she would mutter when she needed to express the full extent of her disgust.

But papá and mamá were determined to make the experiment work. Papá quickly gave up his place in the double bed and came to sleep in our room. We were thrilled, but for mamá it was a very different experience. Sharing a bed with grandma, with her face covered in gunk, must have been like sleeping next to a block of provolone cheese.

Worse still, grandma refused to set foot in the kitchen, because, as she saw it, she was a guest and the kitchen is the domain of the hostess. This did not, of course, stop her from commenting on the food mamá put on the table. While grandma was there, the usual dynamics of dinner changed completely. Usually, when mamá served dinner, papá would altruistically take the first bite, as a good husband should; I would mount a passive resistance and the Midget would swallow anything that was put in front of him like a hippopotamus in Hungry Hungry Hippos. But grandma's presence disrupted everything, resulting in conversations like this:

'What's this?' grandma would ask, poking at the brownish stew on her plate with a fork.

'It's goulash,' said mamá, a slight tremor in her voice.

'Goulash is a Hungarian dish,' papá explained, only for grandma to catch me out.

'And do you know what the word "goulash" means in Hungarian?'

'No, grandma.'

'It means warmed-up leftovers!'

Because although grandma stank of face cream and used too much hairspray, and although she was snobby and scheming, she was also intelligent and refined and she had a tongue like a cat-o'-nine-tails; she invariably stung you in more places than one.

Papá and mamá did their best to ward off disaster. Whenever it looked as though things might come to a head – when, for example, they allowed grandma to take over the television so that we couldn't watch *The Invaders* or cartoons, not even *Superpower Saturday* – they tried to make it up to us in order to preserve the delicate equilibrium. There were sudden offers to play Risk, promises of new comics and trips to the cinema. They offered us everything they had to hand and anything else was entered into the debit column, but by the time the sun set on Saturday, papá and mamá had frankly run out of credit. There was nothing left in the *quinta* for them to give us and we were beginning to suspect that a lot of the debts they had already run up would never be paid.

Then came dinner, and with it, the goulash.

Shortly afterwards we heard the half-time whistle. The home team retired to the dressing room two-nil down with a sense of impending disaster.

We said goodnight to mamá almost guiltily. We left her to the mercy of the lions. And of the provolone cheese.

We had always known that mamá and grandma Matilde didn't get on, but we had never seen them together over an extended period. At birthday parties, there were always other distractions, at least for us. In this respect, that weekend was a revelation. Mamá was clearly suffering from a Matilde overdose.

Against all our expectations, mamá turned out to have kryptonite of her own.

36

MONSTERS

It took a long time for us to get to sleep. What with papá having to sleep in our room, me and the Midget having to share a single bed and mamá in the clutches of grandma Matilde, it wasn't easy to relax. Under cover of darkness, the accusations flew.

'Grandma is unbearable,' I said.

'You think so?' papá asked, half-asleep.

'Grandma's got jars of smelly gunk in her handbag,' said the Midget, 'and she sprays Flit in her hair.'

'What if we wait for grandma to fall asleep and bring mamá in here with us?' I asked.

'You mean the two of you are prepared to venture into the monster's lair?'

'There's no such thing as monsters,' yelped the Midget, shrivelling like a prune behind me.

'There are some monsters I quite like,' I said. 'I feel kind of sad for Frankenstein. And Dracula in the old movies is funny. But the Mummy is scary.'

'Which one, Boris Karloff?'

'The one in *Titanes en el Ring*. Ana took me to see the film and I had to sleep with the light on that night.'

'Turn on the light!' whined the Midget.

'One time, when we were on holiday in Santa Rosa de Calamuchita, I thought I'd been bitten by a vampire,' I said. 'Do you remember me coming to wake you up?'

'I don't actually.'

'I found a strange mark on my neck, it looked like two bite marks right next to each other. The whole house was dark, everyone was in bed, the wind was howling . . .'

'Turn the light on!'

'And I went in and I was shaking you and crying "Papá, papá, I think a vampire bit me".'

Papá was laughing now.

'And you wouldn't even listen, I swear . . .'

'There's no such thing as monsters!'

'Oh, there is such a thing as monsters,' said papá, 'but usually they don't have fangs or bolts through their necks. A monster isn't someone who looks like a monster, it's someone who acts like a monster.'

'López Rega,' I said.

'For example.'

'Onganía, the Walrus.'

'That's two.'

'And grandma Matilde.'

'Hold on a minute! Don't go comparing apples and oranges!' said papá.

'Grandma's not a monster, she's nice!' the Midget protested.

'There are First Division monsters and then there's the rest,' said papá.

'But she's horrible to mamá,' I said.

'That doesn't mean she doesn't love her.'

'You can't love someone and be horrible to them.'

'That's not true. Lots of people are horrible to the people they love most.'

'Well, people like that must be crazy.'

'Grandma's not crazy!' wailed the Midget.

'I know it doesn't sound logical, but that's the way it is,' said papá. 'There are people who try to control the people they love, or try to make them feel insecure or inferior or unworthy. They can be very hurtful, but they're sad people. They're afraid of being abandoned, they're afraid of not being loved.'

'Grandma's afraid mamá will abandon her?'

'In a way.'

'Well, in that case, she doesn't know mamá.'

'On that point we can agree.'

'Of course grandma knows mamá, stupid!' yelled the Midget. 'She carried mamá in her tummy!'

I asked papá about grandma Matilde's life (people usually assume their grandparents were always as old as they are now) and he told me some things. What he told me then, and what I learned when I was living in Kamchatka, I'll move onto next.

37

THE ICE MAIDEN

On the essentials, all the histories agree: grandma Matilde was not mamá's mother.

I'm not denying that she was mamá's biological mother. As the Midget had pointed out, Matilde had carried mamá in her womb and that was all the labour required for her to earn the title. But the histories point to a more subtle distinction. A woman can conceive, gestate, give birth to and suckle a child; ensure the child is clothed, fed and educated, attend school concerts; she can choose a university, put a roof over the child's head and walk her down the aisle to the altar that marks the beginning of her adult life. Most women who accomplish these things will, in fact, be fully qualified mothers. It is, however, possible for someone to fulfil all the requirements without showing the slightest enthusiasm. Someone who keeps up appearances for the sake of appearances but without the passion we consider inseparable from the task of motherhood.

My grandfather was a timid, conscientious man, overshadowed by my grandmother's histrionics and consumed by the need to accede to her every whim. Everything points to the fact that he lived simply to make money. When he had made a lot of money, he wanted to retire and enjoy it, but my grandmother wouldn't let him; the very idea seemed to her grossly irresponsible.

If grandpa felt any affection for his wife, he suppressed it, because grandma didn't believe displays of affection had any role in the marital equation. And his love for his daughter he measured out with an eye-dropper, invariably behind grandma's back, since she considered affection to be tasteless and inimical to a good education. My grandfather died at the age of forty-eight when mamá was seventeen. Though he was still a young man, the combination of too much work and too little love often proves toxic. When his body finally cried enough, he left two thriving businesses – a Chrysler concession and a garage – and hefty accounts in various banks. For her part, my grandmother considered that her husband had fulfilled his part of the deal and got on with her own life.

After his death, grandma was rarely at home. She travelled a lot, mostly in Europe. When she was in Buenos Aires, she would go out every day, to have tea, to go to the theatre, to play canasta, or on a 'date' with one of her long list of suitors – many of whom were young enough to have dated mamá. Grandma made no attempt to be discreet. Young men would call and collect her at the house, or ring the doorbell and leave flowers, chocolates, necklaces. In the beginning, mamá often opened the door to them, but she finally gave up and after that, opening the door became the sole responsibility of grandma's maid Mary.

Grandma was too smart not to realize that many of her suitors saw her as a good catch – properties, businesses, bank accounts – which is why she never accepted another proposal of marriage. But she wasn't sensitive enough to notice how much the age of her suitors bothered mamá. My parents had already told me that, whenever mamá had boyfriends over, grandma liked to make a dramatic entrance, wearing a dress copied from Brigitte Bardot or Claudia Cardinale. The quarrels between grandma and mamá were noisy, loud and futile. Grandma would fiercely defend her right to dress however she pleased, go wherever she pleased and see whomever she pleased.

Grandma, I think, saw mamá as a rival and it was a competition she was not inclined to lose. Mamá only wanted a mother.

It was at this point that mamá decided marriage was her only way out. Her famous fiancé was short, boring and almost penniless, ensuring grandma wouldn't flirt with him. But then papá showed up: he made mamá laugh, he listened to her, he loved rather than judged her and mamá realized that she had found much more than a way out.

According to papá, the night she brought him home to dinner to meet the family, mamá was a bundle of nerves. Throughout the meal, papá, in spite of grandma's insistence, refused to call her Mati, but addressed her as señora, a word that stung grandma since it reminded her of her position and her age. But grandma could not ignore the enthusiastic blessing the rest of the family bestowed on papá. With the exception of grandma, everyone else had noticed how happy mamá was when she was with him.

I realize that this portrait of grandma Matilde is hardly flattering. But she is much more than the monster I once thought she was; she is also the saddest person in this story. Maybe this is the moment to say that – if they do not know about her grief – everyone these days knows who my grandmother is. They have read about her in the newspapers, seen her on TV, supported her struggle and that of the 'mothers of the disappeared' on the Plaza de Mayo. I would not have believed it myself had I not witnessed her transformation, watched her grow old and full of light. It was she, in Kamchatka, who told me many of the things I've just told you. My grandmother, the woman who admitted she had never been able to be a mother to mamá, became her daughter, as though mamá had given birth to her. My grandmother says that mamá saved her life.

And I'm not talking about that Sunday night when the Midget tried to kill her.

38

THE DEADLY SURPRISE

By lunchtime on Sunday, mamá and papá had already been forced to admit defeat. It was obvious that there was no way grandma Matilde was going to stay, given that she clearly found the *quinta* about as hospitable as the Amazon jungle. Nor could they imagine her allowing us to stay in her house, full of jars of face cream, cut-glass animals and immaculate rugs. As for me and the Midget, though we knew nothing about their plans, our opinion of grandma Matilde was unequivocal. The only time we saw the grown-ups was at mealtimes. The rest of the day we spent as far away from her as possible.

We had a light lunch, after which papá planned to drive grandma back to her house. I remember a conversation about the state of the country which shocked me because grandma Matilde's opinions seemed wildly radical. If it were up to her, she said, the government would disband the army, lynch the bankers and distribute the wealth of the country equally between everyone. (This was what grandma used to be like: regardless of the circumstances or the subject of the conversation, grandma had to be noticed; she had to be more extremist, more charming, more youthful, more frivolous than anyone else.) The only problem, she admitted, was that, if the government did these things, she would have to do without champagne, and well, champagne is so *delightful* . . .

The Midget, who had already left the table by then, came back and whispered to me that the reverse diving board still wasn't working: there was another dead toad floating in the pool. Exasperated, I asked for permission to be excused and was refused. Mamá wanted me to help her clear the table – something grandma could easily have helped with if she had been a different grandmother – and by the time we had finished, I'd forgotten about the toads and we were already saying our goodbyes. Grandma, stinking of face cream, kissed us and asked if we had seen her handbag. The Midget, the epitome of politeness, said, 'I'll get it.'

The sound of the Citroën had already faded by the time I went out to the swimming pool. I couldn't see anything. I looked carefully, dragging the net across the surface. There was no toad. I shouted to the Midget to tell him he'd been wrong. He said he wasn't, there had been a dead toad but that he had recovered the body himself.

'Where did you put it? Let's bury it.'

'We can't.'

'Why not?'

'Because it's gone.'

'Have you buried it already?'

'I put it somewhere.'

'What do you mean you put it somewhere?'

So he told me.

Mamá was up to her elbows in lukewarm water, washing the dishes very slowly as though being forced to live with grandma had sapped all her strength. When she saw me in the kitchen she asked if I would help her to dry, that way it would get done more quickly. I said sure, of course I would, but first I needed to tell her something. Something important.

'The Midget played a practical joke on grandma,' I told her.

'Saints alive!'

'Have you noticed how sometimes there's a dead toad floating in the pool?'

Though she still had her back to me, mamá froze.

The Midget was hiding behind the back door, watching, more outside than in, keeping a safe distance.

'What did he do with the toad?' mamá asked in a tone of voice that suggested that she was about to use the Glacial Stare.

'He put it in grandma's handbag. Just now. She's just gone off with it.'

Mamá turned to face us. I could feel the Midget go rigid behind me, he was ashen.

She stared at us for a moment, looked from him to me, back to him, back to me and then she burst out laughing.

'She'll have a heart attack!' said mamá, tears running down her cheeks, still flushed from the steam.

I gave a sigh of relief. The Midget, sensing that his death sentence had been commuted, appeared in the doorway, doing the stupid little dance he always did when he thought he was the cleverest kid in the universe.

'She'll have a heart attack!' mamá said again, wiping her face with a tea towel.

Just then she realized the significance of what she had said. She thought about grandma's high blood pressure, the fatty goulash, grandma's morbid fear of strange animals. Grandma, she remembered, kept her keys in her coat pocket rather than in her handbag so it was likely that she would not open it until she was on her own and needed one of her jars of gunk. She realized that 'she'll have a heart attack' might be more than an expression of surprise: it might be prophetic. When she rushed into the living room, the Midget, assuming she intended to kill him, took off.

Mamá grabbed the phone, dialled, hung up, redialled, hung up again. She hoped grandma would hear the ringing as soon as she got home and answer before she had a chance to open her handbag.

The Midget was nowhere to be found.

Much later, I found him in the grounds, hiding behind a tree next to the fence, as far from the house as he could get. He refused to move until mamá came to him with a white flag and a promise that, for the second time in his short life, she would let him live.

39

ACCIDENT AND EMERGENCY

The hospital was only a few blocks from grandma's house. It was an old but well-maintained building that stood on a corner, though it was not in fact a hospital. According to papá, it was a clinic.

'A hospital is a place where everyone is treated free of charge,' said papá breathlessly, as we rushed through the front doors and up the steps, taking them two or even three at a time. 'This is a clinic. Clinics are not public, they're private. If you want these people to cure you, it'll cost you an arm and a leg.'

An expression the Midget would have loved if he hadn't been sound asleep in papá's arms.

The accident and emergency room was on the left. Actually it looked more like a crowded corridor than a room. There were people waiting to be called – I remember a man in a grey shirt with a blood-soaked tea towel wrapped around his hand – there were metal drip-stands everywhere, making it difficult to get through, boxes of supplies and fat nurses with faces that would turn milk.

Grandma was at the far end of the room, lying on a stretcher. The buttons of her blouse were open and you could see her bra – it was disgusting. She was hooked up to a drip and a bunch of machines that made pinging noises and had colour screens. She also had tubes up her nose. I figured she was supposed to breathe through them, but grandma was breathing through her mouth, almost gasping.

Something had happened to her hairdo. It still had the same shape, the same size, the same artificial shine, but it looked out of place, as though the top of her skull had been rotated several degrees so that it completely covered one ear while the other ear was uncovered.

'What are you doing here?' grandma asked when she saw us.

I turned on my heel and headed for the door but papá grabbed me by the scruff of the neck and pulled me to him.

Mamá ignored this daunting question and took grandma's hand in hers. 'What did the doctor say?'

'A lot of rubbish, like doctors always do. Just stay calm, señora. Your condition is stable, señora. We won't know anything until we know something, señora. I don't know why they don't give me a pacemaker. And they're planning to discharge me today!'

A possible reconstruction of events might run as follows: papá dropped grandma at her front gate and waited until he saw her go inside before turning the Citroën around to head back to the quinta. Grandma went in via the garage door and, stepping into the kitchen, decided to make herself some tea with honey when suddenly she heard the phone ringing at the far end of the house. She wondered who could be calling her at this hour. As she headed towards the living room, handbag still over her shoulder, she decided to take off her false eyelashes and put them back in their case.

The case was in her handbag.

When mamá dialled for the nth time and the phone was engaged, she knew that something had happened. She tried again a couple of times and then made us go out and stand by the gate so we could let her know the minute we heard the rumble of the Citroën in the distance. When papá arrived, she made him let her drive, piled us into the back like sacks of potatoes and shot off back towards grandma's house.

Luckily it was Sunday night and there was no one else on the roads at midnight. Of the journey itself, I need only say that there was a point when I thought that the entire frame of the car was about to disintegrate and we would be left hurtling along, sitting on the bare chassis.

Mamá had a set of keys to grandma's house. She rushed through the door and found the lights on, the handbag lying on the floor, the phone off the hook and the murder weapon lying green and stiff on the rug. Since there was no sign of grandma, mamá assumed she had managed to get out of the house by herself and decided to try the private clinic where grandma had been treated while grandpa was still alive.

According to Néstor, the trusted chauffeur of whose virtues we had heard so much, grandma had called him and in two seconds managed to explain the situation. (By the time they had finished talking, grandma was not able – or could not be bothered – to hang up the phone, which explained why it had been permanently engaged.) Néstor acted swiftly. By the time he arrived at her house, grandma was waiting for him at the door. He helped her to walk to the reception desk of the clinic. Grandma began banging on the counter and, with her customary theatrical flair, said, 'You'd think they'd get a move on, *che*, I'm having a heart attack here!'

It was not as serious as that, but her fear was genuine. Grandma, kept in for observation, lay on a trolley, waiting for the results of her tests.

Mamá gave papá the keys to grandma's house and told him to go back, turn off the lights and tidy the place up. The order was unspoken, but papá understood: she wanted him to get rid of the murder weapon so that grandma wouldn't find it there when she got home.

So papá headed off, carrying the Midget, who was still asleep – or pretending to be asleep to avoid the wrath of the grown-ups.

'Why don't you all go?' asked grandma. 'I've already sent Néstor to fetch Luisa. She should be here any minute. I think I'd prefer that. The *quinta* is so far away and by the time . . .'

'I am not leaving here with you in this condition. I wouldn't dream of it!' mamá said firmly. 'Which doctor did you see?'

'That one over there, with the face like an enema bag,' said grandma.

Mamá went to talk to the doctor.

If I'm not mistaken this was the first time me and grandma had ever been alone, one on one, face to face. It was hardly the most auspicious timing. The place made me feel uncomfortable. Everything smelled of disinfectant and sweat-stained sheets. Every sound was metallic, things being dropped onto instrument trays. On the trolley next to grandma, the man with the tea towel around his hand was having stitches put in. Lying there, half-dressed, tubes distorting her features, the dignity she wore like a crown deserting her, it looked as though she was dying.

'You're so serious,' she said between gasps. 'Your mother was just like you . . . always serious . . . She would look at you . . . like she was judging you . . . the conscience of the world . . . strange girl . . . doesn't do any good . . . being serious . . . gives you wrinkles . . . You think too much, don't you? You're thinking right now . . . thinking I've lost my marbles . . . well, maybe you're right . . . God only knows what they're . . . putting up my nose . . . pure oxygen . . . I can feel the bubbles . . . inside my head . . . champagne!'

Grandma tried to laugh and almost suffocated. 'You know where my house is?' she said, gasping.

Of course I knew where her house was.

'But you know how to get there, you know the address?'

I knew the address; I knew how to get there.

'Good. If anything happens. Well, you know. I'll be there. When they let me out. All these tubes and wires. I'll be there.

Anything at all. I'll be waiting.'

I nodded emphatically like a puppet. I needed grandma to stop talking. I was terrified she was going to suffocate. Mamá and the doctor weren't here. They had gone outside. It was all down to me.

'Can I tell you something?' grandma asked. 'Something I've never told you?'

She lifted her hand and straightened my hair. A hand with a tube snaking out of it. 'I love you very much,' she said.

This was the first time I had really met my grandma, the handbag-wielding monster with an overdose of oxygen in her bloodstream as a result of one of the Midget's practical jokes.

By the time we saw each other again, I was already in Kamchatka.

Playtime

Estoy muy solo y triste acá en este mundo abandonado.
Tengo una idea, es la de irme al lugar que yo más quiera.

(I am so sad and lonely here in this desolate world.
I have an idea, I want to go to the place I love best.)
Tanguito, 'La Balsa'

Third Period: Language

Noun. 1. The faculty, particular to Man, of using articulated sounds to express oneself: 'The invention of language'. / *Speech.*
2. The system of communication specific to a particular community or country.

40

ENTER LUCAS

Lucas showed up one afternoon in the Citroën with mamá. We were waiting for him. Or rather, we were ready for him. In the days before he arrived, me and the Midget had turned the *quinta* into a fortress calculated to repel the invader.

Mamá had announced his arrival a couple of days earlier. 'There's a kid coming,' she told me, just like that, out of the blue. 'He'll be staying with us.'

'You're going to adopt him?'

'No, you silly goose. It's for a few days. He needs a place to stay.'

But I didn't believe her. This information was coming from the same source who had told me that grandma Matilde's visit was purely social, when in fact it was part of a devious plan thwarted, among other reasons, by the providential appearance of the kamikaze toad. How could I be sure that this was not another of mamá and papá's tricks? Maybe they would just wait for us to get used to the presence of the interloper before admitting his true status as a permanent fixture – their new son. The appearance of this 'kid' implied that they weren't satisfied with us. We weren't enough for them. We didn't measure up. They needed something more.

'You see what I'm saying, Midget? You'll see, I bet he'll have blond hair. I bet he'll be this perfectly behaved kid who always remembers to say 'please' and 'thank you'. How much do you bet that he never wets the bed?'

The Midget swore undying loyalty to me and volunteered for battle.

The first thing we did was to barricade our room. Our aim was to prevent it from being occupied by the interloper: if mamá and papá wanted a new son, he could sleep in their room. We made signs so there would be no doubt as to who owned what. The sign on our bedroom door read: 'Hideout of Harry and The Saint'. There were signs on the headboards of our beds too – and on the outside of the wardrobe door. Lest there be any doubt, we divided the space inside the wardrobe in two, half for me, half for the Midget. (Not that we had anything we needed to put there, but you never know.) We sealed up the drawer of the bedside table with bits of sellotape, which of course meant that we couldn't open it either, but it was worth it for the sake of the message it sent. The Midget attached Goofy to his bed with a piece of string but, worried that this might not be enough, asked me to make a sign that he could put on him. We hung the last sign on the window screen facing outward. It read 'Beware of the Dog', in English, just like in the Merrie Melodies cartoons. Underneath the words we stuck the only picture of a dog we had: Superman's pet dog Krypto; he didn't look very fierce but he had superpowers. In case of emergency, me and the Midget agreed we would hide under our beds and bark to give the impression there was an actual guard dog. We practised a couple of times and everything. The Midget sounded like the little puppy he was.

Our preparation extended to the grounds of the *quinta*. We removed the crosses we'd made out of lollipop sticks that marked the places where the toads were buried; after all, the interloper might easily turn out to be a grave robber. As for the reverse diving board, we decided to say it was already here when we arrived and we didn't know what it was for. We needed to divert his attention from the swimming pool, away from our rescue mission designed to produce future generations of intelligent toads. The experiment was too important to be jeopardized. If interrogated, we would give only the essentials: name, rank and serial number. Vicente, Simón. International Spy. Number 007. (This was the only number the Midget could remember easily.)

All of this went against everything I had promised mamá. When she had told me that this kid was coming, she had asked me to help keep the Midget from getting upset.

'You know how he can be, how easily he gets upset by anything new, anything strange. Right now, he's handling things pretty well, the poor thing. Don't you think?'

I nodded but I was thinking about how the Midget had started wetting the bed again and had begged me not to tell on him. How could I possible refuse her? This was why I didn't feel any remorse about breaking my promise to mamá: it had been extracted under duress.

When Lucas showed up, all of our plans proved to be futile.

I was hiding out in the tool shed. From here I could see the place where the Citroën was always parked (behind the lemon trees) without being seen. Stationed in the driveway, the Midget was supposed to warn me when they were coming and then go to the bedroom and lock the door until I knocked: three quick taps followed by two slow ones; that was the secret code. We had stored provisions in our room so that we could hold out there for as long as necessary: ham, cheese, crackers and – obviously – milk and Nesquik.

From the start, everything went wrong. The Midget got bored waiting at his post and went inside to watch TV. Mamá parked the car between the lemon trees and, instead of sizing up the enemy and then running back to the house, I sat there in the tool shed, open-mouthed until I heard them calling me at the tops of their voices.

Lucas was the biggest kid in the world.

41

A HOUSE POSSESSED

Lucas dressed the same way all my friends did: jeans, Flecha trainers and a really cool orange T-shirt with a motorbike and the words 'Jawa CZ' on the front – only it was size XXL. Lucas was a giant. He was over six feet tall, which made him quite a bit taller than papá and mamá. He was carrying a light blue bag with a Japan Airlines logo on it and a sleeping bag. He was really skinny, with arms and legs as long as the spiders I'd imagined finding in the mysterious house. It looked as if he'd been stretched on a rack just before he came and wasn't really used to his new size yet. Because he walked like he had springs inserted into the soles of his feet. And he had three or four black hairs on his chin that looked ridiculous. He looked like Shaggy from *Scooby Doo*, but creepy: Shaggy possessed by an evil spirit, a victim of voodoo; the sort of Shaggy who'd eat your eyeballs and suck your brains out through the empty sockets.

I had no choice but to come when mamá called me. By the time I joined them, most of the introductions had been made. Everyone was smiling, everyone except the Midget who barely came up to Lucas's waist.

'This is Harry,' said papá.

Lucas held out his hand and said he thought Harry was a really cool name. People who are possessed always try to make out like they're nice. I shook his hand so he'd think I'd fallen for his trick.

'Boys, this is Lucas.'

'Lucas what?' asked the Midget.

Papá, mamá and Lucas exchanged looks, then Lucas said, 'Lucas, just Lucas.'

Then papá suggested he show Lucas around the *quinta*.

The Midget wanted to go with them, but I signalled for him to stay behind. We let the grown-ups head off and we rushed into the house, in a race against time.

In a matter of seconds we tore down all the signs. The Midget didn't really understand why, but faithful to his oath of obedience, he carried out my orders without a word while I tried to explain the inexplicable.

We had been duped. Lucas wasn't a kid. He was a grown-up disguised as a kid, an impostor, a guard they had hired to keep an eye on us while papá and mamá were away. Had it not been for the attempt on grandma Matilde's life, we would have been left with her; at least we would have known what to expect. Now we were at the mercy of a complete stranger – a stranger with legs like springs and arms like wires who moved like no one we had ever seen before. Whatever Lucas was, he certainly wasn't human but he could mimic human movement. This was the mystery we had to solve. Was Lucas who he claimed to be, who papá and mamá believed him to be? Or was he some messenger from the dark side intent on enslaving us, our own personal *Invader*?

Reduced to silence by the weight of these doubts, the Midget handed over the signs, picked up Goofy and started hurling it across the room. He liked the noise the string made when it pulled taut and Goofy stopped in mid-air. But he didn't fool me. I could see through his charade, I could tell how scared he was.

Just as I was about to ask him, mamá and Lucas appeared at the bedroom door.

'Lucas will be sleeping in here with you guys,' she announced.

Hands in my pockets, I squeezed the signs we'd torn down into little balls.

'I can sleep in the dining room if you'd rather,' Lucas said to mamá, noticing our discomfort.

'You'll do no such thing, there's a terrible draught in the dining room,' said mamá, and left the room as though nothing had happened.

The moment lasted for centuries. (All time, I believe, is simultaneous.) The Midget was hugging Goofy, Lucas was hugging his sleeping bag and I was squeezing bits of paper. It was as if, without anyone suggesting it, we were all suddenly playing a game of Statues.

It was the Midget who broke the ice. In his little head, he decided on the only way to settle his doubts and immediately put it into practice. He laid Goofy on his bed, brought both hands level with his face and crooked his little fingers several times.

Lucas, who thought this was some sort of greeting, dropped his sleeping bag and imitated the Midget, crooking both fingers over and over.

'Hello, Simón Vicente,' said Lucas.

'Hi, Lucas Just-Lucas. Do you know how to make Nesquik? Come with me, I'll show you.' And the Midget headed off in the direction of the kitchen, with Lucas bringing up the rear.

In a fraction of a second, the Midget had confirmed that Lucas was not one of the Invaders, and welcomed him into the human faction.

I was not so gullible. I knew there were different kinds of Invaders.

I threw the balls of paper into the air in a fit of anger and went and hid in the wardrobe.

42

IN PRAISE OF WORDS

In the beginning, words served to name things that already existed. Mother. Father. Water. Cold. In almost all languages, the words that define these fundamental truths are similar, or have something of the same music to them. Mother is "umm' in Arabic, 'Mutter' in German, 'maht' in Russian. (All land is land.) On the contrary, words that describe similar human emotions, like fear, do not sound the same anywhere. 'Miedo' is not the same as the English 'fear' nor the French 'peur'. I like to believe that we are more alike in our positive experiences than in our negative ones, that what binds us is stronger than what separates us.

Every language is a way of imagining the world. English, for example, is sharp and precise. Spanish tends to be baroque. It is obvious that they have adapted to the needs of the peoples who speak them, because both have stood the test of time. From time to time, academics accept new words that have already been tested in everyday speech, or accept as correct constructions they previously considered ungrammatical. These new words are leaves on a tree that is already lush with foliage, and the new constructions are the pruning, which helps it to grow; but the tree is still the same tree.

Despite the already advanced age of human languages, it is possible to think of things which do not yet have names. For example, there is a word for the fear of confined spaces: claustrophobia. But there is no word for the *love* of confined spaces. Claustrophilia? Could the monks of Kildare, whose skill as copyists saved much of Western culture, be called claustrophiliacs? Can a miner or a submariner be called claustrophiliac?

My family maintain that I was claustrophiliac from the time I learned to crawl. I would look for small, dark places and squeeze inside: a dog kennel, a wardrobe, the boot of a car. Since I never cried, I would remain hidden until someone noticed I was missing and set out to look for me. If I'd fallen asleep, as I did most of the time, the search might last for hours. If I was still awake, they would quickly find me, because they would hear me laughing. Obviously I must have liked hearing lots of people shouting my name.

Most people argued that my claustrophilia was the result of the ten months I had spent in my mother's belly. According to this theory, these dark cramped spaces reminded me of the sanctuary of the womb I had been so reluctant to leave. There were other theories – though they were often no more than jokes. For a while, after they had to drag me out of the barrel of an old cannon in the museum in Los Cocos in Córdoba, there was a theory that I had suicidal tendencies.

I was growing and the cannons were a little small for me. But from time to time, when I was really bored or particularly angry, I would still seek refuge in a wardrobe somewhere. I would make myself comfortable among the piles of clothes and listen intently. Inside a wardrobe you can hear everything. It acts as a sound box for the whole house. You discover layer upon layer of noises: the cistern in the bathroom, the hiss of the immersion heater, the TV in the distance, the hum of the fridge, the movements of everyone in the house, the conversations you're not supposed to overhear. On humid days, you could even hear the creaking of the wood of the wardrobe itself.

140

The afternoon Lucas arrived (or 'Lucas Just-Lucas' as the Midget called him) all I could hear was my own heart beating. It was like a train hurtling along a track, the engine about to explode. My chest hurt as though a fist were thumping on my ribs from the inside. I was furious! I felt I had been tricked by my parents and betrayed by the Midget. I decided that I would repel the intruder, even if I had to do it alone. I wanted to think about how I would go about it, but I couldn't concentrate. My heart was making too much noise.

Señorita Barbeito says that the heart is a muscle. It expands and contracts. As it beats it makes the sound 'b-b-buh-bum'. No, it's not 'buh-bum', it's 'b-b-buh-bum'; the 'b' that starts it off is slower; as with any machine, the initial motion is the most difficult and therefore lasts longer. According to Señorita Barbeito, the fact that it is a muscle suggests that it can be controlled. But the heart is a complicated muscle and has a tough job to do. Most muscles respond to direct, conscious commands, but the heart is automatic rather than manual, like the cars they have in America. You have to work out how to shut off the automatic switch and set it to manual, if only for a short period. It's a difficult thing to learn, because the body doesn't come with an instruction manual (if it did, it would save us a lot of time and trouble), and there's no off switch or key or lever to switch from one system to another. It's like *Airport* – the book, not the film (I haven't seen the film, but mamá lent me the book): the plane is in danger, the real pilot is unconscious and you have to take over the controls even though you've no idea how to fly a plane, and let yourself be guided by the voice of the guy in the control tower, or, in my case, by the (imaginary) voice of Señorita Barbeito. Books about planes in trouble were very popular back then. There was *The President's Plane Is Missing*, in which, at some point, the hero says you should always look carefully at a girl's mother before getting hitched, that way you know what she'll look like in twenty years' time and decide if she's worth it. This seemed to me a perceptive remark and

I jotted it down in my mental notebook, intending to make use of it when the time came.

By the time I thought about it, my heartbeat had slowed. I wondered if that was because I hadn't been thinking about my heart, because I was thinking about something else. You think about something else, you get distracted, you follow the thought and while you're doing it you forget that you were panicked, and when you forget to panic, you calm down again. It was like the thing that worked for me with my breathing, when my chest felt tight and it felt like I couldn't get enough air into my lungs. I thought I was suffocating and that made me suffocate all the more. So I'd turn on the TV or make myself a *café con leche* or read a book and drift off to Oz or Neverland or Camelot and after a while I'd discover I was breathing normally again. You had to pretend to ignore the problem if you were to get through it, otherwise it was like surrendering. It had worked with my lungs; now it was working with my heart. Well done, said Señorita Barbeito's voice inside my head. An almost perfect landing. Now, you can climb out of the cockpit and everyone will be cheering and clapping. You're a hero, Harry. (I called myself Harry even when I was thinking. Papá had been very clear – our real names had to be kept safely under lock and key. The slightest slip could be fatal. We weren't even allowed to use our real names with each other. Papá called me Harry. Mamá called me Harry.)

Houdini must have been a claustrophiliac too. Or maybe there was a lot of stuff going on around him that made him panicked or angry and he had to climb inside trunks and vaults and glass boxes so that he could think about something else – something silly – until he could calm down and decide to come out and face the world again.

43

LUCAS HAS A GIRLFRIEND

That night I got up to go for a pee (I thought about taking the Midget with me, but it was too late, he'd already wet the bed) and nearly killed myself. Lucas was lying right in the middle of the path in his sleeping bag. Since the sleeping bag was too small, or he was too big, the only way he could fit inside was by rolling into a ball. He looked like a (giant) baby kangaroo inside the pouch of his (giant) mother.

Stepping around him, I noticed he'd left his clothes on a chair. The moonlight streaming through the venetian blinds gave his orange T-shirt an otherworldly glow. I dared myself to touch it. The motorbike and the writing that said 'Jawa CZ' felt weird, not like fabric, it was sort of rubbery. I'd never seen a T-shirt like it. I squinted so I could read the label inside. 'Made in Poland.' What had Lucas been doing in Poland? It was a weird place to go, even for tourists who go to Europe. Tourists go to Madrid or Paris, or London or Rome, but Poland? It would have been better if it read 'Made in Transylvania', because at least then it would have made sense. Lucas would be Renfield, Dracula's one acolyte who hadn't yet been turned into a vampire. But Poland was just mysterious. It sounded like spies and double agents and zither music, like Anton Karas's music for *The Third Man*. (My knowledge of central European geography was sufficiently vague back then that I was capable of getting Poland and Austria mixed up.)

And what about the light blue Japan Airlines bag? How could Lucas be so young and have travelled so much? And why did he always go to weird places? Japan was a case in point. I couldn't think of a single reason why anyone would want to go to Japan, except maybe if you were James Bond and M sent you on a mission and you were in the book called *You Only Live Twice*. (Grandpa had a complete set of Ian Fleming's books in his house in Dorrego, in editions that had photos from the Bond movies on the covers.) Was Lucas some kind of secret agent? And if he was, did papá and mamá know, or had he tricked them the same way he was trying to trick me? I needed to know more.

And there was Lucas's wallet, sticking out of the back pocket of his jeans. I waited a couple of seconds (well, not too many, I was about to piss myself) to make sure that Lucas was sleeping soundly. Then I carefully took his wallet out of the pocket.

Not much money. No ID. I expected this: Lucas would want to conceal his true identity, he wouldn't want anyone to know his real name wasn't Lucas Just-Lucas, or Lucas Thingamajig. There were a couple of bus tickets and a programme for a cinema on the Calle Lavalle. The programme was dated 1973. Why would Lucas keep such an old programme? The answer was in the film itself: *Live and Let Die* with Roger Moore, Yaphet Kotto and Jane Seymour. The first movie with Roger Moore as James Bond. Lucas was keeping this as a reminder of his own initiation as a spy – he was soppy.

Just then he moved in his sleep; he was dreaming. I hid the wallet behind my back. When you're about to be caught doing something and you need an explanation, you never come up with anything plausible. The only excuses I could think of were rubbish, like I was going to wash his jeans to welcome him or that I was looking for change for a 100 peso note (at 3 a.m.!) but luckily, I didn't need an explanation. Lucas went on sleeping.

That was when I found the photo. The girl was wearing a white miniskirt, and a black blouse that she held open with both hands so I could see her boobs as she stared tenderly out at me. If proof were needed to confirm my suspicion that Lucas was a sentimental spy, this was it. This girl could have been a Bond girl in any of the movies. Lucas wanted something to remember her by during his missions so he'd come up with the cunning idea of printing her photo on the back of a calendar from Kiosko Pepe, Santa Fe y Ecuador. Simple, but brilliant. Grown-ups do really weird things to hide their sex stuff. Mamá's cousin Tito used to hide his copies of *Playboy* and *Penthouse* in a pile of *Hot Rods* and car magazines. Papá, who only read newspapers, law books and the *Palermo Rosa* for the racing form, had a copy of *Lady Chatterley's Lover* in his office. If Bertuccio, with his obsession with books for grown-ups, hadn't alerted me, I wouldn't even have noticed that he had that dirty book stuck between his volumes of the penal code.

I put the wallet back where I'd found it and rushed to the loo. OK, if I'm being honest, I wrestled for ages with the temptation to keep the photo for myself, but in the end I thought it was better if Lucas didn't notice anything out of the ordinary (in any case, I could take it any night I wanted to) so I put it back in his pocket. This way, Lucas wouldn't know that I knew; now I had the upper hand again.

Someone should invent toilets with slanted sides. Women are always complaining because we splash but aiming your thing is harder than it looks.

44

I AM FOUND OUT

Papá and mamá left early the next morning. To make up for going away, they promised to swing by our house and pick up some of our stuff. We bombarded them with requests. We wanted the whole world and then some. Mamá tried to impose some sort of limits on what we could have, but papá intervened, clenching his fist to make the sign of the Rock so she would relent. He tried to hide it but I saw it. When she gave in to our demands, we were so happy we rocked the car. (If anyone still doubts my description of how flimsy the Citroën was, it was the sort of car that could be jiggled like a cocktail shaker by a ten-year-old boy and his five-year-old brother.) But even this sudden joy didn't entirely compensate for the feeling that we were being abandoned, left in the enemy's clutches.

The plan was to steer clear of Lucas. At first it was easy, because we had stuff to do. While mamá was taking a shower, I took the Midget's mattress outside in a stealth manoeuvre so that it could dry in the sun. Mamá noticed anyway and asked what it was doing there but we told her we'd taken it outside to do somersaults. She gave us a suspicious look, but she said nothing more. I let the Midget know mamá was getting suspicious and that he had to take extreme precautions. From now on, there were to be no more drinks before bed. Not a drop. 'No Coke?' said the Midget. No Coke, I confirmed.

'What about water?' No water, no soft drinks, I said. 'No milk?' 'Not with or without Nesquik,' I said, believing I had exhausted the full range of beverages the Midget drank. It wasn't a joke, I explained, mamá was on to him and if he wasn't careful, he was in for the Glacial Stare, the Petrifying Scream and the Deadly Pinch. So there wasn't even a peep out of him when I told him to wash the sheets, thereby eliminating the evidence of his crime.

As for me, I'd decided to begin a regimen of intense physical training. I needed to get fit so that I could start my career as an escape artist as soon as possible. This was easy to say, but for me it amounted to a real achievement. Let's just say I'd never been particularly sporty. At school, when they made us run, my chest would tighten and I'd feel as though I was suffocating, and every breath sounded like a train whistle in my chest. I didn't even like football – Argentina's national obsession. My relationship with the ball was cut short at an early age. Once, while I was kicking a rubber ball in the street, I cut my ankle on a broken bottle: I had to have six stitches and still had the scar. A couple of months after that, in Santa Rosa de Calamuchita, I kicked my first proper football into the air and it hit a branch with a beehive on it. That was the end of my interest in sports and the beginning of my unshakeable empathy for cartoon characters who fell off cliffs, had pianos land on their heads and were chased by angry swarms of bees: this was why I always preferred Wile E. Coyote to the Road Runner; Sylvester to Tweety Pie and Daffy Duck to Bugs Bunny. When I got lectures about the importance of sport, I remembered the blood and the scratches and I said to myself however healthy sport is, claustrophilia is healthier.

My plan of action included several laps of the grounds of the *quinta*, working on my biceps and sit-ups. To help motivate myself, I had drawn up a graph with the exercises marked on the x axis and the date on the y axis, beginning today. All I had to do was mark down which exercises I'd done, and how many.

I survived the first lap of the grounds pretty well. As I passed the laundry room I saw the Midget, rubbing soap on the sheets where the stain was, looking appropriately serious and determined.

The second lap was agony. The Midget was still rubbing soap on the same spot.

I never finished the third lap. Seeing that the Midget had abandoned his task was a small comfort, but it was a consolation. Almost joyfully I rinsed out the sheet.

Lucas grilled steaks, and he let us eat in front of the TV. To be fair to him, his steaks were better than mamá's. There was no fat, even around the edges.

That afternoon I made another attempt at exercising, but by then I'd lost my motivation. Looking at my graph, I was ashamed to see how little I'd actually done. Two and a half laps around the grounds? Eight sit-ups? There were worms out there fitter than I was and they probably had bigger biceps. I felt flushed and twitchy, my whole body ached and tingled with pins and needles; I went back to the house in the worst possible mood.

And found Lucas reading my book about Houdini.

I must have looked daggers at him, because he shut it carefully and gingerly set it down on the table as though it were a flask of nitro-glycerine or one of the little crystal animals that grandma Matilde was always so careful with.

'You interested in magic?' he asked, trying to cover up by seeming curious.

'Houdini wasn't a magician. He was an escape artist. Magicians are just liars. They pretend they've got magic powers but they haven't,' I snapped at him as I angrily snatched up my book. But obviously I wasn't particularly happy with my comeback because, halfway to my room, I turned around and said. 'Your name's not really Lucas, is it?'

In the silence that followed my question, Lucas dropped the innocent air he'd had while talking to me, like someone taking off a disguise. A new gleam lit up his eyes, something cunning. Until then, I'd thought I was dealing with a kid trapped in a body that was too big for him. Now he looked like an old man trapped in a brand-new, hardly used body.

'No, my name's not really Lucas,' he said. I thought he was about to reveal his identity. This was the moment of truth, like in the movies. But I was wrong. 'And your name isn't really Harry, is it?'

I didn't answer, just went to my room. To be honest, I was angry with myself. I had given up whatever advantage I'd gained from looking through his wallet. I'd allowed him to catch me unawares. How did he know I too had a secret identity? The only thing for me to do was to stay poker-faced and deny everything. But I didn't know how. I slammed the door and threw myself down on my bed.

I was woken by a loud noise, it sounded like rain. Then I heard the Midget shouting. It seemed unlikely that it was actually raining since I could still see the sun shining through the window. And the Midget was howling with joy, the voice echoing through the corridors of the *quinta*.

When I opened the door, I saw him splashing around like Gene Kelly in *Singing in the Rain*. The house was flooded. The corridor was full of water, pouring through the drain in the bathroom floor. The house was obviously built on a slope so that the water was flowing towards the dining room.

The tank was overflowing and Lucas didn't know how to turn it off. Papá and mamá had gone out of their way to tell me how, because I was little, so obviously wouldn't already know, but they hadn't realized that Lucas, even though he was trapped in a giant's body, didn't necessarily know all the stuff that grown-ups know. So the tank was overflowing (that was the 'rain' I had heard) and Lucas had rushed outside and was turning all the taps he could find and that's when the Midget yelled 'It's flooding' and went into the bathroom and tried to stop up the grille in the floor with a mop, so the water

149

started flooding out of the toilet. In desperation, Lucas had rushed back inside and started twisting all the taps and levers he could find, and by now the Midget was enjoying the whole mess – 'What a glorious feeling/I'm happy again'– and that's when I showed up.

I turned off the stopcock like mamá and papá showed me. Then me and the Midget went out to the swimming pool to see how the reverse diving board was working (it looked promising, there were no dead toads), leaving Lucas alone in the house.

Life may not be fair, but it has its moments.

That night wasn't too bad. Papá and mamá brought back my game of Risk, my sketchpad and the *Dennis Martin* comic I hadn't had a chance to read on the last night before we left. Dennis Martin was a bit like James Bond, but I liked him better: he was Irish, he had long hair and he always gave girls yellow roses. The Midget got his cuddly toy Goofy back, his red plastic cup with the teat (which he wasn't allowed to use, at least at night, as he had made a solemn promise) and the pyjamas he said gave him sweet dreams. No one remarked on the state of the house, which suggested everything was fine, although I overheard papá say to Lucas that there were roadblocks on the roads and that they'd have to change their route every time.

Over dinner, we all laughed about the water tank overflowing. The Midget made out it was worse than it was, saying that the water had been up to here and that he'd been swimming and everything. Lucas blushed red as a tomato, half-ashamed and half-amused and confessed that I'd saved his life. Then he tried to grab the salad bowl, but I got there first.

45

I AM DELIVERED UP TO A TRIBE OF CANNIBALS

Maybe because they thought we were going to flood the house again, or maybe because they were afraid that next time we'd set fire to it, papá and mamá decided that me and the Midget should go back to school. This would have made me happy, except they wanted to send us to a different school.

Their argument – against which anything I said was futile – was that they didn't want us to get out of the routine of going to school. In that case, I insisted, I want to go back to the same school, the same year, the same class.

'That's not going to be possible yet,' they told me, 'it's too dangerous.'

'It's not dangerous for me,' I said, 'I didn't do anything.'

'Roberto didn't do anything either and look what happened to him,' said papá, going all psycho on me.

It was a long drawn-out battle and of course I lost. I offered to study at home at the *quinta*: nothing doing. I screamed, I sobbed: nothing doing. I gave them the cold shoulder: nothing doing. When mamá and papá agreed on something, they were immovable, like a brick wall with no cracks. They were determined that we should not turn into little savages.

To make matters worse, San Roque turned out to be a Catholic school. The weekend before the fatal Monday was spent giving us an intensive course in Christianity. It was one thing to fake it during mass, which, even if it felt like an eternity, only happened on Sundays, but it was something else entirely to fake it from Monday to Friday, for hours at a stretch. First thing Saturday morning, we practised the prayers we'd already learned and after that mamá started explaining Catholicism to us.

'God created the world in six days and on the seventh day he rested.'

'How can he rest if he's God?' the Midget wanted to know.

'Then he created Adam, the first man. He made him out of mud.'

'Wouldn't it have been easier to use plasticine?'

'He breathed on the mud, a magic breath, and Adam was alive. But God did not want Adam to be alone and decided he should have a mate.'

'I get it, "Here comes the bride".'

'Stop being silly. So God created Eve.'

'Eva Perón?!'

We spent all of Saturday afternoon trying to commit to memory stories that sounded like titles from a B-movie festival: Samson and Delilah, David and Goliath, the Ten Commandments. The Midget loved the bit where Moses brought down the plague of frogs and he forced mamá to admit that if God had really asked Noah to save two of every animal on Earth, then there had to be a stuffed Goofy and a plastic Goofy on the Ark.

On Sunday we went to mass and realized that everything we'd learned was from Book One, which was called the Old Testament.

After that came Book Two, the New Testament. It was a lot less interesting than the Book One (Brothers killing each other! Burning bushes that talked! Prophetic dreams! Floods! Seas that parted! Lots of special effects!) but it was more moving. Jesus was the son of a carpenter and he preached love and peace and understanding among men. He was against violence and he despised money because the Earth had riches enough so that all men might eat, have shelter and live well: it was just a matter of getting things organized and learning to share. His ideas made a lot of people nervous – politicians and economists and religious leaders – because Jesus didn't respect their authority and they were afraid their followers would lose respect for them and stop obeying them. So they killed him – in a horrible way. Exactly like the picture I'd set fire to. And to make matters worse, it was pointless, because what Jesus said still made sense even after he was dead.

The rest of the stuff about Christ was a bit pernickety and seemed pretty random – about priests being more important than nuns, for example. (The Midget wanted to know why religious orders had fathers and brothers, but no uncles or cousins.) About priests not being allowed to get married. About not being interested in worldly things. And the whole business about the Host: every time you eat it, you're eating the body of Christ, which is pretty much like being a cannibal. I know it's only a gesture or a symbol – mamá explained that a thousand times – but it still sounded a bit simple-minded to my mind, like the primitive tribes that eat their victims' hearts thinking they can absorb their wisdom. Grandpa used to say that there's no slower process on Earth than the getting of wisdom. The two things that take ages to get, he'd say, are wisdom and a phone line.

Mamá ironed our school smocks (mine was blue like the cards in Risk), papá and Lucas went out to get pizza, and me and the Midget sat on the edge of the swimming pool watching a toad swimming round and round, too stupid even to realize that salvation was at

153

hand in the form of the reverse diving board. We shouldn't have got involved, because the whole idea was that the toads were supposed to learn for themselves, but we were touched by all the effort it was making and in the end we scooped it out with the net and put it on the board.

We all need a helping hand sometimes.

46

AMONG THE BEASTS

We got to the school early. Papá and mamá introduced us to Father Ruiz, the headmaster. He seemed nice enough, though pretty short-sighted, given the thick glasses he wore. He already stank of BO even though it was still early. He led us out into the playground and told us to wait there until the school bell rang. The Midget went over to look at a mural depicting the life of San Roque and I sat on a concrete bench while papá and mamá moved off a little way with Father Ruiz to talk. I heard some of what they said, thanks to my auditory powers, heightened by hours and hours spent hiding in wardrobes; Father Ruiz was explaining that we'd be included on the register and in the daily roll call, but that they didn't need to send any documentation to the Department of Education, so there was nothing to worry about.

When the bell rang, Father Ruiz went to find the Midget and mamá sat down next to me. She lit up a Jockey, the last one in the pack and, in her best 'Rock' voice, asked me: 'What's your name?'

'Vicente,' I said, dully.

'And why are you only coming to school now?'

'Because we've only just moved to the area.'

'What does your papá do for a living?'

'He's an architect. He works for a construction company called Campbell and Associates.'

'What about me?'

'Housewife.'

Mamá exhaled a large cloud of smoke. She looked tired. She had never been much of a morning person. When she spoke again she didn't sound like the Rock any more.

'It's not that bad. You'll make new friends.'

'I don't want to make new friends, I want my old friends. The ones you took away from me!'

At that moment Father Ruiz reappeared and I got to my feet. As I walked over to him, I heard mamá scrunch the pack of Jockeys into a ball.

When Father Ruiz opened the door to my new classroom, none of my classmates was there. They were all up in front of the blackboard, huddled down like a rugby scrum, killing themselves laughing.

Father Ruiz launched himself into the scrum like a bulldozer, shouting 'Get back to your seats' over and over, pinching their sides. It was obvious he'd had a lot of practice breaking up crowds. He bulldozed until there was only one person left – a skinny boy in a windcheater, a green scarf and a woolly hat, who refused to budge.

'Did you hear what I said?' Father Ruiz barked. 'Get to your seat.'

The only answer he got was gales of laughter from the rest of the class.

The 'boy' was actually the school's model skeleton dressed up to look like one of my classmates. At least it was definitely a skeleton. I wondered just how far Catholics took this cannibalism thing.

Father Ruiz blushed, then finally burst out laughing. (He was obviously more short-sighted than I'd thought.) He pulled the clothes off the skeleton and thanked my classmates for their generous donation of old clothes. Most of them booed, except for the ones who owned the clothes, and they simply turned pale.

He stood me at the front of the class and explained that I was new to the school. He gave a little welcome speech, emphasizing how awkward people feel arriving at a new school where everyone knows everyone else and asked them to open their hearts to me. His words were received in a respectful silence. Headmaster or not, Father Ruiz was a good man and everyone who had dealings with him clearly knew that. But the atmosphere of calm he had managed to instil shattered into a million pieces when, at the end of his speech, he announced: 'May I introduce Haroldo Vicente.'

Haroldo! A yelp came from somewhere at the back of the class.

I closed my eyes. I wanted to die.

This was something I hadn't foreseen. With a respect for my wishes, my parents had tried to preserve the name 'Harry' in the world of my new school. 'Harry' is a diminutive of 'Harold', which in Spanish is 'Haroldo' – a stupid name which, as someone at the back of the class worked out, happens to rhyme with all sorts of rude words. Soon, thirty little monsters in blue uniforms – like the Blue Meanies in *Yellow Submarine* – were all pointing and laughing at me, even though I'd never wanted to be Haroldo. I wanted to be Harry but now they'd all got in on the act and started rhyming everything I said. It was like I was in a musical with no music, with everyone speaking in rhymes. All we needed now was for the school skeleton to get up and dance on the walls and the ceiling like Fred Astaire in *Royal Wedding* until someone pulled him down by the green-striped scarf.

47

I LEARN TO BREATHE

I felt like one of those characters in comics that have a little black cloud floating over their heads that follows them around and every now and then shoots out bolts of lightning. I spent the whole day playing Hangman by myself, not paying attention to anything that was said in class. I'd always been a good student, but right now I was prepared to boycott the whole thing: I wanted to get a Fail in every subject so papá and mamá would have no choice but to take me out of this school. Eventually, the kid I was sharing a desk with noticed me playing Hangman, a boy called Denucci who couldn't figure out the rules (how could I guess the wrong letter in a word when I already knew the answer?) and couldn't figure out why I hanged myself in game after game after game.

After school, papá and mamá were waiting for us. We all walked back to the *quinta* together because they wanted to show us the way. The Midget ruined my perfect bad mood by babbling on enthusiastically about his day: he loved the new school.

'My teacher says I have beautiful hair. And she said I'm really nice. And she said that Simón is a lovely name. Sandra is a lovely name. My teacher is called Sandra. Why didn't you call yourself Sandra, mamá? Did you see the picture of San Roque? He's got a dog! Can I get a dog?'

Papá, who was in a good mood, commented that San Roque also had wounds all over his legs and asked if the Midget wanted the wounds too.

'No, cos the dog might lick them, like San Roque's dog does and then I'd have to get a ninjection so I didn't get rabies. When I grow up, I want to be a saint, but only if I can be a healthy saint.'

'Like San Atorium,' said papá.

'Essactly,' said the Midget.

Lucas didn't get back to the *quinta* until late, by which time we had already had dinner. He couldn't think of anything better to do than ask me how my first day at the new school had been. This was the perfect excuse for me to get up from the table and storm off into the garden, slamming the door behind me. The grass was still damp from the brief, torrential shower that afternoon. The wind shook the branches, showering down droplets that stung my face.

School had upset my routine, but I didn't want to abandon my fitness regime. Although I was worn out and angry and had eaten too much, I started on a lap of the grounds. This time I barely managed one lap before I collapsed onto the grass by the kitchen window. I was panting. From inside I could hear music being played loud, some guy with a nasal voice singing 'How sad Venice can beeee/ When you return aloooone/To find a memoreee/In every paving stooone.' I thought I could see mamá in the kitchen. To hide my feeble condition, I tried a few press-ups. I managed two. Two! The breath was whistling in my chest when I heard the door slam. It was Lucas. He was running. Around the grounds. Alone.

The strange thing was not that he had come out to run so soon after accepting mamá's offer to make him something to eat, it was the fluid ease of his movements when he ran. Lucas, with his scrawny, lanky frame, all knees and elbows, who looked like Groucho Marx when he walked, could run effortlessly, steadily, gracefully, as though his body had been designed for speed. And just to rub salt into my

159

wounds, he did three laps of the grounds without even breaking a sweat.

'The secret is the rhythm,' he said, running on the spot after every lap. 'It has to be completely regular. You run at a set pace and you breathe at the same pace. You breathe in through your nose, deep into your belly, then you breathe out. Not from your chest, from the pit of your stomach. If you do that, you'll never get tired.'

'Never?'

'You want to see me run four more laps?'

'Can I run with you?'

Lucas adjusted his rhythm to mine. We jogged slowly, me imitating the regular swing of his arms, breathe in for a count of four, breathe out for a count of four, to the privet hedges at the far end of the grounds, then back, breathe in, two, three, four, and out, two, three, four. I wasn't wheezing any more. Running like this put my lungs on auto-pilot; they worked the way they were supposed to work, in time with the rest of my body, without me stupidly interfering.

I asked Lucas if he had been running like this since he was little.

He told me that it was something he had learned to do. Anything worth knowing, he said, had to be learned.

I pointed out that there are some things we know how to do when we're born.

'But we have to learn how to do them well,' he said. 'For example, everyone breathes, but a lot of people don't know how to breathe properly. When they're born, babies instinctively know how to swim, but you have to help them develop it. Everybody moves, but they move awkwardly: you need to refine it. Lots of things are like that. We're all born with the right equipment, but we're not born with instructions for how to use it.'

'I never thought of that,' I said. 'What other things do we have to learn?'

160

'When we're born, we make noises, but we have to learn to speak.'

'And to sing.'

'Exactly. And to think.'

'And to feel.'

'Feeling is important,' said Lucas.

By the time I'd thought about it, we had already done three laps.

We were coming back to the house. The music was deafening. Matt Monro singing: 'Can't take my eyes off of you' in terrible Spanish.

We went into the dining room, sweating, happy, to find papá and mamá dancing while the Midget pranced around between their legs. As soon as he saw me, he wanted me to dance with him and mamá asked Lucas to dance. But Lucas said no, no, no, his mouth full of bread, lapsing back into his usual awkwardness (dancing is something else you have to learn) while papá scratched his head, looking at the empty glass on the sideboard and said: 'Che, who drank my wine?'

48

AN UNFINISHED SONG

When we're born, we're also able to hear, but we have to learn to listen.

From an early age, my experience as a denizen of wardrobes taught me to evaluate sounds. Early on, I realized how deceptive sounds could be. I was surprised to discover that what I thought was the sound of an insect crawling over a piece of wood was, in fact, the sound of my mother sweeping the floor and was obviously not coming from inside the wardrobe, as I had thought, but from downstairs in the kitchen.

What we can hear is dependent on the acuity of human hearing: it's something that can be measured and the results are the same for everyone. But what we can make out from what we hear depends on how we listen, something which is completely individual. In listening we use our experience; listening taps into our fears, our desires, and into the deepest recesses of our subconscious. In listening we use the language common to all those who speak it, but which is also utterly individual. If 180 million people speak Spanish, that means there are millions of personal variations of Spanish, each with its own vocabulary, syntax, mistakes and silences; a monologue defines its author as reliably as his fingerprints.

The twists and turns of language are more obvious in the lyrics of songs than almost anywhere else. Wrapped up in music, words learn to dance. Sometimes they dance close to us, sometimes they move away to do a pirouette, leaving us with one hand hovering in the air. At such times we hear not what they mean, but what we imagine they mean. One of my classmates at San Roque, a little guy called Rigou, used to giggle to himself at every mass during the same hymn, because what he heard was not 'Gladly the Cross I'd Bear', but 'Gladly, the cross-eyed bear'. And in the Christmas carol, he thought 'Sleep in heavenly peace' was something to do with 'heavenly peas'. National anthems are like a Rorschach test for anyone. When the class had to stand up and sing 'To My Flag', Ottone – a tall kid who smoked cigarettes in the school toilets – used to howl 'when the sad enslavéd Homeland/Brady broke his bonds', never stopping to wonder who on Earth this Brady person might be, not realizing that the line is actually 'when our sad enslavéd Homeland/Bravely broke its bonds'.

The Midget knew almost nothing about the history of Argentina. He could barely identify Sarmiento (bald guy), San Martín (big-nosed guy) and Belgrano (the guy in the knickerbockers), and he wasn't really up to memorizing lines like 'Thus in the high radiant aurora / The arrow-tip evokes the gilded countenance'. But he could appreciate the energy and the passion of these songs and he loved listening to them even if he didn't understand a word. It happens to grown-ups too. In *Gilda*, the Rita Hayworth movie set in a casino in Buenos Aires, a crowd celebrating the end of the Second World War suddenly starts singing 'La Marcha de San Lorenzo' to honour both the Allied Forces and the original Sergeant Cabral. The words aren't important, it's the spirit of the song that matters: it sounds joyous and triumphant and that's all they care about. The Midget went about things in much the same way without knowing it. Whenever he was happy, he sang the national anthem.

That night he was really happy, partly because of the dancing and partly because of the glass of wine he'd drunk; I had forbidden him

163

from drinking before bedtime so he wouldn't wet the bed, so he was dying of thirst. We finished dancing, cleared the table, brushed our teeth and went to bed, with the Midget still singing 'Hear, mortals, the sacred cry: "Freedom! Freedom! Freedom!"' I wasn't really paying attention because I was still trying to wheedle information out of Lucas. As long as Lucas let me continue my interrogation, the Midget could sing and jump up and down on his bed as much as he liked. In the half-light of the bedroom, the rumpled sheets, the pyjamas and the sleeping bag encouraged secrets.

'How old are you?'

'Eighteen.'

'Where are you from?'

'Didn't you hear what your father said? The less you know about me, the better.'

'May the laurels be eternal . . . '

'Well, from the city or from Gran Buenos Aires?'

'Neither.'

'You're Polish!'

'Where on Earth did you get that idea?'

'Your T-shirt is from Poland.'

'My grandparents brought it back for me.'

'I suppose they brought you the Japanese knapsack too?'

'That too.'

' . . . those we fought for and won . . . '

'Do your parents live here or in Poland?'

'Here.'

'Where?'

'Wrong question.'

'Where? Go on, tell me.'

'In La Plata, but that's all I'm saying.'

'Do you live with them?'

'Wrong question.'

' . . . those we fought for and won . . .'

'Did they throw you out?'

'You're crazy.'

'So what are you doing here, then?'

'I'm on a secret mission.'

'Liar!'

'You see? Even when I tell the truth you don't believe me.'

'Did you move out so you could live with your girlfriend?'

'What girlfriend?'

'Don't play dumb. I saw her.'

'Saw who?'

'The photo. You've got a girlfriend and I saw her boobs!'

'Let us live crowned in glory . . .'

Bonk!

When we turned round, the Midget had disappeared. With all the bouncing, the mattress had flipped over and there was no sign of my brother. It was as if he'd been a victim of spontaneous combustion, like Countess Cornelia de Bandi Cesenate in Verona in the early eighteenth century: she burst into flames and in a flash she was reduced to ashes. For a minute I thought maybe this was why kids weren't allowed to drink wine.

But the Midget hadn't disintegrated. His face appeared on the other side of the bed, between the mattress and the wall. He was scratching his head where he had hit it when he fell and looked as if he was about to cry. Lucas and me were staring at him with funny looks on our faces, a mixture of panic and surprise, because he smiled and said: 'I killeded myself!' Then he climbed back onto the bed and started singing the national anthem again at the top of his voice: 'Great big Nesquiks in their bodies/As they march they make milk shakes . . .'

At this point mamá and papá rushed in, startled by the loud bang. What they saw left them speechless. I explained that the Midget

165

was drunk. Papá asked why he was singing about milkshakes. We all ended up singing the national anthem together, falling about laughing.

Mamá covered the Midget in kisses and was trying to explain that the actual words were 'Greatness nestles in their bodies/As they march they make things quake'.

'Don't,' papá interrupted. 'I think his version is better.'

Papá was right. When you're five, 'Great big Nesquiks in their bodies/As they march they make milk shakes' is better because there are some things you're too little to understand.

49

IN WHICH I DISCOVER THAT SOMEONE I LOVE VERY MUCH IS NOT PERFECT

Lucas became my personal trainer. Our sessions were unpredictable, because he spent more and more time away from the *quinta* and sometimes he'd get back really late, but on these occasions he always left me a 'training schedule'. When he got back, the first thing he'd do was ask me for what he called 'a debriefing': had I carried out the plan? If I had, had I completed it or only partially completed it? Which exercises had I left out? I'd tell him everything, in detail.

Lucas, on the other hand, never told me where he went. Every time I asked, he'd stop me with an unequivocal: 'Wrong question'. Sometimes he'd come back so exhausted that he'd climb into the sleeping bag and go to sleep without even having dinner; me and the Midget would creep into the room on tiptoe, careful not to wake him. From time to time he would ask mamá or papá or both if he could discuss something with them, and their talks always took place where they could be sure we couldn't hear them. But from their body language, it was clear that they were plotting something. By now I realized that mamá and papá knew about Lucas's secret mission and that in some way they were helping and supporting him.

Lucas's idea was for me to do some basic physical training before launching my career as an escape artist. Houdini had an advantage over me in that he had been a keen runner and a swimmer from an early age, and I had to make up this gap in our physical capacities. While I was training, Lucas suggested, we could plan out a series of escapes of increasing difficulty.

So he could plan, I offered him total access to my Houdini book. The first time he accepted it with an almost solemn gesture, indicating that he realized how precious it was to me. He read it very quickly and gave it back, suggesting I make notes on the most important bits, writing down questions whose answers went beyond what was in the book: for example, it was important to increase lung capacity gradually. Houdini could hold his breath for four minutes underwater. Four minutes! So I noted on a piece of paper: '*Houdini holds breath 4 minutes*', and slipped it between the pages of the book.

The questions had to do with things we needed to find out. One of the subjects we needed to study was how locks worked, from the simplest to the most complicated, obviously focusing on padlocks. Another one was something mamá mentioned to me, the importance of calculating how long it would take me to escape from the chains or the ropes so I would know how much air there needed to be in the trunk. This note read: '*How much time?*'

Sometimes I'd find myself doing embarrassing things in front of Lucas, the sort of things I'd only ever do when I was with Bertuccio: picking my nose and wiping the snot on the nearest available surface, or staring at a photo of a girl in a bikini as though I could undress her with my eyes. I lost the ability to censor myself, maybe because Lucas was an easy-going guy and sometimes I'd come home and find him watching *Scooby Doo* with the Midget, both of them breathing through their Nesquik. Some things about him I found weird, like him shaving every day (which was pointless since he didn't have a beard, apart from the four hairs on his chin which sprouted again, black as ever, after a couple of hours) or his obsession with reading the newspapers. These were grown-up things, but he did them with the same artlessness as he ran laps or read my *Dennis Martin* comics: Lucas never tried to hold back, except when we persisted in asking him the wrong questions.

In any case he gradually told us things, drip by drip. The stuff about his grandparents was true. They'd been to Europe and to Japan and they'd brought him back the knapsack and the T-shirt and a lot of other things. When he talked about them, his voice was more high-pitched, like he'd been breathing helium. His papá and his mamá still lived in La Plata, but he didn't see them anymore. Seeing in my eyes the question my lips refused to utter, he gave me the same explanation papá had given when he told me Bertuccio couldn't come to the *quinta*: he didn't visit his parents so as not to put them in danger.

He supported Estudiantes, but he wasn't really a football fan. And when all this was over, he planned to study medicine. He wanted to be a paediatrician. He'd had offers from lots of sports clubs to compete as an athlete, but he was indifferent to his abilities; he was flippant about them, as though he didn't want to be enslaved to a gift he hadn't asked for.

I kept up my exercise programme, and astonished my family not only by giving up fizzy drinks but by my sudden fondness for fruit. (Healthy eating was part of the plan.) But Lucas noticed that I was too impatient for his gradual plan and decided to speed things up a bit. He taught me some knots and showed me a technique for escaping: the knots he had learned while he was camping out. The technique was something he'd seen on TV and had managed to work out for himself. It involved being in complete control of your body while you were being tied up. If your wrists are being tied together, you have to keep them stiff and not give in to the pressure of the knot. Once you're all tied up, you just relax your wrists and then you can wriggle one hand out of the ropes. The same thing works with the ankles and even the torso – you just puff out your chest and hold your breath while you're being tied up; then, when you breathe out, the volume of your body is reduced and the rope goes slack.

Lucas offered to demonstrate. In the tool shed there was an old length of rope. I tied his hands behind his back as tight as I could; I pulled and pulled until I thought I might hurt him. He didn't protest. When I'd finished, he turned around, took two steps back, his hands hidden behind his back.

'How can you possibly like Superman?' he asked.

I stood, frozen. The concept that there were people who didn't like Superman had never occurred to me.

'Why? Don't you like him?'

'Not really, no.'

'What's wrong with Superman?' I said, immediately defensive. The question was rhetorical, but Lucas took it seriously.

'The colours of his costume are horrible,' he said quickly, as though he had a long list of things. 'Bright red underpants? Please . . . ! And the stuff about his secret identity doesn't make sense. Why can't he just be Superman all the time? That way he could do twice as much justice. And the bad guys in *Superman* have no style – you can't compare Lex Luthor to the Joker or Catwoman, or the Penguin or Two-Face . . . !'

'I knew it!' I said, pointing a trembling accusatory finger at him. 'You're a *Batman* fan!'

'Batman's a thousand times better!'

'But he's got no superpowers!'

'That's exactly why he's got style. Superman's powers are a gift from the gods. He's always the same; he's two-dimensional and never learns anything. Batman's just a guy like me or you. He suffered a

170

terrible tragedy when he was a kid and that's what makes him who he is now. Besides, he's a lot more intelligent. And he's more creative. And he's got a really cool car. And the Batcave is awesome.'

'Superman's got the Fortress of Solitude.'

'So what? He never uses it.'

'He does use it!'

'When?'

Silence.

'When?'

I couldn't think of an answer. Maybe because I didn't have time.

Before I had a chance to open my mouth, he threw me the rope he'd just wriggled out of.

50

SHAME

Whether it was from sheer resignation or whether I had adapted to my new environment, going to school ceased to be the torment it had been at first. I came to quite like San Roque school and was amused by the differences with 'my' school back in Flores. At San Roque we had prayers at assembly every morning, we had the catechism class, we had different teachers for each subject, rather than one teacher who taught everything, and there were no women teachers. Some of the teachers were called 'Father' and some of them were called 'Brother', a distinction that, like the Midget, I never fully understood. A 'Brother' is sort of like a doctor who's got his degree but decides not to do his residency: he's got the qualifications but he's not allowed to practise.

After a while I gave up my self-imposed boycott on learning. At first I only bothered to learn the absolute minimum, just enough not to get into trouble – the Vicente family had to be discreet and what better camouflage than academic mediocrity. But the teachers' enthusiasm for their subjects was contagious and the atmosphere, which was always friendly, made you want to get involved. One day I found that I'd put my hand up to ask a question. The teacher praised me for my curiosity and told me I could ask questions whenever I wanted. After that I left Hangman for break time, when Haroldo

Vicente would retreat into the shadows again, protected by his vow of silence.

The staff were a colourful collection of creatures. González, the school secretary, wandered around in a cloud of chalk-dust like a dragon breathing smoke. He was always the first to arrive and the last to leave – if he ever did leave – his whole life was San Roque. (Once a kid in seventh grade asked him the make of the tape recorder in the Secretary's Office and González said: 'Automatic Rewind'. The biology teacher, who told us to call him Don Francisco, had an anthropological worldview summed up by the phrase: 'Man is an animal that eats and excretes.' The maths teacher, Llamas, always wore the same clothes: a white teacher's gown with nothing but a vest underneath, even on frosty mornings. Señor Andrés, who taught Spanish, had a peculiar way of testing us on our lessons. He'd get us all to stand up with our backs to the wall, all around the classroom. He'd throw out a question and if a boy hesitated even for a second, he'd say 'Next!' and pass the question over to the other side and the mortified boy had to go back to his seat: it was terrifying and exhilarating, like an intellectual version of dodgeball.

He was the youngest of the teachers, and the cleverest. Most people use their intelligence as a weapon, but Señor Andrés had the intelligence of someone who could have aimed high but had settled for a quiet life. As a result, he was always in a good mood and he loved to surprise us with strange facts, puzzles and stories with riddles that he would leave us to brood over. Language, he would say, is the sieve of human experience; we only understand something when we articulate it. As I tell this story now, I'm tempted to believe him.

What most intrigued me about Señor Andrés was the way he looked at me – eyes half-closed with a knowing smile – as though he knew more about me than I knew about myself. At the time, I assumed that Señor Andrés knew my secret and this was his way of letting me know that he knew. The fact that he tolerated my apparent lack of interest only seemed to confirm my suspicion that Señor Andrés knew I was the victim and was making allowances for my extenuating circumstances. Now that I can articulate it, now that I am putting my story into words, I wonder whether Señor Andrés knew that all time occurs simultaneously; whether, when he looked at me, he could see not only who I was then, but who I would be; whether he saw not only Haroldo, but Kamchatka too.

In the olden days, teachers were venerated. People would walk for miles to hear them speak, in search of knowledge about the physical world or the laws of logic, about the humours of the body and the celestial sphere, about the cycles of nature or about ancient history, treasuring every word with the fervour of those who know that, unlike secular powers, wisdom does not decay with time. Other teachers, like the monks of Kildare, devoted themselves to the preservation of wisdom, convinced that no one could raise a building when the pillars have been lost, copying down their ancestors' every idea, every intuition – whether sacred or profane – in books filled with exquisite marginalia. (The path of wisdom through the Dark Ages, from the Greeks to the Arabs, and from the Arabs to the medieval copyists, is evidence of a tolerance among men, across epochs and between cultures that we would do well to learn from.) Others, with missionary zeal, brought their teachings to places where they believed they were needed, as though bringing the gift of fire to a world that has known only cold. Many of them accompanied colonial missions, but they cannot be held responsible for the destruction that followed; it would be unjust to blame Aristotle, who was his teacher, for the conquests of Alexander the Great.

My native country, Argentina, is going through its own Dark Ages. The land is owned by feudal lords, who keep for themselves the lion's share and pay tithes to some distant king. The streets are overrun by criminals stealing food they can get by no other means and by soldiers who claim to protect us. Our cities are filthy and foul-smelling and in their darkest corners breed the germs of future epidemics. An army of indigents delves through piles of garbage looking for something to eat or something to trade. And hundreds of thousands of children eat little and badly, growing up frail, their minds prematurely exhausted while, on the other side of the fence, they watch as grain is harvested to be sent to mouths elsewhere.

These days I think a lot about the teachers at San Roque. They may have been a little plodding, but they erected an effective barrier against the violence of the outside world which never once crossed the threshold of the school; from other accounts, I know that at the time many schools degenerated into savagery, wielding the only language they knew to express themselves. I am certain that none of these teachers (except maybe Señor Andrés, though I couldn't swear to it) knew the effect they had on me. But I remember them: I see them in the teachers of today, whose barricades bear the scars of greater and more insidious battles. The fact that they go on working day after day is a constant affront to the powers of this world who foster ignorance, for they know that it is a prerequisite of their power: they need the stupid, the lazy, the docile.

The main reason that teachers these days are abused, paid paltry salaries and given chimerical tasks is different, more contemptible and as a result is never mentioned. A teacher is someone who chooses to spend his life nurturing in others the spark that was nurtured in him as a child, to give back what he received a hundredfold. To the powerful of this world – who as children were given whatever they wanted and now take whatever they want – the reasoning that underpins this selflessness is obscene. It is a mirror in which they do not want to see themselves, and so they smash it to spare themselves the shame.

51

IN WHICH I BECOME
A MAN OF MYSTERY

At first my new classmates ignored me. Father Ruiz's speech had failed to take account of the unquestioned principle that governs juvenile societies: the newcomer, the 'new boy' (as though he had just been born), is always a second-class citizen at least until he proves otherwise. Though they were not spiteful, my classmates observed this unwritten rule by ignoring and mocking me. At break time they would shout out the name of the game they were going to play, a game I was never invited to join, a performance with an audience of one. And at the beginning of the day, during roll call, one of them (always a different one, in that much they were organized) would wait until the teacher called 'Vicente, Haroldo' and then whisper to me 'Haroldo Vicente what?' as though I had two first names but no surname.

What gradually defused this charade was my uncommunicativeness. The usual reason such games are fun is because the 'new boy' is desperate to be accepted. I, however, had several good reasons not to want to join their little tribe. I kept my distance –

in part, because of papá and mamá's insistence that I should not give anyone a clue that might lead to them finding out who we really were, which ruled out almost every subject of conversation. Even mentioning Superman might be a clue if someone went and talked to Fernández, the guy who ran the newsstand near my house in Flores, since he could attest that I religiously bought *Superman* comics every fortnight. In part it was sullenness. I felt cut off from my classmates in the same way that mystics and superheroes are cut off from the rest of humanity. I missed my old friends, who were a lot cooler than these guys. As far as I was concerned, none of the boys at San Roque was fit to tie Bertuccio's shoelaces. I spent my whole time comparing them to him: Bertuccio would never play a prank like that, Bertuccio is a much better player than he is, Bertuccio would never have got sent out of class, or if he was he'd go kicking and screaming until he had to be dragged by the scruff of the neck.

But the chief reason for my indifference only gradually occurred to me. Who would worry about being accepted by a bunch of ten-year-old kids when he's got a grown-up friend who's eighteen years old? Compared to Lucas, my classmates all seemed like silly, stupid babies. Lucas was my Green Lantern, my sun and my radioactive spider: the true source of all my powers. While they were kicking a ball in the street, I was practising sailors' knots. While they were stuffing themselves with chips, I was doing four laps of the grounds of the *quinta*. While they were watching TV, I was practising holding my breath in the bath. (Mamá was eternally grateful to Houdini for getting me to do something she had never got me to do: take a bath every day.)

After a while they stopped whispering, stopped making fun of me, stopped pretending. It was obvious that none of it had any effect on me. I had done nothing to try to be accepted, not so much as a smile. In fact, I'd even turned down an invitation from Denucci to

177

play with his trading cards. It was at this point that they started to wonder about my true identity. Why did I sometimes forget to say 'Here' when my name was called during roll call? Why did Señor Andrés let me off that time, when I didn't know the answer and shouted 'Next!', taking the words out of his mouth. Why did I always go off by myself at break time, with a piece of paper that I started scribbling on if anyone came near me? Was it possible that all these things obscured some mystery?

They offered me chewing gum and sweets. They offered to trade cards with me.

I always said 'No'. At first as a safety measure but later because I enjoyed it. There's nothing in the world more fun than being a man of mystery.

52

MISTER CORPUSCLE

And yet through all this there was one friend who kept me company and never said a word. Don Francisco put me in charge of Mister Corpuscle, the school skeleton. My responsibilities included making sure that he was in the classroom at the beginning of biology lessons and putting him back in a dusty corner of the Secretary's office afterwards. Since the Secretary's office was on one side of the playground and my classroom was on the other, I had to push him as the rickety wheels on the wooden base squeaked across the tiles and his bones clacked against each other, making music like a xylophone.

I was not absolved of my responsibilities when it rained, and on such occasions I used an old umbrella that also lived in the Secretary's office. Since it was difficult to hold the umbrella and push at the same time, I always ended up giving it to Mister Corpuscle. I'd put the handle into his bony hand and balance the rim of the umbrella on his skull – and we would dash through rain and storm so that he wouldn't be late for his big entrance.

The best thing was that biology didn't come before playtime; it came before Señor Andrés' class. Since I had to walk Mister Corpuscle home, I had permission to leave the classroom and thereby miss precious minutes of the Spanish class; this way I avoided numerous opportunities to be called up in front of the rest of the class to be tested on the pluperfect or the perfective aspect.

Our walk back to the Secretary's office was always slower. Sometimes I'd pretend to be tired, stop halfway and sit on the concrete bench that ran all the way around the playground. Mister Corpuscle never complained. He seemed to enjoy this little breather as much as I did, this moment devoted to contemplation before he was again abandoned among the maps and the compasses and the boxes of chalk. We made a strange couple, me sitting there, him standing, staring in the same direction. Over time we came to trust each other and I found myself talking to him, nothing out of the ordinary, just stuff about the class we'd just been in (he didn't have much respect for Don Francisco, though he was very fond of him), stories about Bertuccio, that kind of thing. When we were together, I never felt alone: he was a master of the eloquent silence.

I spent much of my time in exile in Kamchatka alone, isolated by eternal snows. Eventually, you find yourself saying aloud things that, until then, only echoed in your head – I hate this fucking cold, I must remember to buy deodorant, who the hell is calling this hour? – and eventually you accept that silence is an aria scored for one voice. Throughout those years I often felt that I wasn't talking to myself, I was talking to Mister Corpuscle: I could sense him in the shadows of my cabin, listening with his usual patience, offering tea and sympathy through my sorrows, staring out through empty sockets that had seen everything.

53

THE FORTRESS OF SOLITUDE

Lucas thought I was making a mistake. That I was missing out on something. If life had dictated that I had to go to this school, why not at least enjoy the good bits? I told him that, given that my classmates were all dumb, there were no good bits. He stubbornly argued that that was impossible; that, if only because of the laws of probability, there had to be at least one cool kid: one in thirty wasn't much to ask for. I figured that even if this was true, I was better off the way I was. After all, what was the point in making friends with someone who might disappear at any moment, never to be seen again? I was angry enough about what had happened with Bertuccio, even though I still hoped I would get to see him again soon.

Lucas understood, but he said that my logic was flawed. Don't you make friends when you're on holiday, friends who might live in Salta or Bariloche, even though you know that when you go home you won't be able to see them? And don't you have fun with them in spite of that, in spite of knowing that it will end? In conclusion, he offered me what he believed was irrefutable proof. If I was right, if it was sensible not to forge new ties, to make new friends in times of change and uncertainty, then what were he and I doing here, at the foot of a poplar tree, practising knots in the weak winter sunshine?

It was impossible to fight with Lucas. He avoided all confrontation – something that was usually my style – but it was not out of cowardice or lack of conviction, it was simply a different way of making a stand.

Lucas knew how to listen, and when he thought it was his turn to speak, he outlined his position clearly and carefully: he never became bitter or aggressive, neither when his position was weak nor when – as now – he obviously had the advantage. And even when he had come up with one irrefutable argument after another, he always left the door open so that the other person could make a dignified exit. I took this route, arguing that it wasn't the same, that he was my trainer and I was his pupil; we were master and disciple, Lucas was Master Po, I was Grasshopper: a kind of relationship that was permissible in times of change and uncertainty. Then he smiled, his fingers moving restlessly over the rope, and said that our relationship was about to come to an end because the knot he was about to show me – he called it a buntline hitch – was the last thing he had to teach me.

From now on we would be equals. And everything we lived through, whether it lasted or not, we would live through together.

My first attempts as an escape artist were a disaster. At first, feeling bold, I told Lucas to tie the knot tighter and tighter around my wrists. As a result, after a few minutes it cut off the circulation to my hands and my arms went numb. It felt as though I was missing an arm – or worse, it felt like having two sandbags strapped to my sides. Then I started to get the hang of it; I kept my wrists stiff while he was tying the knots. When I relaxed the rope slackened a bit, but then I started to pull and tug and the ropes burned my arms and all I succeeded in doing was pulling the knots tighter. The trick was to be relaxed. When I stopped obsessing about the escape, my heart stopped racing, the blood stopped pulsing in my hands, making me supple rather than stiff and, with a bit of effort, I was free. Lucas suggested I think of a poem or a song or something I could recite to myself while I was doing it, to take my mind off the knots. I promised I'd think about it, but for the time being, given that I wasn't in a padlocked trunk at the bottom of the sea, I'd prefer to chat to him – which had the same effect.

I remember one of those conversations vividly. We were out in the gardens. It was about five o'clock in the evening, the time the sun sets in the winter. Papá and mamá still weren't back from their daily expedition into the jungle of Buenos Aires. The Midget was in the house, and though I couldn't hear him, I could hear the TV, which was reassuring. Lucas tied my hands while I worked at keeping the muscles in my arms tense, so as to offer the greatest resistance.

'If you can get out of that in less than a minute, you're Houdini,' he said as he adjusted the final knot. 'If you can get out in two, you're Mediocrini. If it takes you longer than that, you're Disastrini.'

I asked him to stand on the other side of the tree. I didn't want him to see me as I struggled with the knots.

This was the moment when I needed to relax, to breathe out, let the rope go slack; the moment when conversation should have helped take my mind off the fears and anxieties conjured by my conscious mind. Feeling I needed to find something to talk about, I went back to the subject that had been nagging at me for days. I had been losing sleep trying to think of a convincing proof for the superiority of Superman. Lucas's attack had taken me by surprise, and I had been preparing my counter-attack ever since.

'Superman can save more people in less time.'

'Sure,' said Lucas from behind the trunk (it was as though the tree itself was talking to me), 'but most of the time he's too busy saving Lois Lane and Jimmy Olsen.'

'Superman is global – he can get to anywhere on the planet in a matter of seconds.'

'That's true. But have you ever seen him dealing with a disaster outside the USA? Have you ever seen a poor person in a *Superman* comic? Have you ever seen Superman take on a Latin American dictator? And this guy is supposed to work for a newspaper!'

It had been a mistake to choose this subject: Lucas was thrashing me and knowing I was losing made me angry, and the anger made me tense and the tension made the rope bite into my wrists like a rabid dog. To make matters worse, he was already up to one minute. Now I couldn't be Houdini. With a bit of luck, I might still be Mediocrini.

'Besides, there's a structural problem in the storyline,' Lucas said, merciless now.

'Huh?'

'Superman can move at super-speed, right? And when he flies around the Earth at a thousand miles an hour he can make time run backwards, right?'

Reluctantly, I admitted this was true. 'One time Lois Lane died and Superman went back in time to stop her from dying.'

'But if he can do that, why can't he go back years and stop the planet Krypton from exploding and his parents from dying?'

This left me speechless. I'd never thought of it this way. Was Superman, as Lucas seemed to be insinuating, an ungrateful son and a traitor to the people of Krypton? If Lucas was right, did that mean Superman was so stupid that the idea had never occurred to him, or did it mean he was so selfish and insensitive that he preferred to cut himself off from his past life so he could be the only superhero?

'Twenty more seconds and you're Disastrini.'

It came to me out of the blue, a brainwave flying the flag of victory. Don't ask me how, but suddenly I had the answer to the riddle, the evidence that would prove that I was right and Lucas was wrong, and prove that Superman was not only a good person but the greatest superhero of them all. I opened my mouth, prepared to shout it from the rooftops. I barely recognized the voice that came from my throat as my own: it sounded hoarse and squeaky, as if the rope around my arms had crept up and was now around my throat.

'Superman can only go back in time here, in this solar system, because he gets his powers from our sun. If he flew back to Krypton, he'd lose his powers so he wouldn't be able to do anything. It's not like he doesn't want to save his parents. He can't. He can't save them, get it? He just can't!'

I stopped squawking and fell to my knees. I was exhausted.

Obviously my voice surprised Lucas too, because he came out from behind the tree, crouched down and untied me.

'I can't feel anything,' I said, my voice faint.

Lucas rubbed my forearms so fast it burned. He was nearly as fast as Superman.

'What if they don't come back?' I asked in a whisper. 'Papá and mamá – what if they never come back?'

He put his arms around me and started to rub my back as though my back had gone to sleep too.

We stayed like that for a while. Before we realized it, it was dark and the cold air prickled our noses.

The afternoon wasn't a complete waste. At least we agreed on the fact that, from time to time, Superman did fly to the Arctic Circle and shut himself away in the Fortress of Solitude.

54

THIS YEAR'S MODEL

Words, like all things, exist in time. Some fall into disuse and end up imprisoned between the pages of old books, where nobody ever visits them, like pensioners in old folks' homes. Some change through their lives, losing some traits and gaining others. Take the word 'father', for example: the dictionary definition is concise and firmly rooted in biology (a man or male animal in relation to its offspring), but the characteristics we associate with the word are very different. Nobody thinks of a father simply as a male animal; the word conjures the image of a lovable man who is a part of his children's lives, who protects them, loves them and guides them. But that definition, which most people would agree on, is more recent than we might think. It might be older than the combustion engine, but it's more recent than the printing press and much more recent than the concept of romantic love. Didn't Romeo and Juliet reject their fathers' authority to be faithful to an emotion they considered more sacred than blind obedience?

What we understand by the word 'father' is very different from what, for centuries, the word meant. The Book of Genesis makes no mention of what Adam and Eve were like with their children. It doesn't even indicate how they reacted when Cain murdered his brother Abel: that the text is silent on the subject suggests bewilderment rather than grief. With a similar fatalism Abraham, who for decades had cried out to heaven that Sarah might bear him a son, agreed to sacrifice Isaac, the child he had so longed for, to the very God who had granted his prayer. In the Bible, Yahweh, the Father of humanity itself, is extraordinarily ambivalent to his creatures: twice he almost wipes them off the face of the Earth (with the Flood and again when the people of Moses began worshipping false idols), and both times he repents at the last minute. He only ever unconditionally embraces the human race when he finds himself overcome with love for David, his favourite; it is the first time that he refers to himself as the Father of Man.

In other traditions, the role of the loving father is also the product of a gradual development. The Greek gods father demigods and heroes right and left, but they don't seem to feel anything for their progeny beyond a vague sense of responsibility; many of them seem more sympathetic to certain mortals than to their own offspring. Saturn, as Goya had revealed to me, went to the extreme of eating his children. Laius tried to kill his son Oedipus, though in the end it was he who was murdered. The first great portrait of a father–son relationship appears in *The Odyssey*, but the glory goes not to Odysseus but to Telemachus, who praises the image of his father during his long absence, which begins with the Trojan War. Homer introduces us to Telemachus in the palace in Ithaca; there he is daydreaming, his heart consumed with grief: 'He could almost see his magnificent father, here . . . in the mind's eye.'

King Arthur never gets to know Uther, who sired him. On hearing the prophecy that his own son will dethrone him, Arthur does as Herod did and orders the death of every newborn male child in the kingdom; on this occasion Mordred survives, but when he grows to be a man he dies after being run through by his father's lance. In Shakespeare, it is the children who show devotion (Cordelia for example, or Hamlet, who owes much to Telemachus), a devotion their fathers do not seem to deserve. The best characters in Dickens are orphans: David Copperfield, Pip, Oliver Twist, even Esther Summerson, raised by an aunt who openly curses the day the girl was born. We know nothing of Ahab's father, or Alice's or Dr Jekyll's; they seem to have appeared in the world just as we meet them, like Venus rising from the shell.

This does not mean that our current concept of what a father is did not exist in other times. A seed can be found in the New Testament, in the parable of the Prodigal Son: a father is he who has the kindness to give the best of himself to his children, the wisdom to leave them free to learn from their own experience; the patience to wait for them to attain maturity; and the goodness, when they return, to welcome them with open arms and invite them to sit at his table once more. This notion of the father tempers that of the Olympian, authoritarian father of the Old Testament, in whose image all patriarchs are made, from Lear to Adam Trask in Steinbeck's *East of Eden*. In the course of a single book, the balance of power shifts dramatically. In the beginning, fatherhood in the Bible is synonymous with power. By the end, it is centred on love.

Until quite recently, children were born into a world that seemed predetermined and unchanging. Their parents were who they were – shepherds or soldiers, hunters or miners – and remained so until the day they died, categorized into classes and castes that bore witness to an immutable social order, which they accepted without even wondering if there might be some other place for them. Fathers were expected to be distant, authoritarian. They cared for their children as a wolf might, providing them with food and shelter, protecting them from predators. By the time their children could walk, they had taught them to communicate through language, to use their hands – whether working with a plough, a lance or a printing press – believing that their children would go on doing so until the time came for them to teach their own children. That was all, and it was a lot.

That world no longer exists. My grandfather belonged to the last generation of fathers in the classical sense of the word: early in life he chose a career and he stuck with it to the end. He faced down storms and fires and drought (I choose these images because it is difficult for me to separate my grandfather from the land he worked), but he never suffered a crisis of identity. My father, on the other hand, first opened his eyes on a world whose certainties had crumbled. As a result, he did not need to be stern (since boundaries were more fluid now) or distant (because this new world had eliminated all distance) with us, which was a good thing. But at the same time he played out the adventure that was his life in front of us – one adventure that was far from resolved. I'd like to think that, in the long run, this too will prove to have been a good thing, but it's too early to tell.

My grandfather was a distinct, unique man. My father was many men: the fool and the soldier, the donkey driver and the fan of *The Invaders*; the cool father and the rebellious son, the saviour and the lover; the professional lawyer and the defender of hopeless cases. I'm not saying that these things were irreconcilable, simply that they were conflicting elements that existed within my father and were constantly struggling towards resolution, never more so than after March 1976, when the country he thought he understood began to slip away beneath his feet. It is easy to think that my mother was not similarly conflicted, because she had fashioned a mask that perfectly concealed her feelings. But it was obvious that she cowered in the fearsome shadow of grandma Matilde, another member of a generation that never confessed to having any doubts – at least not until it was too late.

55

I FIND MYSELF IN THE MIDDLE OF A 3-D MOVIE

After the setbacks of the first few days, our stay at the *quinta* took on a veneer of normality. At first sight, the only thing that appeared to have changed was the sets. We were all still playing the same roles – only the screenplay was different. Me and the Midget still went to school. Papá and mamá went off to work. Even Lucas, a foreign body introduced into the family, had been assimilated: one more son who slipped into a pre-existing long-established family dynamic. Over dinner, he might talk about the news with papá and mamá while playing with a ball made of crumbs of bread, firing it between the goalposts I created with my hands; Lucas had become an equidistant centre, a point of perfect equilibrium. He even kept his toothbrush in the same glass as the rest of ours.

On the face of it, the fact that our new life went smoothly seemed to be a triumph over the Midget's obsessions and phobias. My little brother had been placed in a special rocket, wearing only his favourite pyjamas, with Goofy in one hand and his training cup in the other, and launched towards another planet. It was a disruption that would have been upsetting to any kid his age; but for the Midget, who was abnormally attached to the rituals and objects that made up his world, the break must have been all the more traumatic. There had been no room on the spaceship for *his* bed, *his* school, *his* LEGO; nor had there been room for my toys and my games which provided his daily diet of destruction, no room for the armchair where he did his little dance every time the TV announcer said 'Coming up next: *The Saint*'; and there had been no room for the blue and red tricycle he was almost too big for. And yet, in the zero gravity in which we now found ourselves, the Midget floated like an experienced astronaut. There was the small problem of his bedwetting, but that was a secret and the two of us were working to resolve it. Papá and mamá knew nothing about it, and from their point of view, the Midget's adjustment to all these changes had been simply remarkable.

In one way or another, all of us were trying hard to see the silver lining; as Manolito puts it in *Mafalda* when he breaks Guille's toy car and then shows him how to use one of the cogs as a spinning top: 'It's all about finding the little victories in the big defeats.'

At the same time I sensed there was something unnatural about the Midget's new-found normality, but it was only a hunch. I didn't know, for example, that our parents' decision to send us back to school was the cornerstone of this edifice: they thought that, in spite of the differences in how they operated, the familiar routine of school smocks, studying and playtime, might serve to counterbalance the silence of the cosmic void in which we found ourselves floating. What calamities might have befallen us had they not stopped by our old house to collect the Midget's fetish objects, my comics and my game of Risk, we will never know, but given the inherent risks involved in making the trip, it was clear just how far they were prepared to go to keep us happy. Even while we were living as fugitives, they were determined that we should have some semblance of a normal life.

When they were with us, they took pains to pretend that they were the same as ever, but it took hard work and courage to feed this illusion. From time to time they would let slip some hint of how worn out they were by the constant pretence that life was perfect: it might be by saying something intended to reassure us that they weren't really worried, or laughing a little too hard, like actors not used to their roles. I noticed these things but kept right on playing the part that had been allotted to me in this drama. But sometimes something happened that took me aback.

In quiet moments, some detail would come unstuck from the background and rush towards me. It was as though I was seeing things through the 3-D glasses they give you in the cinema to watch *House of Wax*. Papá's moustache, for example: it was supposed to make him look older and more serious, but sometimes I'd see it, like the smile of the Cheshire cat, floating in the middle of the living room even after he had already left the house. Or the smart suits mamá had taken to wearing whenever she went out, so unlike the jeans and the bright colours she had always worn at home. Sometimes I'd see a skirt and a blouse floating in the doorway, clinging to an invisible body even though the sound of the Citroën meant that mamá had already gone.

My mind was playing tricks on me, and its sense of humour revealed what all of us were carefully trying to conceal: that we were trying to be other people, living a borrowed life as we floated in a sky that was getting darker and more impenetrable. I knew by now that someone or something had forced my mother to resign from her job at the university, although she still had her job at the lab. I knew by now that someone or something had taken over papá's office and he now worked in a different bar or café every day, to throw whoever was trailing him off the scent. One time he met up with Ligia, his secretary, under some filthy bridge. There were people there digging through the rubbish, and at some point a police car went past and

192

they had to duck out of sight, but the only thing that bothered Ligia was that when papá handed her a petition of habeas corpus, it was usually covered in coffee rings.

These and other bits of information filtered back to me, but only fragments, pieces of a jigsaw puzzle I couldn't fit together; I was so much in denial that I didn't even have nightmares. For a long time I thought that my parents told me these little things because they believed I wouldn't understand the bigger picture – whatever it was they were not saying, whatever they were hiding from me. Now I think that they did it deliberately, knowing that by the time I put the pieces together and could finally see the picture in the jigsaw puzzle, I would be safe, far from the danger that, right now, threatened us all.

56

NOT SINGLE SPIES,
BUT IN BATTALIONS

The moment I entered the house, I realized I was not alone. I kept moving, impelled by the inertia of coming home (throwing my schoolbag onto a chair, letting my worried fingers toy with the top button of my school smock), but the evidence hit me quickly like the clip around the ear mothers give to children throwing a tantrum. The house always smelled of dust, dirty socks and last night's dinner. Now it smelled of something different, something sweeter and more natural. I found a TV guide on the table. We never bought the TV guide. This one was open and someone had underlined their favourite programmes in blue pen. As for the rest of the living room, I was more disturbed by what was not there than what was: someone had erased all traces of our existence, the slippers on the floor, the half-eaten box of biscuits, the comics, the Midget's drawings. (By now he was drawing haloes over everything. The cows had haloes. Secret Squirrel and Morocco Mole had haloes.)

The first thing I thought was that I should warn him. The Midget was still outside, checking for dead toads in the swimming pool. It might be too late for me, but I still had time to warn him: all I had to do was scream 'Run for it!' (In my imagination dramatic moments were always dubbed in Mexican, like cop shows on TV.) The Midget would run away, climb over the privet hedge and run to the spot on the road that papá showed us when he was explaining 'action stations'. If papá shouted 'action stations', we were supposed to run to the village and ask Father Ruiz to hide us, probably in the church itself because everyone knows that fugitives are allowed to hide in churches and claim sanctuary.

'Hello, darling. Are you home?'

Mamá emerged from the kitchen carrying a little bowl of wild flowers.

'What are you doing here?' I said loudly to overcome the thunderous b-b-buh-BUM of my heart.

'I got home early today. Where's chubby?'

At that moment the Midget came in. Hardly had mamá set down the bowl of flowers than the Midget hugged her, almost knocking her over.

'Hello, darling. How was school?'

'Inndsmsp!' said the Midget, his face still buried in mamá's skirt.

'What?'

'I need some soap. We're going to make statues out of soap!'

'That sounds like fun. I bought milk.'

These were the magic words. The Midget did the short version of his little victory dance and rushed into the kitchen.

'Wait a minute, I'll open it for you.' Mamá turned her attention to me. 'What about you, how was your day?'

I shrugged my shoulders and followed her into the kitchen with the Midget.

'What about my *Superman* comic?'

'It's in your bedroom, where it should be.'

'And my slippers?'

'Have you looked in the wardrobe?'

'They're never in the wardrobe.'

'They are now.'

Mamá tore a corner off the milk bag with her teeth and spat the little piece of plastic into the sink. This calmed me a little. For a minute I thought she'd been replaced by an Invader, a *Doppelgänger* identical on the outside but programmed to do typical mother things like tidying the house, putting things in their proper places and decorating the place with flowers.

'There's a film on I want you to see. It's on TV on Monday.' She put the sachet of milk in its plastic holder and handed it to the Midget.

'What's the film? *The Sound of Music?*'

Wrong question. Mamá still hadn't got over the disappointment of taking me to see it in the cinema. I fell asleep.

'This is how you make Nesquik,' said the Midget, who loved to explain the process as he made his Nesquik, as though we were trainees.

'Is it a horror movie?' I asked. The last time mamá had made me watch a film on TV it was *The Miracle of Marcelino*.

'No, silly.'

'You put in three teaspoons,' said the Midget, filling his cup with brown powder.

'It's called *Picnic*.'

A film about a picnic? It sounded boring.

'It's not boring,' said mamá, who could read my mind, or at least my expression. 'The music is wonderful, and there's fight scenes in it, and I know you like them.'

'Then you pour the milk from way up high.'

'Is there anyone famous in it?'

'William Holden. The one who was in *The Bridge on the River Kwai.*'

The Bridge on the River Kwai was boring (at least it was then, it got better later) and it ended badly (that hasn't changed), and I didn't like films that ended badly (that hasn't changed either).

'The guy who was in *Stalag 17*.' Mamá didn't give up easily.

Stalag 17 was brilliant. It was about these guys who escape from a German POW camp. I like films about escapes.

'And then you stir, but not too much, otherwise there won't be any little lumps. The little lumps are the best bit,' said the Midget, taking his first sip.

'Lucas?'

'He said he'd be back around seven. I was fired from the lab today. Do you want me to get you a cup?'

I nodded mechanically.

Mamá took a cup down from the cupboard and pushed it across the counter to me.

'It might be nice to go down to the farm for your grandfather's birthday. What do you think?' she said, looking for another teaspoon in the drawer. The Midget never lent his spoon. He liked drinking his Nesquik with the spoon still in his cup.

'Does papá want to go?' I asked suspiciously.

'I'll talk him into it. After all, it's his father. He has to stop acting like a prick around him.'

'You said "prick",' the Midget noted.

'I'm allowed to say it, because I'm me,' mamá said pedantically.

'So you're allowed to say "prick" because you're a grown-up?'

'And you're not allowed to say "prick", even when you're repeating what I say. Stop being a smart aleck.'

'What do you mean they fired you?'

Mamá looked at me with a mixture of resentment and admiration, shielding her face behind a cloud of cigarette smoke. She hated being forced to talk about things when she didn't want to, but she grudgingly acknowledged my skilful manoeuvre. Having just told

197

the Midget not to be a smart aleck, my question put her between a rock and a hard place; now she wasn't allowed to act the smart aleck either.

'They fired me, that's all there is to it.'

'But why? Were you terrible at your job in the laboratory?'

'I'm a stupendous lab technician. And I'm a stupendous teacher, just like I'm a stupendous mother.'

The Midget noisily sucked his Nesquik through his teeth, approvingly.

'You're a terrible cook,' I said.

'Nobody's perfect.'

'But why did they fire you, then?'

'Politics.'

At that moment an angel passed. According to grandma Matilde, when there's a sudden silence in a conversation it's because an angel is passing.

Then the Midget shouted: 'Look, mamá, look!' He showed her his cup. The teat of his cup had snapped and was now attached by a thin thread of plastic.

'That's because you're always chewing on it, you little prick,' I said.

'Don't you start!' said mamá.

'He called me a prick first!'

'That doesn't mean you have to repeat it!' mamá snapped, but with no real conviction. The Midget was genuinely upset and she didn't want to make things worse.

The three of us stood there, staring at the Midget's cup, the Midget with his arms around mamá, me leaning against both of them. There was nothing much to be said. It was impossible to fix. And buying another one, even one exactly the same, was unthinkable. My brother had never accepted the concept of the production line. For him, no two objects were the same. In general we avoided allowing him to make decisions about what to buy, because it could take him an hour to choose a pair of clackers when to us they all looked identical. We'd tell him until we were blue in the face that they were all the same and he would swear that they weren't. The funniest thing was that, privately, mamá admitted that the Midget was right. He had science on his side. Although they might look identical, no two cups are actually the same. No two cars are the same. No two lamps, no two railings and no two moments are ever the same.

57

A PIECE OF BAD NEWS
TURNS OUT TO BE GOOD

In the days that followed, we observed the phenomenon of mamá as housewife as both privileged witnesses and innocent guinea pigs.

Mamá had never been a housewife. Mamá was a terrible housewife. Whether the former was a consequence of the latter, or the latter the result of the former was a problem as philosophically taxing as the chicken and the egg.

But my view is completely objective. I have hundreds of exhibits to enter into evidence.

Once she put a chicken in the oven without taking the plastic bag full of giblets out of it.

Once she tried to iron a nylon shirt with the iron on full blast and burned it to a crisp.

Once she wanted to paint my bedroom and she painted over the wallpaper.

Once she filled the blender all the way up to the lid and then she turned it on.

Once she turned on the oven without looking inside first and set fire to the chopping board.

Once, half-asleep, she put the Midget's school smock on him without taking out the clothes hanger and sent him off to school with the hanger still inside.

Papá dealt with these things magnanimously. Partly because he loved her, partly because mamá was perfect in every other way, and partly because, even if she was a terrible housewife, he was no better at playing the handyman (once our toilet was blocked for six days and in the end I took the plunger and fixed it myself, because papá couldn't go near it without throwing up), so he was in no position to cast the first stone.

But all of these disasters were the work of a different mamá, a mamá who spent as little time as possible in the house, and when she was there, spent her time doing the things she enjoyed, like watching movies on TV, doing crosswords or reading for hours in the loo.

Now everything was different. With no work at the university or the lab, mamá had no choice but to spend her days at the *quinta*. How many films can you watch in a day? How many crosswords can you do? How many hours could she spend sitting on the toilet reading *Stability and Flux in Thermodynamic States?*

For a couple of weeks I could work out every single thing that had gone on at home while I was at school. For the Sherlock Holmes in me, it was easy: all I had to do was follow the trail of cigarette ash. The ash beside the radiogram indicated that she had put on music while she was working. The ash on the marble countertop in the kitchen meant she had been smoking as she washed the dishes. The ash next to the outside sink meant that she had been hand-washing clothes, even though it was freezing cold. The ash by the drain in the bathroom floor meant that she had been sitting on the toilet for long enough to have had to dispose of her cigarette – I lifted the grille and there was her cigarette butt, floating on the water.

There were other, more subtle, clues. For a while I thought that the burn mark on the windowsill was getting deeper. Had mamá set down a lit cigarette in a place where someone – a previous tenant, some other mamá – had left one before? Was there a moment during the day when mamá stopped cleaning, whirling around like the white tornado in the Ajax commercial, and stood here, looking out at the garden, with a cigarette burning away next to her? What could she have been looking at? (It was a pretty view, calming even, but not in any way exceptional.) What had the other people who had briefly lived in the *quinta* stood here looking at?

I thought maybe the house was taking hold of mamá. These things happen, especially in Stephen King books. The man who had smoked the first cigarette (to me it had to be a man, but that was pure intuition) had met with some tragic fate. He must have been related to Pedro, because Pedro was a kid like me and kids don't smoke. I imagined it was Pedro's uncle, an uncle he really loved – it would have made more sense to think of it as his father, but I ignored this possibility – whose death had plunged Pedro into a terrible depression that China and Beba hoped to tempt him out of with Havanna biscuits. Having his life cut short meant that his soul was still wandering the Earth. It's common knowledge that when someone is betrayed or murdered, their ghost can't rest in peace, it roams around looking for justice. (There are ghosts that look for vengeance, but they end up in hell, like Hamlet's father. He didn't realize that you can't purge a sin by asking someone to commit another sin; justice and vengeance are two very different things.) So the ghost of Pedro's uncle still haunted the *quinta* and possessed whoever spent the most time in the house – in this case, mamá – who, without realizing it, started doing the same things the dead man used to do, like smoking a cigarette, standing by the same window, victims of the same daydream. It occurred to me that maybe Pedro's uncle might be buried here, in the grounds of the *quinta*, with no cross or headstone to mark the grave. One day me and the Midget would go to bury another dead toad and we'd dig up a skeleton wearing threadbare clothes, and in his pocket would be a half-smoked pack of Jockey cigarettes. (This is the problem about thinking about something else to take your mind off something. It works for a while, but in the end you always come back to the thing you were trying not to think about, only now whatever it was is worse.)

One afternoon, me and the Midget got home from school to discover that the Ajax white tornado had run out of puff: last night's dirty dishes were still on the table; our pyjamas, our slippers and our dirty clothes were on the floor where we'd left them; the ashtrays were overflowing and there were cigarette butts floating in a coffee cup. Mamá was sitting on the sofa, cigarette in hand, feet up on the coffee table, the tin of Nesquik between her ankles, watching TV.

'What I don't understand,' she said, without even bothering to say 'Hi' or 'How was your day', 'is this thing about not being able to move their little fingers. How come a civilization sophisticated enough to design interstellar spaceships, can't work out how to move their little fingers?'

'It's a manufacturing flaw,' I said, sitting next to her. 'It can happen to anyone. Achilles' heel was vulnerable because his mother held him by his foot when she dipped him in the river Styx.'

'Where are the clean cups?' asked the Midget, emerging from the kitchen with a carton of milk.

'There aren't any. Pour the milk into the Nesquik tin, there's not much Nesquik left anyway,' said mamá, without taking her eyes off *The Invaders*.

And that was how we got mamá back. After days and days of trying, she had to face the facts: it was as physically impossible for her to do housework properly as it was for the Midget to pick something up without breaking it. Laboratory or no laboratory, ghost or no ghost, mamá was still mamá.

This, in case you didn't realize, was the good news.

58

A PICNIC IN THE RAIN

'Where are you off to?' mamá asked me later that night. I stood there, my mouth open, my book under my arm. What kind of question was this? It was nearly ten o'clock, we'd had dinner, I was carrying a book (one about King Arthur that I'd borrowed from the school library) and my body was clearly pointing in the direction of the hall that led to the bedrooms. Where could I be off to, except to bed? Then I remembered. It was Monday. Mamá, with suspicious conscientiousness, had just cleared the table. She was carrying a plate of biscuits and was clearly heading in the direction of the living room, where I could hear the theme music to *El Mundo del Espectáculo*. Tonight they were showing *Picnic*. We had a date. I was trapped.

Not that I didn't see the advantages of the situation. It was a rare opportunity to have mamá all to myself. If there was a romantic movie on, papá scuttled away faster than a cockroach when you turn the light on. Without mamá there to stop him, the Midget knew he could bounce on his bed until he was exhausted or had split his head open. So it was just me and mamá. And the biscuits (called 'Ladies' Lips' – delicious!).

But there were disadvantages too. Mamá's taste in movies, for a start. If previous experience was anything to go by, I was doomed to two hours of agony. Or, in the case of *The Sound of Music*, more than two hours.

In general, the movies mamá liked left me cold, or worse. But what was worse was the seriousness of mamá's relationship to the cinema. Everyone likes films, but not so much that they keep a photo of Montgomery Clift on their bedside table. When she was in a cinema, mamá behaved the way the Midget behaved in church. Her every emotion was amplified. She took everything in with wide eyes and a sweet tooth. Sometimes, though she didn't realize it, she'd be sitting there with her mouth hanging open: in the dark of the cinema she didn't care if she looked stupid. On the subject of the cinema, she was an evangelist: she was determined to convert me to the faith, to infect me with her enthusiasm for this religion, patiently explaining to me how the experience of sitting with other people in a darkened cinema watching light play on a huge screen was something mystical and profound. Like all evangelists, she made me feel awkward. I never really understood the intensity of her faith. I was happy to go to the cinema, but, to me, the chocolate-covered peanuts you bought in the foyer were as important as the film.

Every trip to the cinema with mamá became an ordeal. On one hand, I had to avoid falling asleep at all costs. The second half of *The Sound of Music* was one of the best naps I've ever had, but it came at a terrible price. Mamá made me feel that it was some sort of betrayal. It was as if I'd insulted her family. (Maybe we were distantly related to the von Trapp family and no one had told me?) On the other hand, I had to be diplomatic when giving my opinion. She told me that *The Miracle of Marcelino* was a lovely film and she didn't take it very well when I told her that it was the most horrible film I'd seen in my whole life. I tried to explain that I'd said it was horrible because of the horror of what happens in the film, not because I thought it was a bad movie, but it was too late, the damage was done. She greeted this comment coldly. I slept with the light on, but even so I dreamed of a big wooden Christ chasing me down endless corridors, trying to nail me to his cross so that he could be free.

In spite of my reservations, *Picnic* wasn't that bad. There was this little village and this pretty, curvy girl, Kim Novak, who seemed like the saddest woman in the world in spite of the fact that her boyfriend was this rich guy. Then this other guy shows up, William Holden, who's much nicer than the rich kid, but hasn't got two pence to rub together. As you'd expect, Kim Novak and William Holden fall in love. He makes her feel happy and she makes him feel like the richest man in the world. What I didn't really get was how they went on and on about how young they were. They didn't look young to me. They were at least as old as my parents, maybe older.

During the first ad break, mamá replenished the supply of biscuits. During the second break, she stayed with me, talking vaguely about the film and how it was different from how she'd remembered it. I couldn't really work out what she was getting at, given that she was being pretty inarticulate by her standards; I assumed she was complaining about having to watch the movie on a black and white TV, with bad reception and ads for Gargantini wine every five minutes.

Eventually we got to the picnic part of *Picnic*. Everyone was there: Kim Novak, her family, her boyfriend, her boyfriend's rich father, the spinster teacher and the guy who's always trying to marry her and, of course, William Holden. I remember a scene where William Holden is dancing beside a river, which I thought was funny because he was obviously supposed to be a good dancer and it was the dancing that won Kim Novak's heart, but I thought the way he danced was embarrassing and ridiculous. It was so funny that I almost had the nerve to say so, but when I looked at mamá I saw she was crying – I mean, really crying – her face was all wet like she'd just got out of the shower, but she didn't make a sound, while her shoulders rocked like the chassis of the Citroën.

I asked her what was wrong. 'What's the matter, mamá? Are you OK?'

She nodded but kept on crying, never taking her eyes off the TV.

'Mamá, I do like the film, honest, I swear I do.'

At that point the teacher, Rosalind Russell, rips William Holden's shirt and makes him look like a fool, and I wondered if mamá was crying because she knew that bit was coming, because sometimes with a book or a film you feel sad in advance because you know that something bad is going to happen, like it did with me and the Houdini book, and that reassured me for a bit. Then mamá hugged me and she didn't say anything, at least not until the film was over, and it was a happy ending (why was she crying then, why all this rain?). She gave me a wet kiss and said goodnight, goodnight, my darling, and left me sitting alone on the sofa watching the news. Presidente this, Armada that, new economic measures, the military government's tireless struggle against traitorous subversion, evil guerrillas, the province of Tucumán, the dollar, same old same old.

59

THE MOST
TREACHEROUS SEASON

Winter complicates everything.

Light clothes have to be taken out of circulation and winter clothes dusted off – long-sleeved shirts, pyjamas, scarves and mufflers, woolly gloves and hats and anoraks. They all smell of mildew and they itch (even the new clothes papá and mamá had bought me in a shop called ¡Verguenza! Mimito that made me look like the Michelin Man). You have to dig through the wardrobes, looking for eiderdowns and blankets that weigh down the bedsheets, so that when you're tucked up it feels like you've got a boulder on top of you. You have to light electric fires and gas stoves and the first time you light them they always smell of scorched Earth. You have to close the windows, check the doors so draughts can't sneak in, look for cracks and put up weather strips. You have to turn down the fridge so the milk doesn't make your teeth hurt. Having a bath becomes a torture, because it's so cold, because the towels are never completely dry and because of the mist that makes it look like you're taking a steam bath; this means that, as well as itching, your clothes stick to your body.

The air stinks because it's yesterday's air, last week's air, going round and round like a horse on a merry-go-round, carrying the smell of sweaty socks from the bedroom to the hallway, the smell of soup from the kitchen to the living room, the smell of mud from the living room to mamá's bedroom. Everyone in the family catches everyone else's colds until the last person collapses in a heap and it starts all over again.

Going outside is painful. The days are too short. (There's nothing more depressing that getting up in the dark to go to school.) The rain turns the roads into quagmires. We can't even play in the puddles because our rubber boots are back at our real house and papá and mamá never get around to keeping their promise to buy us new ones. Me and the Midget pretend that winter doesn't exist, but the fallen leaves are rotting to become a stinking slime under our feet, there are no toads any more, and half the time I don't even understand what the Midget is saying. With his scarf wrapped round and round his face he looks like 'Son of the Black Mummy'.

It's the same as always – or almost. Because this winter, something is different.

People lock up their houses early, double-lock their doors, put on the window locks, close the shutters and padlock them. There are lots of strange bugs going around this winter, they say, lots of diseases. They prefer to breathe musty air, prefer familiar smells to unfamiliar ones because a new smell means another organism and an unfamiliar organism is a stranger and no one has the time or energy to get to know strangers. It's winter, there are lots of strange bugs going round, lots of diseases. When people come knocking, they pretend they're not at home, or shout through the closed door. Postmen wonder if they will ever see a friendly face again. Even phone calls are cut short as though callers feel sorry for these words forced to travel along telephone lines exposed to frost and hail and rain, because it's not healthy to talk this winter, there are lots of strange bugs going around, lots of diseases. When people talk, their breath comes out in clouds of vapour, which isn't good because it makes it obvious that you're talking; it's better to talk indoors where the air is warm and your breath doesn't come out in clouds and you can say I'm hungry, I'm lost or what's on TV, without fear of being betrayed by winter.

60

HEAVEN HELPS ME
HOLD MY BREATH

During these dead afternoons, I took really long baths so I could practise holding my breath. My aim was to be able to spend four minutes underwater, one of the many feats that had made Houdini a legend. While I was underwater, the Midget timed me using mamá's watch. Not that he knew how to tell the time yet, but he could tell how many times the little hand made a full circle. The Midget didn't count in minutes; he counted in circles.

'When I grow up, I want to be a saint,' the Midget said, sitting on the toilet seat and playing with the watch. Mamá's conditions had been very clear: keep your hands dry and keep away from the bath.

'How many times do I have to tell you? Simon Templar isn't a real saint!' I protested between deep breaths.

'But San Roque is a real saint.'

I nodded as I exhaled.

'There are lots of saints. The other day, during the long mass, they must have mentioned about a thousand of them, remember? San Roque, pray for us, San José, pray for us . . .'

'I'm ready.'

'Wait until the little hand gets to the twelve. San Martín, pray for us. San Pedro, pray for us . . .'

'Hey . . .'

'Go!'

I went under. Below the water I could still hear the Midget who was talking as if I could still hear what he was saying.

With practice I had learned a couple of little tricks. When you're worried or nervous, you can't hold your breath as long. But when you distract yourself – and stop thinking about what you're doing – you can hold it for longer. Since the bottom of the bath doesn't offer much in the way of distraction, I had arranged my own show. I had two toy soldiers. One of them was huge, it must have been twenty centimetres, a medieval knight dressed head to toe in armour. He wielded a mace until the Midget lost it. The other one was tiny, maybe six centimetres and completely blue. Papá bought it for me in one of those incredible supermarkets that were starting to pop up all over the place, called Gigante or Jumbo or something, where they even sold toys. This one had his arms stretched out in front of him, because he came with an underwater tow sled like the one James Bond has in *Thunderball*, which, needless to say, the Midget had broken, wearing a pair of flippers that *I* broke from moving them up and down all the time. The good thing about these soldiers was they could play out all sorts of stories. Since his helmet had a crest in the middle, the knight could be Ultraman, and given that the little soldier had his arms stretched out, he could be flying, he could even be Superman, or . . .

Time to surface.

' . . . pray for us. San Jorge . . .'

'How many did I do?' I gasped.

'The hand didn't get all the way to twelve, it got as far as here.'

'Forty seconds?' It was embarrassing. I had to prepare myself

212

better. Breathe in, deep, deeper. Breathe out . . .

'San Mateo, pray for us . . . That's all I can think of! Tell me more saints!'

I shook my head and kept practising.

'Tell me, or I'm not helping anymore.'

'San Felipe.'

'That's the name of a wine, silly.'

'But before it was a wine, he was a saint.'

'Pray for us . . . Another one!'

'San Carlos . . .'

' . . . de Bariloche, pray for us!'

'San José.'

'I said him already.'

'Well, make some up, then.'

'What do you mean?'

'You can use words that start with San . . . San Atorium, for example . . . Let's go again!'

'Wait till it gets to the twelve. San Atorium, pray for us . . . San ChoPanza . . . is San ChoPanza OK?'

'It's fine, come on.'

'Go!'

I go under again. The Midget continues his litany.

Superman swims to the deepest depths of the ocean. He's received a message from Jimmy Olsen saying that Lois Lane has been kidnapped by Lex Luthor and is trapped in an underwater cave, and there's a big rock over the mouth of the cave that looks just like a bath plug. He has to get her out before she uses up all the oxygen and suffocates. Eventually, Superman gets to the cave and, using his super-strength, he moves the rock. (All of this happens with a soundtrack: my mental orchestra is always poised for the climactic scene.) Then he realizes he's been tricked: there's no sign of Lois Lane, she was never there in the first place. The stone wasn't blocking the entrance to a cave; it was blocking a deep chasm capable of swallowing everything, a bit like an underwater black hole that could swallow the whole ocean in a matter of minutes. He has to seal up the opening before all ocean life perishes . . . and with it the thousands of people in the city of Atlantis only a few miles away. (In my fantasies, I measure things in miles.)

Superman struggles with the terrible weight of the rock-plug. Against him is the power of the underwater black hole called Abyss Sinnian, whose power grows with every passing second. He is desperate, and then he sees that someone else has shown up. It's Ultraman! There is hope! He asks Ultraman to help him move the rock back into place. Only then does he find out that Ultraman has been hypnotized by Lex Luthor and is actually there to stop him from saving Atlantis! Super and Ultra (they sound like two kinds of petrol) wrestle with each other. Can Superman stop him in time to replace the rock-plug and save all ocean life? Will he be able . . .?'

Time to surface.

'San Dal, pray for us . . .'

'How many did I do?'

'One turn. Tell me some more saints!'

'San Dwich, San Itation, San Ity! I did a whole circle!'

I jumped out of the bath, splashing water everywhere. (For the curious, I should say that when I took a bath with the Midget present, I did it in my underpants. By that age my concept of modesty was fully developed.) I wanted to tell mamá about my feat. I'd held my breath for a whole minute! Now – ever the optimist – all I had to do was keep practising. If it had only taken me a couple of days to hold my breath for a minute, then in a week I'd be able to hold it for two and within two weeks I'd be able to hold it for four. Simple logic, as mamá liked to say.

I opened the bathroom door. From the doorway I could see mamá

214

in the living room talking to someone on the phone. She had her head down, like she was talking to the floor.

'. . . ten o'clock then. Yes, I know it. I've got blonde hair and I'll be reading a book . . . about physics. Sure: *Stability and Flux in Thermodynamic States*.'

'Saint Salive!' the Midget screamed from behind me.

At that moment mamá saw me. The scream must have scared her because when she looked at me, her eyes were sunken.

I closed the door and got back into the bath.

For the next dive I played out the story again, right up to the Super–Ultra battle. I didn't get to find out the end that time either. I don't think I ever found out how it ended.

61

ON THE ART OF
THE *MILANESA*

As with all really simple things, *milanesas* are hard to make properly. If you don't believe me, you only have to take mamá's efforts as an example.

Mamá did everything wrong. For a start, she didn't cut off the fat or the little bits of tendon, which meant that as soon as you put the meat into the frying pan it shrivelled into a ball – Quasimodo *milanesas* were her speciality – and as a result they weren't evenly cooked. And she never sieved the breadcrumbs, leaving big lumps in with the crumbs so that her *milanesas* looked like they were dipped in rocks. Sometimes, you'd get a piece of eggshell in your teeth that had fallen in when she cracked the eggs.

'*Milanesas* are better if you tenderize the meat,' I said, making a dash for the cutlery drawer. I'd seen one of the spiky wooden hammers for tenderizing meat in there somewhere.

She looked at me suspiciously as she busied herself with the frying pan, the oil, the cooker. As far as mamá was concerned, there were no gradations, no such thing as 'low' or 'medium': she always turned the gas up as high as it would go.

I found a chopping board and got down to work. The idea is to pound the meat so it becomes tender, that way you don't end up cutting through the breadcrumbs to find shoe leather inside.

Bam. Bam. Bam.

'It tastes better if you put some stock in with the beaten egg,' I said, still hammering. 'It gives it flavour.'

'Why are you hitting the meat?' yelled the Midget. Sitting on the kitchen counter wrapped in a huge towel, he looked like Humpty Dumpty. 'It's already dead!'

'Where did you learn all this from?' asked mamá, intrigued. 'Have you been watching Doña Petrona?'

The Midget laughed. Doña Petrona was a fat woman with knobbly fingers who did cooking on women's programmes on TV. She had an assistant called Juanita and she had a really funny way of talking: she didn't say 'Juanita'; she pronounced it 'Whaa-Nee-Tah', stressing every syllable.

'Bertuccio's mother taught me.'

'Did she now?'

'What's wrong with that? Bertuccio's mother is a genius.'

'You've got a strange concept of what a genius is. Aristotle, Galileo, Einstein and Bertuccio's mother!'

'You're burning the oil!'

Mamá quickly tossed in the first *milanesa*, which spattered furiously in the pan.

'Bertuccio's mother is a fat slob who doesn't know her arse from her elbow!'

'Firstly, she's not fat, she's thin. And secondly, she knows lots of things. She helps Bertuccio with his homework all the time!'

'And why would I help you? You never need any help. I've got a clever son!'

217

'And she's at home when Bertuccio comes home from school.'

'When you get home from school, you switch on the TV and I can't get a word out of you. Whenever I ask you how school was, all you ever say is "fine". What do you need me to be here for?'

'You're burning it!'

'Oops . . .'

Too late. The *milanesa* was no longer Quasimodo; it now looked like London after the Great Fire.

As mamá was staring at her pitiful attempt, I managed to turn the heat down to low.

'How about you try?' she said. 'I have to go.'

I had been expecting this. The phone conversation I had overheard had prepared me for this contingency, and I'd decided to resist it.

'What do you mean you have to go?'

'I have to go.'

'Where?'

'A meeting at work.'

'What work? They fired you!'

'I got fired from the lab, but that doesn't mean I don't have other things to do.'

'What things?'

'Things. You know.'

'Things that are more important than us?' (I was prepared for anything.)

'Nothing is more important to me than you two.'

'Well then, stay here.'

'I can't.'

'Stay, just this once. You can go some other day!'

Mamá took the frying pan off the heat, then rested her hands on my shoulders. She looked me in the eye, bringing her face close to mine (almost close enough for us to rub noses like an Eskimo kiss) and hit me full force with the Devastating Smile.

'Don't ask me to do a bad thing. Not you.'

Mamá, one. Harry, nil.

The *milanesas* were delicious. They were succulent and tender. Papá and Lucas showered me with praise, relieved for once to be spared the bland, often inorganic meals that were mamá's speciality. I must have eaten too many because after a while I had a stomach ache and eventually I threw up.

When I went to bed, mamá still wasn't home.

She arrived back a little later. Papá and Lucas were still up. I heard them talking about roadblocks. Then papá mentioned that I'd had a stomach ache and a second later she was opening the door to my room.

I pretended to be asleep, but it didn't matter. She talked to me like she knew I was faking it – even though I was brilliant, I kept my eyes closed, my body still, my breathing deep and regular, nothing to give me away. She obviously didn't want to wake the Midget because she whispered. I can clearly remember her warm breath on my left ear, telling me not to worry, that everything was going to be OK, that she would always be there (by my side, or in my ear?), that she loved me very much, that of all the scientific experiments she'd done in her life, I was the one that had turned out best. She said she didn't care whether I could hear her prattling on; didn't care that she was dribbling into my ear; didn't even care – get this – that she was behaving like Bertuccio's mother.

She probably twigged because I was smiling.

62

WE RECEIVE AN ANNOUNCEMENT

No one who did not have mamá's persuasiveness, which, though based on her keen intelligence, owed much to her natural air of authority (some, shrewdly, called it seductiveness), could have persuaded papá to go to grandpa's birthday. Since the beginning of the world – which, in this case, means for as long as I could remember – papá and grandpa had never got along.

Relentless hostility was the basis of their relationship. Just as the duellists in Conrad's short story symbolize a constant in a world of change, so papá and grandpa fought whenever and wherever they met – at parties, family reunions, Christmas and christenings – with the inevitability of ritual. Grandma insisted that they had not always been like this, but every time she made this claim, mamá and I would exchange a sceptical glance. Whatever harmony had existed between them dated back to Eden before the Fall; the last time they had hugged was long before Adam asked Eve if there was anything for dessert and she said: 'Wouldn't you prefer a nice piece of fruit?'

They invariably argued about the same things – the car, for example. Grandpa thought the Citroën was little more than a go-kart with a bit of fancy bodywork. Mortally offended, papá took this as his cue to unleash every weapon in his arsenal. They argued about the farm. If grandpa started talking about the harvest, or the livestock or some new fertilizer he was trying out, papá would interrupt him and try to change the subject, but he could never manage to get in before grandpa asked the question he always asked: 'Have you never thought of coming back to live in the country?' And every time Papá would reluctantly answer. There were two answers, one for mixed company and one that included the word 'fuck'.

The most sensitive subject, however, was Argentina. Aside from the name of the country and the colours of the flag, there was nothing on which papá and grandpa agreed. They argued about the army, censorship, the economy, the disappearances, the bombings, the newspapers, the repression, petrol, while grandma heaved loud sighs and mamá took papá's side, though she was more measured than he was – it was important not to crush grandpa and ruin things completely. I found these conversations deathly boring. Broadly speaking, it pretty much boiled down to the fact that grandpa thought the Peronists were a bunch of shits and papá thought they were good people, or some of them at least – not López Rega obviously, or Isabelita, or Lastiri who wore all those different ties, or some of the union leaders like Casildo Herrera, the guy who left Argentina, saying: 'I'm out of here'.

Papá would say grandpa was a gorilla – that's what people called anti-Peronists. The Midget would stubbornly argue that grandpa was a gentleman so as to tease him; papá would say grandpa was worse than Magilla Gorilla in the cartoons. Sometimes, when papá wasn't around, the Midget would pretend to be a monkey in front of grandpa, who thought it was funny, though he had no idea what it actually meant, or why the Midget suddenly stopped monkeying around when papá showed up.

I didn't think politics was anything to take seriously. It seemed to be something that got people all worked up about nothing, a sport that was as loud as it was pointless, a bit like football. Although I wasn't really interested in sport, in theory I supported Boca and Bertuccio supported River Plate, but even then we never fell out, except for the day after a *clásico* – derby games when Boca played River – when one of us would flay the other red raw until the bell rang for first break and it was time for more important things: trading cards, comics, playing Titanes, the usual stuff. This was why I suspected that there was something else at the root of papá and grandpa's endless feuding, something more than the Citroën or the farm or even Peronism, something so important that it had them facing off at dawn, staring down the pommels of their swords. Maybe it was the typical father/son stuff people talk about – the stuff that papá and I would go through when the time came – the conflict between a father's plans and his son's need to assert his own identity, rough edges that are worn away by time if and only if no outside force interrupts the normal sequence of events, if and only if nothing – no country, no person, no sword – intervenes.

In spite of what papá thought, to me grandpa was the best grandfather in the world. You could tell just by looking at him: fat, friendly, given to explosive bursts of tango ('*decí por Dios qué me has dao, que estoy tan cambiao . . .*') and always eager for an opportunity to play with us. Grandpa had a moustache as white as the hair he plastered down with Brylcreem as soon as he got out of the bath so as to temper its natural curliness. He didn't smoke cigarettes, but he liked cigars, Romeo y Julietas, and he'd give me the empty boxes when he was finished with them to put my trading cards in. (I think I liked Orson Welles before I ever saw an Orson Welles movie because he had the same look, like a smoking bear, that I associated with my grandfather.) Any time he saw me with a *Superman* comic he'd say: 'When are you going to stop reading that rubbish? You're a big boy now!' I'd tell him I'd stop reading comics the day he stopped reading pulp westerns by Silver Kane and Marcial Lafuente Estefanía, the sort of lurid novels you can buy at newsstands, and when we next passed a newsstand, we'd laugh, call a truce and buy another two, three, five . . .

Sometimes I'd see him doing something strange. Whenever he got worked up about something, he'd laugh and cry at the same time. He knew it was weird: he tried to explain it to me. He'd be watching *Sábados Circulares*, for example, and the presenter, Mancera, would introduce a choir of poor blind kids and grandpa would listen to them singing like angels and he'd start laughing and crying at the same time. It's not an easy thing to do. It takes a lot more practice than Houdini's four minutes underwater. The difference is, for the four-minute trick, you have to learn to do it, you have to take it seriously, practise like a professional, whereas laughing and crying at the same time is something life teaches you without you even noticing. If life was a movie and someone asked you what kind of movie it was, the best answer would be: it's a movie that makes you laugh and cry at the same time. Grandpa knew that.

We never found out what mamá did to persuade papá, because the news that we were going to Dorrego superseded all other considerations. Me and the Midget immediately started daydreaming. Dorrego meant our grandparents, whom we hadn't seen since the Christmas holidays, but it also meant the farm, horses, the tractor, animals, the library, papá's old toys, the lagoon, the boats and – last but not least – the Salvatierras, the foreman's children, with whom we were always getting into scrapes. One time we found some pots of paint and it occurred to us that, when he got up after his siesta, papá would be thrilled to see the Citroën (the one before the one we had now) painted a brilliant white. I'll leave the rest of that story here to the reader's imagination.

223

In my mind Dorrego meant something else, something that I didn't mention to the Midget – it meant leaving the *quinta* and therefore leaving Buenos Aires. It meant that mamá would not be going anywhere on her own. And it was a way of reconnecting with our own story, which had been in a state of suspended animation since the day mamá had unexpectedly come to school to collect us. Dorrego would not be our house, but it was the nearest thing to it we had left. A place where we would be surrounded by familiar sounds, by the people we knew and loved.

It was a pity Lucas couldn't come.

63

THE RIGHT QUESTIONS

It didn't take long for Lucas and me to reach the limits of what we could say to each other. In the time we spent together, we talked until we were hoarse about everything we were allowed to talk about, given the rules of the game. We talked a lot about the Beatles, our four evangelists; it was Lucas who pointed out to me that there was a Beatles' song for every possible mood (even the most bleak, like 'Yer Blues').

We talked about how pointless most of the things we learned at school were, and discussed the things kids should be taught. Wouldn't students be better off if they were given the opportunity to discover the book that would change their life? Shouldn't we have to listen to the best music, to sing and dance? In learning Geography, shouldn't they start by teaching us how to find our way around? (Nobody much used a compass any more, as though we couldn't get lost.) And as for History, wouldn't it make more sense to start with the present day? If we couldn't make sense of what was going on around us, how could we learn from the experience of those who had gone before us?

(Every now and then, when he recounted more recent memories, Lucas would let slip a plural – 'we were', 'we ran', one time 'we saw' – which made me think that he had also been forced to leave a Bertuccio behind, or a Midget, but obviously I couldn't ask him any questions.)

We discussed our experiences with the female of the species; his, which were many and varied – although he still denied that the girl in his wallet was or had ever been his girlfriend – and mine, which were limited to Mara, the daughter of friends of my parents who was in my after-school English class, whose mere presence made me want to do stupid things. I suspect I made a rather feeble case for the sensitive, intelligent man.

We also talked about comics and TV shows and movies. Lucas asked if I'd ever read a comic called *El Eternauta*, which he was sure I'd love, given how much I loved *The Invaders*. I told him I'd try and find a copy. I remember a Mona Lisa smile lit up his face and he told me that, these days, asking for a copy of *El Eternauta* at a newsstand was also the wrong question. All roads seemed to lead to the wrong question. Back then, we felt as though we were condemned to silence.

I don't know whether Lucas started the game or I did. I suspect it was me. Being the son of the Rock and a fervent disciple of Houdini, I felt a feverish desire to flout, or at least mock, the constraints imposed on me; I wouldn't say I was blind to my conditioning, but I was getting a little short-sighted. Since asking the wrong questions was prohibited, I began to rack my brains to come up with the right ones, questions that could be spoken aloud, in the light of day. I bridled at being told what I could and could not do: people start by forbidding you to ask certain questions and you end up not being able to ask any at all, and a man who has stopped asking questions is a dead man. Pretty quickly, we hit the mother lode. There were basic, obvious questions to which we didn't know the answers. Why is the sky blue? Why is the Earth shaped the way it is? Why is water wet? Why did nature evolve spicy food? Why does helium give you a high-pitched voice like Benny the Ball from *Top Cat*? Why is air transparent? How do LPs store music? Why are saints always shown with haloes? (This was the Midget's contribution.) Why did dead languages die? Why don't people sing rather than talk? How hot is the surface of the sun? – a question that, in the dead of winter, provoked an exquisite nostalgia for summer. The questions kept coming.

We would slump on the grass, our backs against a tree, indifferent to the cold, and sit there for a long time, saying nothing. To the casual observer, it might seem as though we were doing nothing, whereas in fact our senses were working overtime. We could feel the rough bark at our backs, in spite of our thick jackets, feel the smoothness and the damp of the ground we were sitting on. As we breathed in the icy air, we could follow its course through our bodies as it became lukewarm, only to lose it when it became a part of us. Sometimes I thought I could see windows melting. (Glass is a super-cooled liquid; it's just that our perception is like a video recorder set to 'Pause'.) Then one of us, it didn't matter who, would ask a question – Are the hairs on our head antennae? – and the other would come up with another one – Why do we have five fingers on each hand rather than three, or seven, or twelve? – and after that they'd come thick and fast, our breath like white clouds, making us seem like friendly dragons, because everyone knows that good dragons belch white smoke.

Lucas and me didn't even bother trying to answer these questions. Mostly because we didn't know the answers, except for a few that Lucas could explain: for example, he was the one who told me about aquifers. Aquifers are reservoirs or layers of water under the ground that collect rainwater and somehow manage, by rivers and streams, to get it back to the sea; everything is connected. Sometimes he'd come up with an answer that was funny or poetic – saints have haloes so that God doesn't lose track of them when he's looking down on them from above, or, if books were feathers, there'd be no birds, there'd be flying libraries, things like that – but only sometimes, because the game was about the questions. It was about proving that there was no such thing as a wrong question, only wrong answers.

In the days before we left for Dorrego, I hardly saw him. One day he'd leave five minutes after I came home from school and wouldn't get back until long after I was asleep, another day he'd get back early but he'd claim he was exhausted and would go to bed without any dinner. I don't think he wanted to talk to anyone, he was pale and he looked as though he felt like zipping his sleeping bag over his head, returning to the womb, smelling his own smells to make sure he was still alive. I felt frustrated. Like an ant, I felt I needed to store up affection for those times when there would be none, I wanted to have days when there was lots of Lucas to compensate for the shortage of Lucas in Dorrego. It's possible to stockpile affection and carry it around like the huge leaves you see ants carrying around on their tiny little bodies. But I couldn't do it. On Friday night, I waited up as late as I could, but Lucas didn't come back in time.

I did see him for a minute, on Saturday morning. We made so much noise getting ready to leave – I was particularly noisy – that he woke up and came to say goodbye. The Citroën had already set off when he suddenly seemed to remember something and he ran after the car on his long spidery legs.

'Nine thousand, nine hundred and thirty-two degrees Fahrenheit,' he said, his breath misting my window.

'What is?'

'The temperature on the surface of the sun.'

'Look after the toads for me,' said the Midget.

'Don't worry . . . we'll keep each other company.'

Papá and mamá said goodbye again and we drove off.

While we were in Dorrego, I didn't have Lucas, but at least I had something. Every time I thought about him, I pictured him in a trench coat, looking mysterious, enigmatic, darting through the shadows from one doorway to another, his eyes small and bright – like the marbles we played with one time – alert to the possible presence of the enemy. I imagined Lucas trying to make it to a vast,

228

shadowy building without being spotted. Once inside, he took off his trench coat and, protected by his orange T-shirt, he forgot about his secret mission for a while, forgot the danger that awaited him outside, and striding in his seven-league boots, he'd walk up to the desk and say: 'Good evening, *señora*, could you tell me where I might find out the temperature of the sun?'

Playtime

Fourth Period: Astronomy

Noun: the science of stars
and heavenly bodies.

64

DORREGO

The gate rose up in the middle of nowhere. That's how it appeared to my child's eyes, the path wound endlessly around the wire fence until it came to the gate right in the middle of infinite nothingness, because you went through the gate and on the other side there was nothing, nothing but fields and a curved horizon, a green sea on which Christ could have walked in his sandals. Even in the Citroën we had to drive for quite a bit before we reached anywhere. First we saw the olive grove – the trees were only a couple of years old and were hardly as tall as me. (Me and the Midget liked playing in the olive grove, it made us feel like giants.) Then came a thicket and beyond that the tilled fields and the livestock and from there, in the distance, we could make out the mill; the house was close now.

It was nice but it was simple, a one-storey house with a red tiled roof, a living/dining room with huge windows and a fireplace, where, family legend had it, I ate half a beetle when I was a year old. There was a long corridor that led to the bedrooms, to grandpa's study and to the kitchen, which was so huge that me and the Midget played handball against the back wall. We called it the Chickendrome, ever since papá, determined to prove that he was a real farmer, tried to kill a chicken by wringing its neck. The poor bird fell on the tiled floor as though it was dead, then suddenly got up and started scurrying around the kitchen, its neck forming a perfect right-angle, flapping its wings wildly.

There was no swimming pool in Dorrego, but there was a big rainwater tank we bathed in with the Salvatierra kids; if we wanted a proper swim we went down to the lagoon, though even on the hottest days of summer the water was freezing. But for adventure, the lagoon was unbeatable: we fished from the pier or out of boats, we practised ducks and drakes, skimming flat stones across the water, we lashed reeds together to make rafts that we never completed and we patrolled the banks of the lagoon searching for nature's endless surprises: lizards, dead fish, bare bones for which we invented macabre origins. ('We thrive on bones,' writes Margaret Atwood, 'without them there'd be no stories.')

The Salvatierra kids were identical Russian dolls of various sizes. There were two boys, the oldest and the youngest, but the middle child, Lila, was by far the bravest of the three. They were quiet but friendly, with permanent smiles, dazzling as the sun, shining out of tanned faces. They had a sixth sense for devilment, and could sniff out an opportunity for a practical joke as if it was sulphur. Wherever there was something that might be dangerous – quicklime, axes, bulls, a sow with her piglets – we would find them hanging around, waiting for the right moment. Their father would invariably end up hauling them home by the ears. Given that he didn't have hands enough to drag all three of them, Lila had to grab the littlest boy by the ear, and off they'd go, all four of them, like a human daisy chain.

When I was little, their father asked Lila to teach me how to ride a horse. I remember how nervous I was, especially since Lila's horse seemed to want to break into a gallop at any minute. I spent my whole time tugging on the reins to try and get him to stop, until eventually I saw the shadow on the ground that explained why he was in such a hurry. Sitting behind me, Lila was digging her heels into his flanks, trying to goad him. Every time I stopped the horse, she'd dig her heels in again, trying hard not to laugh.

But underlying all the games, I felt an unspoken hostility towards me, an outsider coming from a different world and attempting to annex their territory. With almost animal instinct, they insisted that I prove myself worthy to join their gang and, like a bull faced with a red cape, I blindly tackled every dare – some successfully, others disastrously – and while no blood was shed, there were a few broken bones. And still they kept drawing imaginary lines in the sand which I continued to cross, determined to prove myself worthy at any cost: scratches, threats, plaster casts, I didn't care. But whenever I went back to playing with my city things – my trading cards and my books – they kept their distance, as though afraid to expose themselves to the effects of a magic whose rules they did not understand. They only got involved when they saw me playing at being someone else – a cowboy, or Robin Hood or Tarzan. Playing characters in a story I made up came naturally to them and they threw themselves into the roles with an energy and an imagination that surpassed my meagre stage directions: they were born actors.

I still bear the scars of the ordeals the Salvatierra kids subjected me to. Strangely, I don't remember ever feeling any pain, but I do remember the joy I felt the first time I beat Lila in a horse race – we were riding barefoot and the stirrups rubbed my instep raw – or when I got the highest walnut from the walnut tree, flaying the skin from my hands in the process. On the map of my body, these scars mark out the course of an initiation for which I feel nothing but gratitude. In their own way, the Salvatierra kids understood the Principle of Necessity. If they had not created the conditions that forced me to change, I would still feel like an outsider in Dorrego, an intruder, a stranger.

65

IN WHICH WE VISIT THE FARM AND I BECOME A FOREIGN CORRESPONDENT

The trip to Dorrego passed without incident, given that the Midget slept almost the whole way. There was a reason he was so tired. Mamá had got him up to pee three times the night before so that he wouldn't wet the bed. Unaware of this, I had also got him up to go to the toilet when I happened to wake up in the middle of the night, and papá, not knowing mamá and I had already done so, also took him to the toilet twice. The Midget had done more walking in his sleep that night than he usually did during the day.

Hardly had the racket of the Citroën announced our arrival than our grandparents came out to greet us. Grandpa was as fat as ever; I remember the vicuña poncho he was wearing. Tall and thin, grandma had a natural elegance. She looked like a number 1 standing beside the chubby 0 that was grandpa; together they formed the binary system on which my entire universe was based.

Awake now, the Midget gave grandpa his first present: a box of Romeo y Julieta. I followed, with a bottle of Johnnie Walker Black

Label. These were presents that never disappointed: we knew that grandpa would enjoy them. But even so, he managed to needle papá.

'Would you look at this?' he said, showing grandma the whisky and the box of cigars. 'I don't know whether they're trying to spoil me or bump me off!'

Papá glanced at mamá, as if to say 'You see?!'

Worse still, grandpa took it upon himself to tell us how long it had been since he'd last seen us. He rattled off the number of months, days and hours, having worked it out exactly, or at least that was what he made us think.

'That is a pretty long time,' the Midget admitted.

And grandpa, having persuaded the jury to convict, rested his case.

It was true that we didn't visit often. At 500 kilometres from Buenos Aires, the trip is no joke, especially in the Citroën. Usually, when we hadn't visited for a while, grandma and grandpa would come and visit us, but it was obvious that papá and grandpa's quarrel the last time they had come to visit had been more acrimonious than usual. (The great advantage of a farm is that, if the conversation turns ugly, there are lots of places you can go to get away.) As a result, we hadn't seen our grandparents since.

During lunch, which was fantastic, the conversation was light enough to ensure that there would be no quarrels. The subject of the farm came up, but it was grandpa who quickly changed the subject. The state of the nation was mentioned, but both papá and grandpa agreed that Argentina was becoming a subject best not talked about. Me and the Midget ended up monopolizing everyone's attention: he stood on a chair and performed his version of the national anthem – with the line 'Great big Nesquiks in their bodies' – and I gave a demonstration of the various knots Lucas had taught me using napkins.

Eventually papá and mamá went for a siesta. Grandpa retired to the living room, lit a Romeo y Julieta (there are few things in the world that stimulate daydreaming like the smell of a good Havana cigar) and sat in his chair facing the window. Next to the fireplace, the Midget was talking to the two Goofys, explaining to the plastic Goofy, the newest member of the family, that it was right here that I once ate half a beetle. The Midget had inherited grandma's fondness for recounting memories; grandma was the permanent curator of the Museum of Our Happiness: anywhere she went evoked some memory she felt compelled to share with whoever was with her, even if they had already heard the story a thousand times.

I sank into a big armchair, intent on capturing this moment: my grandparents, the smell of the Romeo y Julieta, the perfect idleness of a Saturday afternoon that seemed eternal. It didn't last long. In that moment the glass seemed half-full, yet a nagging doubt prevented me from draining it.

Maybe that's the way I've always been, from the moment I emerged from my mother's belly and was launched into the world; I know what I want and how to get it, but once I have it in my grasp there is always some part of me that refuses to relax, to enjoy the moment; a part of me that is already worrying about what will come next, about a future that has not yet taken shape. That afternoon remains in my memory as the first time I became aware of my limitations. I can never live entirely in the moment. There is always a part of me that is absent, not where I am seen to be, where I seem to be, a part that is somewhere in the future, waiting for the call 'action stations'.

'When will you teach me how to drive the tractor?' I asked grandpa, who was lost in his own daydream. (When you're a kid, it's impossible to imagine all the things that might be going through the mind of a grown-up who looks as though he's not thinking about anything.)

Grandpa exhaled a plume of grey smoke and said, 'Right now.'

When we were down in the country, grandpa liked to take us around and show us things. Whenever he drove the tractor, I sat up beside him, perched on a metal toolbox. If he went riding (though he was fat, grandpa was an excellent horseman), he always asked for two horses to be saddled. If he went to pick tomatoes, I took another basket and we went together. I didn't ask, but I figured he had done the same with papá when he was little and that my being there helped him forget the void that had been by his side for twenty years.

'So, how are things, *che*?' he asked ingenuously as I was practising changing gears on the tractor. 'How's your friend, the little Chinese guy?'

'Japanese!' I corrected him, as I always did. Grandpa liked winding me up. I must have been in first or second grade when he told me he was psychic and that he had had a vision that I had a Japanese friend. At the time I was stunned, but later, when I became a little less gullible, I realized that it had been a lucky guess. There were Chinese, Japanese and Korean kids in every state school in the country. Probability was on his side. But I never dared question his psychic gifts.

'Chinese, Japanese . . .'

'I don't know . . . he left the school last year.'

'You don't say? What about the other lad, what's his name, Bertolotti, Bergamotti . . .'

'Bertuccio!'

'How's Bertuccio?'

I couldn't get the hang of changing gears. I tried to force it.

'Hey, hey, easy does it, *che*. It takes skill, not brute force.' By now grandpa had realized that something was wrong. He didn't need to be psychic. 'Don't tell me Bertuccio left too?'

At this point I would like to say that I carefully considered the possible consequences of my actions, but that would be a lie. It was like someone had given me a truth serum with lunch; I would have answered any question grandpa asked me, however private or embarrassing the answer.

'He didn't leave. I left. Me and the Midget. We're going to a religious school now. The priest is a friend of papá. Since we started going there the Midget wants to be a saint. Mamá got fired from the laboratory. Papá's law office is gone, some guys stormed in and trashed everything. He worked in bars for a while, but there's too many police now, so he works at home. But it's not our home, it's someone else's home. We're living on a *quinta* now, with a swimming pool and a bunch of suicidal toads.'

Grandpa didn't say anything. For a minute I thought he hadn't heard a word I'd said. I wondered how a foreign correspondent would have put it, the guy who was on the TV every night at midnight, just before the 'moment of meditation'. His voice and his face were funereal, if memory serves; his name was Repetto, Armando Repetto, he had dark hair, slicked back like Bela Lugosi. I could almost hear him intone, in his deep baritone voice: 'The situation of the Vicente family has taken a turn for the worse. Already facing the challenges of living in secret, they are now in financial trouble. Flavia has lost her job and the future of David's work is precarious, raising the threat of insolvency . . . David's father confessed to media sources that he was not surprised, and insisted that he intended to take steps to . . .'

'*Abuelo*, *abuelo*, are you listening to me?'

'Of course, darling.'

'Don't fight with papá, please. Not this time.'

242

66

THE LARVAE

I remember once there was this opossum that drove grandpa crazy. It laid waste to the chicken coop. I have a fleeting memory of blood and feathers and broken eggs. Grandpa laid traps, blocked every hole in the coop, but the opossum kept squeezing through and decimating the hens. Until one day grandpa decided enough was enough and we set out to hunt down the opossum.

I was excited by the prospect of joining the hunting party. It was like a Western. The opossum was a cattle-rustler, grandpa was the sheriff and I was his trusty deputy; I stood next to him as he took down his shotgun and filled his pockets with red buckshot cartridges and I ran over to get Señor Salvatierra when he asked me to. The two boys came, too. Lila wanted nothing to do with the whole thing. Women have better instincts.

We wandered around in circles for so long that for a while I thought the opossum was outwitting us. Finally Señor Salvatierra tracked him down. He stopped about a metre from a tree, stared at a hole in the trunk and announced that the opossum was inside. At first I didn't believe him, but then he pushed the barrel of the shotgun into the hole and fired.

Shotguns sound like cannons. I can't imagine what cannons sound like.

Then he put his arm inside and pulled it out.

Opossums are disgusting animals. On the outside they look like little furry cushions, but inside they're all vicious teeth and claws. Señor Salvatierra threw it on the ground and poked it in the belly with the barrel of the shotgun. This seemed to me a little unnecessary, given that it was obviously dead, but it confirmed what Salvatierra had been thinking.

'She's with young,' he said.

Inside her pouch were several white hairless creatures that looked like little more than larvae, twisting and turning as though stretching themselves.

'What'll happen to them now?' I asked.

Señor Salvatierra looked at grandpa. Grandpa said nothing. He was busying himself unloading his shotgun and stuffing the cartridges back in his pockets with the others.

Manolo, the older of the Salvatierra boys, who was kneeling next to me beside the opossum, said, 'They'll die.'

I gave him a push and he fell on his backside. 'No, they won't,' I said stubbornly. 'If I feed them and keep them warm they won't die.'

'They're too little,' said Manolo. 'Can't you see, they're still suckling? Look at their mouths. You'll never find a teat small enough to feed them!'

'Get on home!' Señor Salvatierra said imperiously. Manolo looked at him resentfully. Why was he being sent home, when I was obviously the stupid one? But he reluctantly headed off, his little brother trailing behind him. Señor Salvatierra quickly took his leave. I stood, frozen, caught between disgust and helplessness, wanting to take the larvae with me but terrified I would hurt them if I picked them up, not knowing how to hold them, where to put them, what to do. Looking up, I saw grandpa watching me, the look on his face was one I'd never seen before – the forlorn expression adults have when they are unable to shield their children or grandchildren from pain.

I didn't even want dinner. I sat by the fire, cradling a cardboard box filled with scraps of cloth, a makeshift mattress for my larvae. After she put the Midget to bed, mamá came over and sat next to me; after a while she told me to sit on her knee, and I did, still clutching the cardboard box. The larvae were sleepy and so was I.

The next morning I woke up in my own bed. For a minute I thought the whole thing had been a nightmare. But mamá, who had been waiting for me to wake up, took me in her arms – I would have been about six or seven then, and still manageable – and carried me out to the bank of the lagoon.

She had buried the larvae there, in the mud bank where the rushes grew. She told me that their bodies would help the rushes to grow strong and supple. Living creatures never completely disappear, mamá told me, when something we love dies, it lingers in the air that we breathe, the food we eat, the ground we walk on. I didn't know what to think, I didn't really understand what she was saying, and I wasn't sure that I believed what little I did understand. But I felt reassured to know that the larvae were close by, somewhere I could visit whenever I liked.

That stretch of the lakeshore was always special to me. I still like to go there when I manage to escape the clutches of the world. I close my eyes and listen to the whistle of the breeze in the rushes; it's the same whistle mamá gives when she's right.

67

GRANDMA'S TIME MACHINE

By mid-afternoon, it was so hot that we began to wonder if the sun had forgotten what season this was. We were ill equipped for such weather: the lightest clothing mamá had packed for me was the check flannel shirt I was already wearing. But grandma said she had some old clothes of papá's that might fit me: a short-sleeved shirt and a pair of shorts, something lighter than my lumberjack outfit. She and I went upstairs to papá's old room, which had been locked to spare it from the destructive talents of the Midget. Papá's room was an entire universe in miniature; a black hole would have damaged it irreparably.

Despite having been shut up, the room smelled clean. It was obvious that grandma aired it regularly. Papá's telescope was still on its tripod next to the window. The bed was made up with clean sheets and everything. There were pennants pinned to the wall above the headboard, reminders of local sports clubs and the sort of philanthropic associations you got back then, the Rotary Club and the Lions Club. On one side of the bed was a small bookcase with a load of children's books all from *la colección Robin Hood*. Through one of the publishing miracles of the Argentina of a different era, papá and I had read exactly the same books. *David Copperfield* translated by a posh lady called María Nélida Bourguet de Ruiz, for example. Papá had a copy of the second edition from 1945 that he bought in 1950, to judge by the name and the date scrawled in his childish handwriting on the first page.

On the desk I found an entire battalion of lead soldiers, ranged against an invisible enemy. On the shelf at head height there was a collection of model cars that, in size and detail, put my Matchbox cars to shame, a collection of model airplanes and a red sailboat whose sail rose to a couple of inches below the ceiling.

'It's exactly the same,' I said as grandma poked around in the wardrobe.

'Exactly, exactly.'

'You could have thrown all this stuff out and had a room for the two of you,' I said, thinking of grandma Matilde, who had boxed up all of mamá's belongings and turned her old bedroom into a showcase for the souvenirs of her trips abroad: hats and *mantillas* and dolls (the most extravagant being a flamenco dancer the train of whose dress was a metre long).

'What would I want with another room?' said grandma, practical as ever. 'Here, try this on.'

She handed me a short-sleeved shirt and a pair of Bermuda shorts. They stank of mothballs, but they were clean and looked almost new. It was weird to think that papá had ever been this small.

'Do you miss him a lot?' I asked as I pulled off my shirt.

'Your father? Of course I miss him. But I'm not crying my eyes out, if that's what you mean. I couldn't ask for any more than I had. And there's nothing that I need that I don't already have. Though I would like to see you all more often. You see, it fits perfectly. Try the shorts on.'

'You could turn it into a playroom,' I said, since I wasn't against the idea of grandma packing all of papá's things into boxes . . . and giving them to me.

'It's already a playroom. For me, it's a time machine,' said grandma as she opened the wardrobe door wide so that I could see myself in the mirror. 'Every time I come in here to clean, I get caught up by something . . . anything, one of those photos, a copybook from school, a shirt . . . and it's like I'm living that moment over again. I can almost hear your papá – his voice when he was a little boy, I mean – yelling down the stairs, always wanting something, a glass of milk, or clean clothes.'

'He does the same to mamá, but mamá just ignores him.'

'Good for her. At least some things have changed for the better.'

Grandma stood behind me so that she could look at me in the mirror. She liked what she saw, apart from my hair, which she tried in vain to curl with her fingers.

'Other things have changed for the worse. The quality of the stuff they make nowadays is terrible. They break the minute you buy them and you have to buy more! Do you think a shirt you bought now would last as long as this has? That's the good thing about memories. They don't wear out from overuse! They don't take up space. And the most important thing,' grandma said, giving me a kiss on the ear that left me half-deaf, 'is that no one can steal them from you!'

68

A TRIP TO ATLANTIS

I don't know whether grandma's paean to how well things were made in the good old days was warranted, but the raft that grandpa had made for papá had survived for more than twenty years. Measuring a metre by a metre and a half, it could fit two adults comfortably or, more usually, three children. Every detail attested to a skilled, or at least a loving, hand: the lacquer to stop the boards from absorbing water, the metal rowlocks, the use of screws rather than nails. Grandpa had found it in one of the sheds, though he had no luck locating the mast that had once stood in the centre of the raft from which, according to papá, flew a skull and crossbones flag that grandma had made according to papá's design.

When grandpa showed up with the raft in the back of the truck, it was impossible to tell who was happier: grandpa, feeling a sense of pride in his craftsmanship, papá, suddenly overwhelmed by memories, or me, excited at the prospect of sailing. We stood for several seconds, barely uttering a sound. Then, as one, we decided that the time was right: the sun was shining, the lagoon was near and we had a raft. Who could have resisted such temptation?

We left our shoes and socks on the bank of the lagoon – and grandpa, since his weight alone would have sunk the raft (it would probably have sunk the *Kon-Tiki*). I begged him at least to get into the water with us, but he wouldn't hear of it; he said he would stay and watch us from the bank. Papá rolled up the legs of his trousers, told me to get onto the raft, and started to push.

And we were off. We headed for the middle of the lagoon, papá using his hands as both oars and rudder. I lay on my belly, leaning over the side, shielding my eyes from the sun as I tried to see the bottom. Grandpa told me that the lagoon hadn't always been here. Years ago, before he bought the farm, he said, it had been a marble quarry. In their eagerness, someone had dug a little too deep and struck an aquifer. Water gushed out like oil wells in the movies and didn't stop until it had filled the whole quarry, leaving the quarrymen to look for work elsewhere. Papá swore there was still machinery on the bottom, huts that had been built for the workers, even trees. (On the other side of the lagoon, next to the Podetti's farm, there were trees whose trunks were half-buried in the lagoon.) He claimed he had seen all this, snorkelling with a breathing tube made from rushes. I listened with a certain scepticism: the story sounded too good to be true. How many people have their very own Atlantis just a stone's throw from their house?

In time I discovered that neither papá nor grandpa had lied. There were two bulldozers covered in moss in the murky depths, a hut with no roof that you could swim through, and tree trunks with tiny fish swimming around the branches. But that first time, out on the raft, I could see nothing, nothing except plants with huge coiled leaves that twisted hypnotically, melting into the darkness of deeper waters.

Papá rowed steadily, occasionally correcting our course. He was already soaking wet, but he didn't seem to care.

Grandpa waved to us from the bank.

'He could at least have got into the water,' I said.

'Your *abuelo* can't swim.'

'What do you mean he can't swim?'

'You think that everyone has a swimming pool to play in? Your *abuelo* has been working since he was a little boy; his mamá didn't have the money to pay for him to go to sports club.'

'So what did he do when you went swimming? Wasn't he afraid? I mean, if something happened while you were on the raft, how would he save you?'

'He had a motor boat moored at the pier. But he claims he was never afraid. I was always a good swimmer. He trusted me. Your *abuelo* believes that the sooner you learn to fend for yourself the better. That's one of the few things we agree on. It's why I taught you how to cross the road and how to travel on your own when you were little.'

'Even though I got lost that time?'

'But after that, you never got lost again.'

Papá was rowing with a purpose. He was looking for a post which, he claimed, marked the centre of the lagoon. It was an old lamp-post, submerged except for the last metre or so. He wanted to see if the things he had carved on it with his penknife were still there, but we couldn't see any post anywhere.

'They must have taken it out. Or maybe it just rotted away. We always used to row out there, me and a couple of friends – Señor Podetti's son and Alberto, one of Salvatierra's cousins. One time, Podetti stood on the lamp-post and started posing like a statue. He posed like Rodin's *Thinker*, then like a rather camp *David*, and then he said: "For my next impression, I'm going to be an angel on a fountain." And he pulled down his trunks and started pissing on us. The little bastard! He was laughing like a hyena, until Alberto and me started rowing and left him standing on the lamp-post. He had to swim halfway across the lagoon to catch us up!'

Papá rowed tirelessly. Tired of trying to see the bottom of the lagoon, I turned onto my back, belly to the sun, and let myself be carried along as papá went on telling stories, memories pouring out of him as though he couldn't turn them off. At some point I stopped listening. Floating is so delicious; like flying, I imagine. I think I might have fallen asleep for a minute or two.

'I'm roasting here,' I said eventually.

'Splash some water on yourself.'

'Can't I just dive in?'

'The water's really cold. It's hard to swim in cold water, your arms and your legs feel heavy and you get tired quickly.'

'OK, well let's play a game then.'

'Me and Podetti used to play a balancing game. We'd stand on either side of the raft, really still, then, on the count of three, we'd rock the raft with our feet, trying to pitch the other person into the water.'

'Come on, let's play that!'

'You're going to end up in the water!'

'You're the one who's going to end up in the water!'

'Dream on!'

'You're just scared of me.'

'Hah! You've just signed your own death warrant. Consider yourself soaked!'

Just standing up was a feat in itself. The raft bobbed and wheeled like a wild thing. We were laughing so much that neither of us could manage to stand.

'Who are you?' I asked, laughing.

'I'm Captain Nemo, who are you?'

'I'm Houdini.'

'Nemo versus Houdini, one . . . No pushing . . . Nemo versus Houdini, two . . .'

'No tickling.'

'Nemo versus Houdini . . . and three!'

It was like ice-skating for the first time, it was incredibly difficult to keep my balance. It was hard enough to stay upright and harder still to try and compensate for the other person rocking the raft.

I was destined to wind up in the lagoon – only a miracle could save me. Or a trick.

Papá was still commentating on our battle ('Nemo dribbles, he dodges, he passes . . .') when I gave him a gentle shove. He was so surprised that he fell backwards like a stone. If I hadn't thrown myself down on the raft, with the sudden disappearance of the counterweight, I would have been pitched over too.

'Incredible, ladies and gentlemen!' I howled. 'Houdini takes him down, Houdini is unbeaten! Nemo has been sunk! It's all over! Put your hands together for the champion!'

I would have gone on crowing like a peacock, but it wasn't much fun until papá came to the surface. And papá still hadn't surfaced.

There weren't even any bubbles. I crawled over to his side of the raft, but a black cloud blocked the sun at that moment and all I could see was black water.

I remembered what papá had said. About how cold the water was, how heavy your arms and legs feel, how difficult it is to swim. What if the cold water had sent him into a state of shock? What if he'd sunk to the bottom, with the bulldozers and the huts and the trees?

I wanted to scream but nothing came out. I suddenly felt cold; my teeth were clacking like castanets, all the heat had drained from my body. That bloody cloud: black cloud, black water. All I could do was prowl from one side of the raft to the other, like a panther in an invisible cage, hoping papá would reappear, that the black cloud would go away, the water would clear and papá would come back from Atlantis.

Suddenly I felt a jet of freezing water hit me. Papá had popped his head above the surface and was filling his mouth with water and spitting it at me – a colourless, odourless variation of Podetti's angel. He thought it was funny, thought he was simply paying me back for playing a dirty trick on him, but the moment he saw me, his smile vanished. I don't know what he saw on my face, what made him turn pale. I suppose he guessed what was coming: I lashed out, punching him brutally, angrily, and he parried the blows with one arm as he tried to put his other arm around me so he could hug me, so he could say I'm sorry, I'm sorry, *querido*, I didn't realize, I swear, I didn't realize. I went on thumping him and he went on apologizing, until finally I was too tired to hit him anymore, but still he went on, saying the words over and over, until he was too hoarse to speak.

The official version was that he fell off the raft through his own stupidity.

We never told anyone what really happened.

69

IN WHICH I PLAY THE SPY
AND HEAR SOMETHING
I SHOULDN'T

Dinner went off without a hitch. It was as though papá had toned down his usual persona, leaving only a subdued version of itself – pewter rather than silver. Even grandpa was surprised when papá did not react to his comments with the usual sarcastic barbs. Apart from the Midget, who kept getting up from the table to toss pieces of bread into the fire, everyone noticed the change in papá. By the time the fruit came, the tension had become so hypnotic that I couldn't tear my eyes away from papá's hands, as he peeled an apple, as he added soda to his wine, as he rolled crumbs into little pellets, trying to work out if his little fingers still flexed properly, if he was still papá or if he had been replaced by a *Doppelgänger* who could duplicate his form but never his spirit.

Grandma got up and began to clear the table. Mamá got up too, and as she scraped all the leftovers onto one plate she gave me the prearranged signal. The first part of my mission was to round up the Midget and herd him into the kitchen. It proved more complicated than expected, because the Midget, having worked out that he could make little dolls using a couple of toothpicks and papá's pellets of bread, was now in the middle of re-enacting a historic court case.

'Let me finish!' he protested as I tugged at him. 'I'm making Joan of Arc!'

'You can burn her later. We have to bring in the pie!'

The idea was that we would lead the procession carrying grandma's pie, singing 'Happy Birthday'. When we got to the kitchen, mamá and grandma were lighting candles as fast as they could.

'There's always a shortage of teachers. It doesn't have to be a permanent thing, but it might be a temporary solution. The important thing is that you suggest it to him. If I talk to him, he won't pay any attention, and if his father tries to talk to him, all hell will break loose. You know how it is. They're as bad as each other,' said grandma, lighting matches as fast as she could.

'Can I light one?'

'Can I light one?' echoed the Midget.

'No!' mama said, and went on talking to grandma as though we weren't there. 'It's the only way they know how to relate to each other. They have to be tough. Do you know what it's like, living with three boys?'

I tried to dip my finger into the meringue on top of the pie, but mamá rapped me on the head with the box of matches.

'Go and stand by the door to the living room, and when I give the signal, turn off the lights.'

'We have to put the fire out too, otherwise it won't be dark,' said the Midget, who was prepared to do anything to save Joan of Arc.

'Don't you go playing with that fire,' said grandma, 'don't you know that little boys who play with fire wet the bed?'

The Midget was speechless. Was grandma clairvoyant?

I did as mamá told me and stood next to the living room door as a lookout. Papá and grandpa were talking in low voices.

'Of course I know it's difficult,' papá was saying; there was a hopelessness in his voice I'd never heard before. 'How could I not know? People are disappearing every day. But we want to stay together for as long as we can. The four of us. Is that so difficult to understand?'

A soft whistle from the kitchen brought me up short. Mamá gave the signal; grandma was right behind her, her face lit up, almost like wax. The cake looked less like a pie and more like a pyre.

I turned off the light and we started singing.

Mamá wanted a photo of the four boys together, but she couldn't take a picture while papá still had his zombie face on. Determined to change his mood, mamá even made the secret sign – the one we usually made to her – clenching her fist to let him know that this time he was the one behaving like the Rock.

'*Abuelo*'s teaching me how to drive the tractor,' I said, trying to help out.

'Tell your *abuelo* he's mad,' said papá.

'That's what he said you'd say, and he said, tell your papá I taught him when he was a year younger than you!'

Papá smiled. We'd got him. And mamá got her photo.

Flash.

70

OF THE STARS

For as long as he has existed, man has gazed up at the stars. The Egyptians believed the heavens were the goddess Nut, separated from her lover Sibû (the Earth) by the god Shu; Nut's feet lay in the west and, through the night, the stars moved along her body. The Chinese, believing their emperor to be the Son of Heaven, made him head of their official religion. The Aztecs identified the god Quetzalcóatl with the Morning Star, otherwise known as the planet Venus. In *The Odyssey*, Homer compares Athena to a shooting star and imagines that the night sky is a dome of bronze or iron, supported by pillars.

If the gods live up in the heavens, then surely they must determine the fates of those below. Fray Bernardino de Sahagún writes that the Aztecs sacrificed prisoners to Venus as it appeared in the east, scattering the blood in the direction of the Morning Star. Van der Waerden argues that the rise of astrology in ancient Greece derives from Zoroastrianism: if the soul comes from the heavens, where it plays a role in the movement of celestial bodies, then it is logical that when the soul enters the human body, it continues to be governed by the stars.

The identification of the heavens with the divine survives even with the advent of science. In 340 BC, in his book *On the*

Heavens, Aristotle argues that the Earth is a sphere. During lunar eclipses, the shadow of the Earth on the moon was always round. The longest chapter in his book is devoted to explaining that the universe is a celestial sphere with the Earth at its centre. Later, in the *Metaphysics*, Aristotle gives a more detailed explanation of his celestial mechanics. The universe, he writes, is made up of a series of nested spheres, each fulfilling a different function, some functions being associated with planets. He no longer justifies the movement of these planets in terms of Platonic Necessity but proposes a physics of motion, of cause and effect. But in following this chain of cause and effect back to the first cause, Aristotle refers to the one who set in motion the first heaven as 'the Unmoved Mover': in other words, God. Certain early commentators considered an Unmoved Mover sufficient to explain the whole system, though Aristotle actually suggests that each planetary sphere has a mover, which implies that for fifty-five spheres there are fifty-five movers, in other words, fifty-five 'gods'. Terrified by the implications of this polytheism, his translators in late antiquity and during the Middle Ages substituted the name of 'God' for the words 'intelligences' and 'angels', without in any way diminishing the power of the original.

There have been those who believed that the heavens govern our lives in ways more overt than those proposed by astrology and theology. The North African tribes that settled in the valley of the Nile noticed that there was a correlation between the behaviour of the river and that of the star Sirius, known to them as Sothis. The rising of the Nile coincided with the first appearance of Sothis on the horizon just before dawn. The Egyptians believed that, during the night, Ra, the Sun-god, journeyed through the underworld, a journey that could be followed by the movements of the stars, which they divided into twelve 'houses'. Later, the day too was divided into twelve houses, resulting in the day we know, divided into twenty-four hours: twelve hours of night and twelve hours of day. Our hours, minutes and seconds are a legacy of Babylonian civilization which used a sexagesimal system because the number sixty has a lot of prime factors. (God made a mistake in not giving us twelve fingers.)

Over the centuries, the course of science moved it further and further from organized religion. Religious persecution of free thinkers for years drove Copernicus to remain silent about his theory that the Sun rather than the Earth was at the centre of the celestial spheres; Kepler was similarly reticent and Galileo paid a terrible price for not being so. But in recent decades, no science has discussed God more than astronomy. Einstein once asked: 'How much choice did God have in constructing the universe?' Stephen Hawking has justified the need to arrive at a unified theory of the cosmos by saying: 'For then we should know the mind of God'. Scientists have described their response to the 'ripples' in the microwave background radiation discovered by the COBE satellite by saying: 'It is like looking at God'. On their lips, the word God relates less to organized religion than to their quest to find an order and a meaning to all of existence; a quest that had once been the province of philosophers and theologians, but is no longer. Obviously they have stopped looking at the heavens.

Sometimes I think that everything you need to know about life can be found in astronomy books. They teach us our place in the universe: we are a chance phenomenon on the surface of a planet which happens to be neither too close nor too far from the Sun, one of many millions of stars. They teach us that the stars, like us, have a lifecycle; the Sun, for example, will die in about 5,000 million years when it has burned up all its hydrogen, at which point it will begin to grow cold and shrink. It is unlikely that the human species will survive this death and thus, just as Moses did not live to see the Promised Land, will not see this incredible spectacle. Our universe will cease to expand within 10,000 million years, at which point it will begin to shrink, to fold in on itself, and time's arrow will run backwards – broken glasses will fly up to become whole, rain will fall upwards, the numbers on the petrol pump will run backwards.

Astronomy teaches us that God, if he exists, acts with great discretion: a gravitational collapse – for example, the universe beginning to contract – can only occur in places that, like black holes, let no light escape and consequently cannot be witnessed from outside.

The books teach us that time is relative and that it passes more slowly near a large mass like the Earth: if a pair of twins is separated, and one is sent across the galaxy at half the speed of light, the twin aboard the spaceship will age more slowly than the twin who stays behind on Earth. Astronomy also leads us to the uncertainty principle, formulated by Werner Heisenberg in 1926, which proposes that it is impossible to know both the position and momentum of a given particle – the more precisely one property is calculated, the less precisely the other can be known. This pretty much destroys any possibility that we can know the future. We can't even measure the present precisely. It takes time for light to travel; consequently the stars we see are not as they are but as they were: when we contemplate the universe, we are not seeing its present but its past. (Time is relative, but more than anything it's weird.)

In the concluding pages of his book A Brief History of Time, Stephen Hawking wonders: 'Why does the universe go to all the bother of existing?' The time when we imagined that we were the centre of this phenomenon is long past, but however infinitesimal, we continue to be a part of the universe and its echoes are present throughout our lives. The answer to Hawking's question, therefore, is the same answer we mere mortals give ourselves to explain our impulse to triumph, to overcome our limitations and strive to create a better version of ourselves before our lifecycle comes to an end, before we grow cold and begin to shrivel, before we gutter out like the Sun.

Five thousand million years. That is how much time we've got to get it right.

71

IN WHICH WE CONTEMPLATE THE STARS AND DISCOVER MORE THINGS THAN CAN BE CONTAINED WITHIN THIS CHAPTER TITLE

According to grandma, star-gazing is almost a family tradition. Papá got the telescope she still keeps up in his room as a present for his tenth birthday. Seized by a brief obsession for astronomy, he named one of the farm dogs Kepler. It's important to think very carefully before giving something a name, because a name points to a destiny. According to the Salvatierra boys, who knew him when he was old, Kepler was not allowed in the house because he constantly trailed a cloud of gas.

When he was engaged to mamá (who had spent time seriously studying astronomy, given that it is a component part of physics), every time they came down to the farm, they would go out into the field after dinner and watch the stars. Grandma used to say that back then, the heavens were full of tourists. According to her, not content to fight over the Earth, the Russians and the Yanks felt they had to flood the sky with capsules and satellites, with dogs and monkeys and discarded rockets and astronauts dreaming of the White House. Grandma swore that one night she had seen a satellite, a story that always made papá laugh.

'Oh, stop calling it a satellite, mamá. It was a shooting star!'

'But the little light was red!'

'The only thing red was the wine you'd been drinking,' interrupted grandpa.

I never saw a sky like the sky over Dorrego – so vast, so black, with stars in an infinite array of size and brilliance. Maybe it seemed vast because the Earth didn't get in the way: the countryside around Dorrego is flat, there are no big cities to blot out the stars with their own clouds of gas, their artificial starlight. (Cities have a terrible tendency to try and imitate starlight, you only have to see them from a plane.) The sky above Dorrego was so vast it was impossible to take in at a glance; you could twist and turn until your neck felt like rubber, scanning the sky from north to south, east to west, then up again without covering half its span. There were stars so tightly clustered that they formed white pools against the night sky; simply gazing at them made you a brother of the first man who first looked up and saw spilled milk.

Before Dorrego, I had always thought of the sky as a black screen on which a handful of scattered stars twinkled vaguely, but were no more enthralling than the ceiling of the Cine Opera. Dorrego revealed the other sky, the boundless dome that sends you rushing to a dictionary for synonyms for 'infinite'; stars that clustered, not into constellations, but into galaxies; stars like swarms of bees which suggested not stillness or permanence but movement, the trail of something, of someone that passed just now, a moment ago, when you weren't looking. A sky that seemed to suddenly reveal the meaning of all things: Man's need to create language to describe it, geography to explain his place within it, biology to remind him that he is a newcomer in this universe, and history, because everything is written in the sky above Dorrego: intimate and extravagant stories, love and loss, the miniature and the epic.

Mamá unfolded a blanket on the grass and the four of us lay down on it. The Midget immediately fell fast asleep; I pulled back his eyelids and shone papá's torch into them but he didn't even move.

'Back when your parents were courting, we always used to come out here after dinner to look at the stars,' said grandma from her armchair, the proud curator of the Museum of Our Happiness.

'Hey, look – a shooting star!' said mamá.

'Where? Where?'

'There, look . . . It's gone now. That's why they're called shooting stars. If you don't pay attention you miss them.'

'What's a shooting star?'

'Sometimes, when you look up at the sky, you'll see a star moving at a thousand miles an hour and . . . zzzzzzt it disappears,' said papá.

'In fact they're not actually stars,' mamá explained, 'they're rocks, fragments of asteroids that burn up as they enter our atmosphere . . .'

'No, no, no . . .' said papá, 'No science, no!'

'Why science no?' protested mamá.

'Because kiss yes.'

He leaned in and kissed her, but I had other things on my mind.

'I can't see anything!'

'You have to be patient. You have to keep watching.'

'Good night, people,' said grandpa.

'Don't go, *abuelo*,' I said and tugged on his arm until he fell down on the blanket next to us.

'And who's going to help me up again?' asked grandpa, laughing.

264

'We'll get the AA to send a crane,' grandma teased him, still stung by his barb about the red wine.

'Your grandson will help you up. He's the strongest of the family,' said papá.

'I'll help you up,' I said, 'but then you have to stay here with us.'

'What if I freeze to death . . .?'

'Is that the Southern Cross?'

'Of course it is.'

'If you see a shooting star,' said papá, 'you can make a wish.'

'What have stars got to do with wishes?'

'I don't know. But I do know that I once made a wish right here, and it came true.'

Papá gave mamá a soppy look and they started playing kissy-face again.

Suddenly the Midget sat up, rubbed his eyes and started yelling: 'I dreamed about a light, I dreamed about a light!'

I don't know how long we sat there: the Midget, on grandma's lap, telling anyone who would listen about his dream, papá and mamá still flirting with each other, grandpa telling me the story of Orion the Hunter, while I lay on my back staring at the sky, trying hard not to blink.

Shooting stars are rocky fragments of meteors that burn up as they come into contact with the Earth's atmosphere. In that, mamá was right. They're also somehow related to wishes; you're supposed to make a wish as soon as you see one streak across the sky. In that, papá was right.

I looked and looked until my eyes were burning, but I didn't see anything.

Maybe that's why my wish didn't come true.

Playtime

Quien sabe, Alicia
Este país no estuvo hecho porque sí

(Who knows, Alicia,
This country wasn't made just because.)

Charly García, 'Canción de Alicia en el País'

Fifth Period: History

Noun. 1. The aggregate of all
events that have occurred in the
past: 'Humanity has progressed
throughout history.'
2. A continuous, systematic narrative
of past events: 'History teaches us
about the most significant events in
the human story.'

72

CONCERNING
(UN)HAPPY ENDINGS

I don't like stories with unhappy endings. That's my problem with *Houdini*, for example. Tony Curtis is suspended upside down in the Chinese Water Torture Cell wearing a straitjacket, his ankles shackled together, and he doesn't have the energy left to struggle. A few last bubbles of air escape from his mouth. Someone screams: a woman, I think. Someone else breaks the glass and the water gushes out all over the stage, splashing the people in the front row. Tony Curtis says a few last words to Janet Leigh and then he dies. It would have been better if he'd been run down by a car, or died in a motorcycle accident like Lawrence of Arabia. (The good thing about *Lawrence of Arabia* is that it starts at the end; that way you get the unhappy bit out of the way at the beginning and the story ends where it should, in the desert.) Houdini dying during one of his escapes because, for once, he wasn't able to get out of his shackles in time, is like a trick of fate: a particularly cruel trick, like the punishments that gods visit on mortals who try to fly or steal the sacred fire. It is a way of saying:

you may well be able to escape from anywhere, Harry, but there's one thing that no one can escape from.

I remember how I felt when I found out that the Robin Hood stories I'd been collecting ever since I could read (if I liked a story, I collected every version of it I could find – I had at least eight versions of *Robin Hood*) had an odd tendency to stop before the end. They usually ended with Richard the Lionheart coming home, giving Robin a pardon, restoring his lands and his title and giving his blessing to Robin's marrying Maid Marian. But in grandpa's library I found another version, a big fat book published by Ediciones Peuser, in which the story continues. According to this version, one of the bad guys sneaked into a banquet and stabbed Maid Marian and her little son Richard. This was terrible, but it wasn't the end. The book ends with Robin Hood, who's sick and depressed by now, arriving at a convent, helped by Little John, looking for medical help. He is taken in by a nun, who suggests that he needs a course of bloodletting. Robin, whose faculties are diminished and who has lost the will to live, doesn't recognize that the nun is actually a woman who's always hated him. Given the perfect opportunity to avenge herself (back then, people accepted that monks and nuns had the same emotions as ordinary people), the woman opens his veins, makes some excuse and leaves the room. By the time Little John decides to go and look for her, it is too late: Robin has bled to death.

I didn't mention my discovery to anyone. I put the book back exactly where I found it, slid it into the gap on the shelf so no one would notice anything different.

But everything was different. For the first time I realized that being a good guy didn't mean you were guaranteed a happy ending. It was as if someone had suddenly abolished the law of gravity: I was no longer connected to the Earth, 'up' was suddenly a bottomless abyss, 'to fall' was a sentence with no full stop.

From then on, even the expression 'happy ending' seemed somehow poisonous. 'Happy' is carefully added to help us to swallow the 'ending', like a bitter pill coated in sugar. Nobody likes to think that they will die. If it were up to us, we'd go on forever like the Duracell bunny.

My belated religious education did everything it could to afford some consolation. Our good deeds could earn us a happy ending . . . after the end. That's why the fat priest cried tears of happiness when Marcelino died: because the kid had a first-class ticket to heaven. That was why Richard Burton and Jean Simmons walked happily to their martyrdom in *The Robe*, because they imagined that in a few minutes they would be in Paradise, whose splendour would outshine even the glories of CinemaScope.

Father Ruiz's explanations were never enough for me – perhaps because, inadvertently, my parents had planted in me the seed of agnosticism. Papá believed in earthly justice – he worked for happy endings here and now. Mamá believed in the principle of causality but only in this world, since it was impossible to know if other worlds existed, still less how things in this world might affect that one. I imagine that they did not want to demean their love for this world by making it dependent on some other world. Everything they did was intended to effect change in this world; the rest, if anything existed, was gravy.

In time I came to understand that stories do not end. This I owe in part to History (which I owe to papá) and in part to Biology (which I owe to mamá) and in part to Poetry (for this last bit, I alone am to blame).

I believe that stories do not end, because even when the protagonists are dead, their actions still have an impact on the living. This is why I believe that History is like an ocean into which rivers of individual histories flow. Everything that has gone before underpins the present; we continue those stories just as those who come after us continue ours. We are bound together in a web that spans all of space – all living creatures are connected in some intimate way: a web large enough to include all those alive today, but also all those of yesterday and tomorrow.

I believe that stories have no end, because even when one life ends, its energy gives life to others. The dead (remember the larvae) simply nourish the Earth so it can be fruitful and feed those above who, in their turn, will give life by dying. For as long as there is life in the universe, the story of each single life never ends; it is simply transformed. In dying, the life-story undergoes a shift. We are no longer a thriller, a comedy, an epic; we are a geography book, a biology book, a history book.

73

CONCERNING
THE BEST STORIES

The best stories are those that fascinate us as children and continue to grow with us, affording new pleasures each time we reread them. (Each time they make themselves new. Therefore, they never end.) Like the songs of the Beatles, seducing us with the yeah, yeah yeahs of 'She Loves You', and carefully leading us – keeping pace with our development – to the point where they can offer us a glimpse of the immensity of time itself in the orchestra's last glissando in 'A Day in the Life'. (The Beatles do not end either. Though the last song on the last side of their last album is called 'The End'– the song in which they say that in the end the love you take is equal to the love you make – it's not really the last song because there's a song not listed on the sleeve, a short, hidden song in which Paul tells us that Her Majesty's a pretty nice girl and someday he's going to make her his.)

I have lots of favourite stories, but the story of King Arthur is special. I suppose that its initial attraction was obvious: I loved the knights in armour, the egalitarianism of the Round Table, the romantic idealism of the knights, the quest for the Holy Grail – the chalice from which Christ drank at the Last Supper. It was always a perfect combination of epic adventure and spiritual quest. As I grew up, I left the children's version of the story behind and began to read the original sources: Geoffrey of Monmouth's *The History of the Kings of Britain*, Sir Thomas Malory's *Le Morte d'Arthur*, the Grail cycle, *Sir Gawain and the Green Knight*. Growing up, in a way, is making sense of contradictions. And so I learned that a man like Arthur may have the best of intentions and still be petty, dissolute and selfish. Arthur committed incest, murdered innocent children and, overcome by private grief, forgot the public good.

But the part that always impressed me most was the end. Sir Bedevere helping the dying Arthur onto a barque full of women dressed in black; among them, three queens, Morgan le Fay, the Queen of Northgalis and the Queen of the Wastelands. They are accompanied by Nimuë, the Lady of the Lake. Seeing Bedevere weep, Arthur tells him that he is going to the Isle of Avalon to be healed of his grievous wounds. The barque disappears as it crosses the lake. The following day Bedevere encounters a hermit at prayer next to a freshly dug grave. He asks the name of the man who lies there. The hermit replies: a man whom some women asked him to bury. Bedevere assumes it to be Arthur and decides to live out the remainder of his life here, in prayer and fasting.

Malory then relates a version of the story in which Arthur does not die but will return when the time is right. As he tells it, the inscription on the tomb reads: 'Here lies Arthur, the once and future king'. But since no one saw him dead, nor ever saw the grave, none can confirm that he died. Malory declines to pronounce on this eventual return: 'I woll nat say that hit shall be so. But rather I wolde sey: here in thys worlde he chaunged hys lyff.'

Now I believe, like Malory, that there is nothing more inspiring than the story of a man who succeeds in changing his life; in this dark world where they say that nobody can change, I can think of nothing more heroic. In 1837, Ralph Waldo Emerson railed against the prophets of resignation: 'It is a mischievous notion that we are come late into Nature; that the world was finished a long time ago.' The world is still not finished. There are still at least 5,000 million years left to go, which is why I am angered by those who claim that all possible stories have already been told, consigning the act of creation itself to the margins, relegating it to the trivial repetition of what has been done before and better, to the crumbs of what was once a banquet. The idea is as reactionary as it would be to say that all possible lives have already been lived, relegating us to the status of second-hand humans living borrowed lives. It strips us of our worth, of our hopes, and makes our passions futile. For our lives are no less important than other lives. On the contrary, our lives appear on the horizon of past lives, the lives that have ceased to be biology and become history, the lives that have cleared the path to this present, which, in that sense, is better than all the past; lives that, just like certain species, trace a path between what was and what is, offer us a bridge across the ravine to the summit of a mountain that is higher than all those that came before, but which is never the last.

There is an image that is often used to underline how intimately the phenomena of nature are intertwined: it suggests that the flapping of a butterfly's wings can set off a chain reaction that can eventually lead a tornado to strike some distant part of the planet. If we grant a butterfly so much power, how much more power has a man who, in taking possession of the life others purport to control, changes it for the better? What tornadoes could be set off by such a change, not only among those closest to him, but in the furthest reaches of the planet? This is why, like Malory, I believe that it is enough that Arthur made good use of his chance of redemption. But when I was little, I preferred the fantastical version of the story, the one that gave me Arthur in Avalon, nursing his wounds and waiting for his time to come again.

For many years, Kamchatka was my Avalon.

74

IN WHICH WE RETURN HOME, TO FIND NOTHING BUT DARKNESS

When we reached the *quinta* at midnight on Sunday, the whole neighbourhood was blacked out. Block after block, everything was in darkness. Papá parked the car 200 metres from the *quinta*, reversing it into the gateway of another house. That way, if there was any trouble he could easily head off in either direction. Mamá and I watched as he moved away, flashlight in hand, along the dirt path. The Midget was asleep beside me, hugging his two Goofys covered in drool. Mamá had time to chain-smoke two Jockeys before papá got back.

'It looks like it's just a power cut,' he said, sliding behind the wheel again.

'What about Lucas?' I asked. That was all I wanted to know.

'Lucas isn't there.'

But, for some reason, papá didn't sound certain. As soon as he'd parked the Citroën in front of the *quinta*, I scrambled out and started looking all over the house for Lucas. Papá was right about there being no electricity. I moved around the house, feeling my way along the walls. When I got to our bedroom, a finger of moonlight slipping through the window made it clear that Lucas was not there. His sleeping bag was also gone. If it was just that Lucas wasn't there, I would have been frustrated because I'd been really looking forward to seeing him, but at least he would come back. The fact that he had taken his things prompted a different kind of worry.

Mamá said that he'd probably decided to sleep somewhere else while we were away. We could hardly blame him. When you're on your own, you get to make your own decisions. But she said I shouldn't worry; if Lucas intended to be away for any length of time, he would not have gone without letting us know.

I wondered if there was a message somewhere in the house, somewhere that, in the darkness, we hadn't found.

I was on my way out to the swimming pool to check on the toads when I saw a light in the near distance.

It flashed on and off, on and off, like a signal.

I threw myself at Lucas and gave him a hug that winded him. He was leaning against a poplar tree. Next to him was his sleeping bag and his Japan Airlines knapsack.

'What are you doing out here? Can't you see it's going to rain?'

'I was waiting for you.'

'What happened to the lights?'

'There's a power cut, the whole area is pitch dark.'

Clearly I must have been none too satisfied by Lucas's answer, because I tried my luck again. 'What are you doing out here?'

Lucas didn't answer. He seemed more interested in papá, who had spotted us and was coming over. This pissed me off. In ignoring me, I felt as though Lucas was breaking a pact and that I therefore had every right to feel upset. But I didn't have time to tell him how hurt I felt. Things happen faster than feelings.

'You got a minute?' Lucas asked papá.

279

Instead of answering, papá sent me inside.

'Go in and help your mother, she's in there all alone with all those suitcases.'

Unwillingly, I did as I was told. When the Midget, who had woken up and was stretching, made some inoffensive comment, I laid into him.

He started whining and went out to the swimming pool where he found a body floating in the water. 'Dead toad! Dead toad!'

For some strange reason, I felt relieved. It was good to have something to do, something to keep me busy. I sent the Midget off to find some newspaper and a piece of string. I went to get a spade.

We buried the toad at the foot of the tree, next to all the others.

'It's not really a hole,' the Midget whispered to the little package that passed for a shroud, 'it's a lift. We put you in here and you go straight up to toad heaven.'

He put the toad in the ground. I started filling in the hole. The Midget made an elegant, painstaking sign of the Cross and ran back to the house.

I was still wrestling with the spade when Lucas came up to me. He had his sleeping bag under one arm and his Japan Airlines knapsack over his other shoulder.

'I'm off, Harry.'

'In this weather? You'll get soaked!'

'Your papá is going to take me to the station.'

'Can I come?'

'No.'

'Why not? I'm nearly finished.'

'I can't wait any longer. I should have gone ages ago, but I wanted to wait for you guys. So I could say goodbye.'

I started hitting the ground with the spade to level it.

'I'm going, Harry. And this time I won't be coming back.'

'Do you really, *really* have to go?' I asked, tamping down the grave with the sole of my shoe.

'Wrong question.'

I knelt down, searching for stones to put on the grave; I didn't want the dogs digging it up in the middle of the night.

'Is this how it's going to be, then? Ciao and I just turn around and walk away? I thought we were friends.'

'But we're never going to see each other again!'

There was a silence, which seemed conclusive. I had my hands full of stones when Lucas said: 'I left my orange T-shirt in the bedroom.'

This felt like the last straw. The only reason I didn't throw the stones at him was because I needed them for something else. 'Go and get it yourself!'

At some point it started to rain, but I didn't notice. I was still on my knees; I was placing the stones in a spiral, starting at the centre and working out in wider and wider circles when I noticed mamá standing next to me.

'Why won't you say goodbye to Lucas?'

'Because I don't want to.'

'You'll be sorry later.'

'What do you know?'

'I know. Believe me, I know.'

'Can't you see I'm busy?'

Suddenly mamá was down on the ground next to me, kneeling on the wet Earth. She put her hands on my shoulders and forced me to turn and face her.

'Look at me. Look at me!' she said, holding my face as I struggled to turn away. 'You can't keep on shutting yourself in. It's horrible when you get hurt, I know, nobody likes it; we'd all like to have a suit of armour to protect us from suffering. But if you build a wall to protect yourself from the world outside, you end up realizing you've shut yourself in.

Don't shut yourself in, darling. It's better to suffer than to feel nothing at all. If you spend your life in a suit of armour, you'll miss out on the best things! Promise me something . . . promise me you won't miss out on a single thing, not one . . . will you promise me that?'

I roughly drew my face away. I was sick of the wrong questions, of suicidal toads, of my mother talking gibberish, which, as you've seen, did not stop when it rained. But if I thought my rejection would force my mother to admit defeat, I was wrong. Even soaking wet, this woman saw motherhood as a test of endurance.

'Do you know the worst pain I've ever felt?' (She didn't wait for me to answer, but just went on.) 'Pain so bad I thought I'd die, I swear. I couldn't bear it. But I had consciously chosen to suffer this pain. I had two choices: I could choose to do what I wanted, knowing I would suffer, or I could choose not to suffer and be left with nothing. And I made the right choice. The suffering I went through was worse than anything I've ever known, but I came through it and I was happier than I've ever been. And I wouldn't change it for anything in the world. Do you know what it was? Do you know what I'm talking about?'

I didn't want to answer, but I was intrigued by this unfamiliar fragment of the family legend. Which story was this one? What had happened to mamá, what suffering? Was there some scar she'd never mentioned?

'I'm talking about you. I'm talking about when I had you, dummy.'

When I got back to my room, I realized what Lucas had been trying to say when he said goodbye. I'd thought he was asking me to go and fetch his T-shirt, but it wasn't that. Lucas knew how much I loved the fluorescent orange, the print that felt like rubber, the incredible drawing of the motorbike. That was why he'd left it on my bed, clean and carefully laid out in all its splendour. He had given it to me.

I ran down the driveway as far as the road, but he was gone.

75

IN WHICH I MAKE MY DEBUT
AS AN ESCAPE ARTIST

Trains lend themselves to daydreaming. It must be something about the jolting, the rhythmic clacking, the drone of the refreshment sellers the same the world over – a lullaby of the post-industrial world. Or maybe it has something to do with the idea of letting yourself be carried away: you pay your fare and surrender yourself to the machine and by the time you realize it – whether you're sitting in a carriage or standing crushed by the crowd – your thoughts have already carried you away. Or maybe such speculation is unnecessary, maybe a daydream is simply a logical extension of the train itself, the very idea of it. After all, several tons of metal hurtling at top speed along a straight line is an idea that could only have occurred to someone in a dream, someone deep in an extraordinary dream, the sort of dream that only a train can produce.

I like it when the train is travelling on an elevated track, because I can see the roofs of the houses. People treat roofs as though they did not exist. They toss all the things they no longer want onto their roofs – rusty tricycles, children's paddling pools, empty bird cages, tins of paint, the skirting boards they never get around to fitting, the tiles left over from a renovation. They also use them to put out of sight those things they don't want to deal with: the washing line of damp clothes that includes an oversized bra, the illicit TV connection, the chimneys pouring out their brazen black smoke. I know you're not supposed to notice these things, that they've been placed there so that they won't be seen, but I like noticing things other people ignore: they speak to me, and, besides, it's not my fault, it's the train's!

On this, my very first train journey, I am heading to Buenos Aires. I leave from the same station that Lucas left from a few hours earlier. The knowledge that I am duplicating his every movement – getting a ticket, waiting for the train, choosing a carriage – makes me feel close to him, but the feeling is fleeting. Once aboard I don't recognize anything or anyone. The carriages seem unfinished, as though someone had taken them out of the oven too soon. There are too many people ignoring each other. The seats are filthy and broken. Worse still, I spot a man who terrifies me. He is holding his newspaper in one hand, and his little finger is suspiciously stiff. When we get to the next station I change carriages, but it doesn't make me feel any better. There are more and more people. I'm drowning in a sea of elbows and armpits. I manage to poke my head above the tangle of limbs, almost throwing myself onto a woman who is still – sleeping – her mouth hanging open. Through the window, the city seems to be running away as fast as its legs will carry it.

The night that Lucas left, I decided that the time had come to prove myself as an escape artist. I had been working out the plan in my mind for some time. To carry it out, I would require perfect self-control. Once I began, there could be no turning back. To the escape artist, this last rule is crucial: when the bolt shoots home, the lid of the trunk closes and there are thousands of tons of water above his head, an escape artist has no time for second thoughts. There is no way back; the only way is forward. Escape is the only option.

The Midget agreed to help, although he was afraid that mamá might not understand the subtle distinction between assistant and accomplice. I had no choice but to resort to bribery. I promised him my *Superman* comics, which were already ruined because the Midget had drawn haloes all over them. (These days he drew a halo over everyone he thought was a good guy. Lex Luthor didn't have a halo.) We headed off for school together, like we did every day. I went with him as far as the gate because he was afraid of getting lost, but before he went inside, I gave him two comics – the down payment; the rest would come later if he held up his end of the deal and didn't say anything about where I'd gone – and I stood there watching until he was inside.

The only thing I hadn't reckoned on was Denucci, a friend from class. He was in the playground, on the other side of the railings, watching me silently. I suppose he must have noticed that me and the Midget didn't go in together. For one endless minute we stood there, neither of us knowing what to do. I saw him look towards Father Ruiz, who was standing at the foot of the steps, greeting the pupils as they arrived, as he did every day. If Denucci said anything to Father Ruiz, my escape plan would fail before it had even begun.

But Denucci did nothing. He stood there, staring at me through the railings, wearing the same expression he did at playtime when he asked me if I wanted to play with his soldiers and I said no. I took one step backwards. Denucci didn't move. I kept walking backwards like a crab; Denucci still didn't move. I had retreated about four metres when he raised his hand and waved. I waved back discreetly. I didn't want Father Ruiz to notice.

Bertuccio always went home for lunch. I planned to confront him as he left school. I was sure he'd invite me to his place and, with a bit of luck, there'd be *milanesas*. Taking trains and buses, I arrived in Flores about mid-morning. All I could do now was wait around until lunchtime. I didn't mind. I could go and see what was on at the cinema – at the Pueyrredón and the San Martín. I could go to Tonini's bookshop and see if they had a new version of *Robin Hood*. I could go to the shopping centre on the Avenida Boyacá and look in the window of the model shop that was always full of Zeroes and Spitfires. My one precaution was to take off my school smock, so it wouldn't look like I was bunking off school. (In my innocence, I thought that a kid wandering around with a schoolbag would look less suspicious than one wearing a school smock.)

I was surprised to find that nothing had changed. I don't know what I was expecting. I think I was looking for some sign that I had been missed, I don't know, for the colours to be more faded, the newsstands closed out of respect (they'd lost one of their best customers, it was the least they could have done), a crack in the façade of the Iglesia San José, I don't know, something! But everything looked exactly the same: the same colours, the same newsstands, with the same guys running them; the same, graceless church.

People seemed exactly the same too. They walked up and down Rivadavia, popping into shops, into banks, into galleries, waiting for buses, crossing the avenue with the brisk air of people with a lot to do, with the purposeful gait of people who had somewhere to be. All this briskness ended up making me suspicious. I stopped feeling that nothing had changed and began to suspect that things looked *too much* like I remembered them. I began to think that maybe this wasn't Flores but a film set, a mock-up carefully created to look exactly as I remembered it, a replica, accurate in every detail but fake, full of actors playing people I used to know: ordinary people, the guys on the newsstands, the old age pensioners, the bankers who looked exactly as I remembered them (they must have used photos and film clips when they did the casting) but actors just the same, nervous because they were playing out the first scenes, the ones where everyone is so busy trying to remember their lines and their actions that it doesn't quite flow. You notice that even simple gestures look forced, exaggerated – the way the person across the street raises a hand to hail the bus, the way that old man takes out his wallet, the affected way those girls are laughing; I had been dropped onto a film set without realizing it, or maybe this was all being played out for my benefit. Whatever it was, I didn't like it.

Waiting for Bertuccio to arrive was agonizing.

When he comes out, I don't go over and talk to him, I just walk in the same direction, keeping to the other side of the street. Bertuccio looks the same as he always did too. The same school smock, the same schoolbag. He's humming softly to himself, but I can't really hear. My idea had been to hide behind a tree and jump out suddenly, the sort of dramatic entrance that would appeal to Bertuccio, but I was afraid I might not see him, that I might miss him as I was trying to hide. Before I knew it, there's Bertuccio, walking along, humming to himself, and all I can do is keep walking, keep looking for a gap in the traffic so that I can cross Yerbal, keep wondering what I'm going to say. 'Hi' sounds too dumb, I've been gone God knows how long and all I can think to say is 'Hi', there has to be something better than that. As we walk, I watch him, observing his every step, his every expression, trying to decide if they look natural or slightly forced, trying to work out if this is Bertuccio or some actor they cast to play him, and before I know it – it's only three blocks – we've arrived at his house.

He rings the doorbell. The buzzer goes, but I don't hear it.

Bertuccio goes inside.

I stand opposite, dumbstruck. I've forgotten to control my breathing. I'm not walking now but my heart is still hammering and the triple 'b-b-buh-bum' sounds like one. I curse myself, I wonder what to do. I remember what I told myself not to forget: don't look back, once you've started, second thoughts are fatal; you have to go forward, to escape.

I put on my school smock again. I cross the street and stand between two parked cars. The idea of ringing the doorbell doesn't even occur to me; my instinct is working again, my natural mastery of time, but I will only realize this in a moment or two. I am waiting for someone to enter or leave Bertuccio's building. A minute later, a woman emerges with a shopping cart; I put on my best schoolboy face and walk in as though I've lived there all my life. The lady holds the door to let me pass. I say 'Good afternoon' and she nods – what a well brought-up boy.

It is Bertuccio's mother who answers the door. I give her my best smile. My 'How are you, *señora?*' sounds too poised, too forced, as though I am not me but an actor playing me, and I'm about to step into the apartment when I ask if Bertuccio is there, purely out of formality. His mother tells me he's not there, that he's gone for lunch at some aunt's house. I stand there frozen – 'Houdini on the rocks', in a bathtub full of ice cubes up to my neck. What do you mean he's not there, I think to myself. I just saw him go in. Did he stop somewhere on the stairs? For an instant, all sorts of strange ideas occur to me – the sort of things you think when you're on a train, that some pervert in the building grabbed Bertuccio as soon as he came in and is hiding him in his own apartment; that Bertuccio decided not to go up to his apartment but to the roof terrace to eat his sandwich instead, because roof terraces are always full of fascinating bits of junk, roofs tell you things – and just then the penny drops.

'That's a shame,' I say. 'I really wanted to see him. Tell him I came by.'

Luckily, the woman sleeping with her mouth open got off before I did. I could sit down, even if it was only for two stops. There wasn't much to see through the windows now. The city was far behind me; the roofs of the houses were looking down on me, almost scornfully, keeping their secrets. I knew that any minute now, everything would be all right; papá and mamá would yell at me because what I'd done was reckless, even dangerous; by now the Midget would have confessed and they would have decided to wait, knowing that

I knew the way, knowing I was always careful crossing the road, knowing – most importantly – that I *would* come back. And maybe they wouldn't yell too much when they saw I was crying. I knew I would cry, my instinct was working perfectly, or my natural mastery of time, which amounts to the same thing. I don't often cry, but when I do papá and mamá turn as soft and mushy as marzipan. When I realized I was going to cry, I relaxed; in a few minutes everything would be all right. I distracted myself watching a blind man playing the harmonica and selling lottery tickets. I wondered how blind people manage not to get ripped off by people not paying them; blind people don't need roofs to hide things away because they can't see them anyway – you know, the sort of thoughts that come to you when you're on a train.

76

IN WHICH WE PLAY RISK
AND I TURN THE TABLES –
WELL, ALMOST

This was the night of the historic game.

After dinner we cleared the dining-room table and papá and I fought it out over a game of Risk: Captain Nemo versus Harry Houdini. To the death, as usual. But this time things didn't go the way they usually did. I started winning. I went on winning. I was thrashing him. It was like I had magic fingers. Every time I threw the dice: six, six, six. The blue forces marched across the planet devouring the watermelon seeds. (That's what I called papá's units.) Then I started conquering entire continents. I held onto them and I started getting new units with every turn. Then I turned in two sets of cards one after the other, the first time three infantry cards, the second time three different cards: one infantry, one artillery, one cavalry. Papá was finding it hard to keep his cool. He was a sore loser, even when he played Whist. If mamá hadn't sat down next to me to referee the game, I think he would have found – or invented – some reason to call the game off on a technicality.

After a couple of hours I had control of forty-one territories – forty-one! – and papá had only one: a territory situated in the top right-hand corner of Asia, bordering Japan and Alaska, a remote, exotic territory, with a name that sounded like the clash of swords.

The only territory papá controlled was Kamchatka. It was here that my armies bit the dust.

Charge after charge, papá fended off my units. My strongest attacks were repelled with stronger counter-attacks. Holed up in this tiny enclave, papá's forces fought back. I recklessly sacrificed one unit after another, quickly exhausting all my troops in Siberia and Yakutsk, China, Japan and Alaska. I had to stop and regroup. Mamá was making frantic secret signals to papá, as though she were the referee, urging him to resign. I don't know why she thought I couldn't see what she was doing. And papá made no secret of his response – he shrugged his shoulders, raised his eyebrows, threw his arms wide, a repertoire of gestures intended to communicate that he was unable to influence the dice to turn things back in my favour.

On my next turn, I marshalled all of my new units around Kamchatka. The disparity between the forces was appalling; a massacre seemed certain. But things went the same way they had the last time, only worse. Every army I risked, I lost. This run of bad luck left me lost for words. It was as though I was cursed, as though our battle was destined to follow the path of other battles: David and Goliath, the 300 Spartans and the Persians at Thermopylae.

Turn after turn, the curse prevailed. The chimes of the clock dwindled from twelve to a single toll that sounded like my death knell.

'You want me to explain?' asked papá, stifling a yawn.

I said something rude and went on playing.

The game went on for hours. Kamchatka versus the rest of the world.

At some point mamá went to bed. At some point I asked for a toilet break and changed into Lucas's orange T-shirt, convinced that this talisman would ensure my victory.

It was futile.

I must have fallen asleep on the table like an idiot, preferring to pass out than accept my defeat. I had a disturbing dream in which I was still on the train trying to wake up from a dream, a dream in which I was trying not to fall asleep, because if I fell asleep I'd miss the station where I was supposed to get off; if I fell asleep I'd miss it; if I fell asleep I would be lost.

The following morning papá called 'action stations'.

77

A VISION

It has rained during the night and in the silence between trains, you can hear the patter of raindrops that have clung to the trees all night, waiting for morning to fall. It is the only sound in the grounds of the *quinta*; the rest is silence.

The raindrops flatten the fallen leaves, which cling together for comfort, making things easier for the toad. The creature hops and slides as though someone had rolled out a red carpet in his honour. The toad notices the house is unusually empty for this time of the morning; the toad can usually tell there is someone, something, from the sound of the radio, a woman humming, a door slamming. Whatever the weather, the woman always comes outside, sits on the bench and, staring at the garden, smokes a cigarette; once she spoke in some language the toad did not understand. But mid-morning has come and gone and there is no sign of the woman, no sound from the radio, even the doors are silent and still.

Emboldened by the silence, the toad hops off his red carpet and onto the tiles that lead to the house. He is grateful that the tiles are wet, but even so they are rough and cold as only something that is not and has never been alive can be and they force him to adapt his movements, unlike the fallen leaves, the grass and the mud which adapt to him; there is something despotic in all things inert, in their tenacious refusal to recognize the existence of the other. But the toad keeps moving forward, his instinct tells him that he can do so, that there is no risk. A couple of hops take him to the birdbath, under which there is a spider's web. The toad feels sure the spider can tell him what he wants to know; since she lives close to the house, attached to the exterior wall, she must have noticed something out of the ordinary, some sound, something that would explain this silence; perhaps the woman said something and the spider understood her strange language. But the spider is nowhere to be seen either. The web is empty but for a raindrop that glistens like a pearl.

The toad knows he has gone as far as he can. He cannot go beyond the doors, and even if they were open and he felt the urge to hop across the threshold, he would not do so because he is no ordinary toad, he is a young, elegant toad, his skin is mossy green (the twin blotches on his back look like eyes) and his instincts are alert, telling him to be careful.

If he could go inside, he would find the house as dark and lifeless as the tiles, but he might find signs of the creatures that lived here until a little while ago. The toad knows (it is in his nature) that life is cyclical, and that some residue remains even when the cycle is complete. Snakes shed their skin, cats their fur, manta rays their teeth. Man sheds used-up objects: he leaves an open Nesquik tin and a dirty glass on the kitchen counter, an open toothpaste tube, unmade beds, their sheets stained with urine; he leaves grandfather clocks, cigarette butts in the ashtrays, comics that have been scrawled on and books borrowed from the school library; he leaves clothes in the wardrobes and food in the fridge.

To go inside would be pointless. Man's things speak his language, a language that the toad does not understand; besides, when their owners discard them they lose their meaning, they cease to be animate, they become impenetrable hieroglyphics, as though they had expiration dates like the tins in the larder, the open can of Nesquik, the food in the fridge, the slowly hardening toothpaste; like books without a reader or clocks without a hand to wind them.

Wisely (as I've already pointed out, this is no ordinary toad, perhaps it has something to do with the marks on his back), the toad retreats, relieved to return to the wet leaves. The touch of the harsh, rough tiles has left his mouth dry; he feels hot and thirsty. The wet leaves cool him, but he needs more; he needs to swim, he can feel his skin crack with every hop, feel the mossy green he is so proud of is growing dull. He must make a decision. The birdbath is ridiculous, it would be like crawling back into the desert in search of an oasis and besides, it's too high. The stream that runs along the boundary of the *quinta* would be ideal, but he would have to hop a considerable distance, and he does not feel up to that just now. Luckily, there is another water source only a few seconds away. He can feel its wetness even from here, minute droplets of water like a balm against his skin.

78

IN WHICH HOUSES CRUMBLE

We were woken with a start. We had to move so quickly, we could take only things that were to hand. The Midget grabbed his two Goofys. I took my game of Risk and the book about Houdini. At first I thought papá and mamá hadn't rescued anything (cigarettes and ulcer tablets did not seem like treasure to me), but I later realized that their impulse had been the same as ours. We grabbed the things that gave us comfort; they had done likewise.

We travelled in silence. The Midget quickly fell asleep: by the time we were half a mile from the *quinta*, he was dead to the world. I felt tired too, but I couldn't sleep. I spent the time staring at the backs of mamá and papá's heads, looking from one to the other, trying to detect some clue to the danger that had forced us to flee the *quinta*, some sign that the Pawnees were not about to swoop down and scalp us. But the back of the head being the least expressive part of the human body (I think it's called the 'occiput' just to make it sound interesting), either there was none, or there was a sign I didn't see.

We spent the day driving around Buenos Aires. The first time we stopped was on some street in a neighbourhood I didn't recognize, though it was quiet, and there was a public phone. Papá kept feeding coins into it and waving his arms like a crazy man. At first me and the Midget laughed (to ourselves, obviously, we didn't want to annoy mamá, who was smoking like a Turk and drumming on the steering wheel) because there's something funny about watching someone waving and gesticulating in front of an inanimate object when you can't hear the conversation. It's as if there's something missing, like a painter trying to paint, not realizing he's forgotten to pick up his brush, or like Wile E. Coyote running in mid-air not realizing he's run off a cliff. But papá kept waving and making horrible faces and feeding coins into the phone and suddenly he was talking so loudly that we could hear what he was saying in spite of the distance. We couldn't make out the words, but we could hear his voice and it was obvious he was shouting, and sometimes, when he found himself yelling, he'd stop and cup the mouthpiece with his hand and he would start talking very slowly, moving from shout to a whisper with nothing in between. When he hung up, he slammed the receiver down so hard he nearly knocked the whole phone booth over.

We weren't laughing any more. When papá slammed down the phone, the Midget flinched and asked mamá what was going on. Mamá smiled, reached back to stroke his leg, and took several deep breaths as though she was about to say something, but she said nothing.

Papá saved her by coming back to the car. He slumped into the passenger seat; the Citroën rocked on its suspension. And even though he knew mamá was waiting for him to say something, he didn't, in fact he didn't even look at her. He looked down at his feet, just like me and the Midget do when mamá is trying to get us to confess to some crime, when we know we've been caught but are trying to postpone the moment when we have to face the music. Mamá had to shake him. The Midget looked at me, as if to ask if papá had fallen asleep. Eventually papá looked at mamá and said in a whisper, like he was still talking into the receiver: 'The safe house has fallen through.'

It was clear that mamá didn't need to hear anything else, because she straightened up in her seat, put the car into first and moved off.

We must have gone round in circles a thousand times before she found a restaurant that was acceptable. They must have been hungry for something special, but driving around in circles like that must have ruined her appetite because in the end she hardly ate anything; she picked at a paella, ate a couple of prawns, slowly slumping over the table like a toy winding down, staring at nothing.

The Midget, on the other hand, wolfed down his food as he always did, and quickly got bored. He knelt up on his chair and I had to keep an eye on him to make sure the chair didn't fall over backwards. At one point, he and the little girl at the table behind us started pulling faces at each other. We knew her name was Milagros because her mother kept saying 'Don't do that, Milagros, please sit still, Milagros'; only a miracle could have made Milagros sit still or her mother shut up. In other circumstances I would have made fun of the Midget, taunted him about having a new girlfriend, but I didn't feel up to it, I felt heavy and sluggish, probably something to do with my digestion. To some extent I felt jealous of the Midget, who could kneel up on his chair, make monkey faces and sing 'Great big Nesquiks in their bodies / as they march they make milkshakes' and no one would say anything. I had to behave myself, sit up straight, eat with my mouth closed, act my age; worse still, I had to watch as papá went on butchering a bloody piece of steak that was probably stone cold, silent except for the sound of his knife on the china plate. All the words papá wasn't saying, Milagros' mamá was saying behind my back; an equal and opposite reaction.

After Milagros left, it was as though an invisible hand suddenly switched off the treble: all the sounds in the restaurant – cups, cutlery, plates, bottles, laughter, voices – sounded dull and muted, as if I was hearing them through a wall. To test my own voice, I asked mamá if I could go to the bathroom. She didn't even answer. Maybe she didn't hear, because even to me it sounded like my voice was coming from the bottom of the swimming pool.

Suddenly the Midget stiffened and pointed at something. To my surprise, his voice sounded perfectly clear when he shouted: 'Look, mamá, look! The vagina!'

Mamá reappeared from behind her curtain of smoke. Papá looked up from his steak. The waiters froze where they stood. Every head in the restaurant turned – the cashier, the diners, the guy selling roses – looking anxiously to see what it was that the Midget was pointing at. Look, mamá, the vagina, see?

It wasn't a vagina: it was the Virgin, an image of the Virgin of Luján, on a little shrine mounted on the wall.

Mamá burst out laughing and papá immediately joined her. Everyone in the restaurant laughed too. The treble was back with a vengeance, in the music of laughter and the clinking of cups, cutlery and plates. The waiter who had come over to ask if we wanted dessert was blushing; he tried to say his piece but he couldn't get the words out.

We didn't have dessert. Mamá didn't even ask. I think she was so desperate to leave that it was an effort just waiting for the bill and paying.

In the car, the Midget was silent. He sat with his little hands clasped in his lap, like someone praying, staring out the window at a strange angle, like someone scanning the sky. I knew what was going through his mind, how literal-minded he could be. The Midget obviously heard papá say: 'The safe house has fallen through'. As we drove around in circles he was staring up at the houses, terrified that whatever disease papá had been talking about was contagious and they too might 'fall through', might collapse, one after the other, like in some Japanese B-movie.

79

THE PRINCIPLE
OF NECESSITY II

It was only much later that I realized that going back to the *quinta* was the worst thing we could have done, something we should have avoided at all costs. That mamá and papá decided to go back anyway gives some idea of how desperate they were.

We spent the afternoon in a playground while papá ran round trying to get change and feeding coins into public phones as though they were piggy banks. At least he was doing something. Mamá looked shattered by having to wait; waiting is the worst, it's a life sentence. After the sun set we felt the cold and realized that we hadn't brought any warm clothes, but we didn't say anything. We did our best to go on playing, though the Midget was starting to look more and more like a 'Blue Period' Picasso and my fingertips went numb from holding onto the freezing chains of the swings. At one point, the Midget pointed to a couple of kids playing on the monkey bars and asked if they were on the run like we were.

We left the car on a street outside the village and walked back to the *quinta* from there. When we were a couple of blocks away, papá passed the sleeping Midget to mamá; he told us to wait where we were and to take care not to be seen. This was easy; it was so dark that by the time papá had walked a few feet, we couldn't see him anymore. Mamá wasn't even allowed to smoke, in case someone saw the burning tip of her cigarette in the dark. I had my Houdini book with me, and while we waited, I tried – pointlessly – to read. The print was just an inky smudge. It's horrible when you want to read a book and can't – it feels sacrilegious, or like a tear in the fabric of the Universe.

It was a while before papá came back. He said we could go inside, that it was safe, but that we should prepare ourselves for what we would see.

They'd taken things, the dining-room table and chairs, the telephone, the TV. The floors were a mess, covered in muddy footprints (it had rained the night before), huge tracks from rubber boots that reminded me of the footprints Neil Armstrong left on the moon. On one wall, where the grandfather clock had stood, was a patch of darkness darker than the shadows: with the clock gone, the filth and grime accumulated over time was exposed. They'd even broken the windows. There were shards of glass everywhere and you couldn't move without hearing the crackle and crunch of glass. It seemed to me a pointless thing to do, though later I realized it wasn't. It was the only way they had found to murder time, to bring it to a halt and thereby stop life itself; in breaking the panes of glass they halted their inexorable downward flow, they had interrupted the process – killed the glass.

They had taken both mattresses from my room and the clothes that had been in the wardrobe. It was as empty now as it had been when I first opened it. Seeing it bare gave me the idea, or maybe reminded me of what I had always intended to do. (The broken windows upset my notion of time.) I picked up one of the Midget's pencils from the floor and, under the words 'Pedro '75' I wrote: 'Harry '76'. After that, I climbed on the night table and put the book back where I had found it, trusting that the dust would hide it, keep it safe until the next escape artist arrived.

Mamá laid the Midget down on their big double bed (obviously, they hadn't been able to take this mattress) and papá put his jacket over him.

'I need to be sure that they'll be safe from all this shit,' papá said, in a deep voice that sounded like Narciso Ibáñez Menta.

'You know the only thing that terrifies me? The thought of never being able to see them again,' mamá said, with a strange gurgling sound in her throat.

I know all this because I was listening. I was outside the house, but I was listening. The windows in their bedroom were broken too.

It was at that moment, just after mamá made the strange sound, that I heard the *plop*. At first I thought it was mamá gargling again, but then I realized it was coming from the other direction – from the garden, from the swimming pool, the 'plop' was the sound of water. I ran to the edge of the pool, imagining that another toad had fallen in and I would have to rescue it. I couldn't wait – we would probably be leaving again soon – and I couldn't afford to trust the reverse diving board, I didn't have time. I had to save the toad right now, because I was tired of dead toads, tired of burying them, sick of waiting; waiting is the worst, it's a life sentence.

I got a surprise. The plop was not the sound of a toad falling into the water, but of a toad hopping out of the water onto the reverse diving board: there he was, up on the sloping plank. I couldn't believe it, it was a beautiful toad, mossy green with two dark patches on its back that looked like eyes, and it was obvious that he had just climbed out because the board was dry except for the wet patch the toad had left when it had hopped out of the water.

We stared at each other for a minute, me standing on the edge of the pool, the toad on the reverse diving board, as though everything that had happened was leading to this moment, the moment that had been written: our two lives coming together for a few seconds, each forever changing the other. Things change when they have no choice, as Señorita Barbeito had told me.

When it got bored with looking at me, the toad gave a hop and disappeared into the grass.

80

IN WHICH SOME LOOSE
ENDS ARE TIED UP

And that's everything. This time it's the truth – or almost.

If I have to, I can fill in a few more details. Bertuccio grew up to be a playwright and a theatre director. He's not what you'd call famous, but he always chose to work outside the commercial theatre; it's good to know that he still holds to the artistic creed that he learned so early, because it makes me feel that something – something worthwhile, obviously – persists in this world in spite of those who try to convince us that nothing lasts and that nothing, therefore, is worth anything.

Papá's partner Roberto never reappeared. Ramiro and his mother stayed in Europe. I don't know anything about what happened to them, though a friend told me that they said they would never set foot in Argentina again.

Several years passed before, opening the newspaper one day, I saw Lucas smiling out at me from an old photograph. He was just as I remembered him, the unruly shock of hair, the pathetic little beard, the radiance that somehow shone through despite the second-rate photo and the cheap print quality. Only then did I discover his real name, from the plea for information printed next to the photo. Only then did I discover that, a few days after I last saw him, he became one of the disappeared. I wondered if he had met up with some old friend after he left the *quinta*; I hoped with all my heart that he had, that someone had hugged him, clapped him on the back, said a goodbye that might make up, if only a little, for the goodbye I had refused to say. It took several more years before I fully appreciated how right mamá had been that night when she tried to persuade me to say goodbye to Lucas, when she explained the importance – and consequently the necessity – of goodbyes. Ultimately, we all realize that our parents understood more than we thought they did; it's a part of growing up. But it is rare that they should be so wise in grief, in the art of loss, in the way they cope with untimely and violent death.

Eventually I plucked up the courage to get in touch with Lucas's family. It was in telling them what had happened during our few short weeks together, that I discovered – it was like an epiphany – the power of stories. Until then I had always believed that the fascination they held for me was personal, almost unilateral. But as I talked, I realized that I was giving Lucas back to his family. All the while I was telling them the story – I did my best to draw it out, to conjure details I had never known – time came together splendidly and Lucas was alive again; Lucas appeared (I like to think this is a story not about *los desaparecidos*, but about *los aparecidos*) and we laughed at his jokes as though they were new, because they were reinvented in the retelling.

Year after year, the family still publish the same photograph, the same plea for information. Now my name is there too. When Lucas's family suggested that they add my name to theirs, I was speechless – something that, you might have noticed, is very rare. I accepted immediately, on condition they allowed me to show Lucas's younger brother something. (As I had suspected, Lucas had a brother about my age.) I stayed up until midnight teaching him the knots that

Lucas had taught me, which I still remembered perfectly. As we practised them together, it felt as though there was something sacred in the movement of our fingers, we were tying together something that should never have been unravelled.

There are lots of things I don't know, things I probably never will know. Who Pedro was, for example, and whether Beba and China were his aunts or what, and how much truth there was to my suspicion that the *quinta* was haunted by a ghost. I don't know who has the book about Houdini, if it still exists. Or what became of Denucci, of Father Ruiz or of mamá's friend who gave us refuge that first night. I'd like to be able to tell them that their generosity helped me to survive during my long exile in Kamchatka.

In all those years I was never without a book from *la colección Robin Hood* that I'd found in grandma Matilde's boxes, or a copy of *The Prisoner of Zenda* that had belonged to mamá when she was a little girl. It was here that I discovered the Princess Flavia, a noblewoman by birth but, more importantly, a woman noble in spirit, her hair as blonde as the sun on the Risk board. I can't explain how I felt when I found out that, even on our island, where we lived as castaways as the country was brutally laid waste, mamá had decided to call herself Flavia as a protest, and as a vindication, because she had never wanted to be the Rock – or at least this world had made her the Rock – this world that starves children to death because it allows others to steal the food from their plates, a world in which you have to be a rock so as not to die of heartache. What else is there? Mamá had never wanted to be made of stone, this was why she instinctively appealed to the things that would help us to survive the dark times – those few certainties that you carry with you from childhood: memories of love, of grief, or simply fantasies, like the fantasy she had had since she was a little girl, a dream she found so embarrassing that she never dared tell anyone about it, because it was childish, because it was politically incorrect – the dream of being a real blonde, of being called Flavia, of becoming a princess.

81

KAMCHATKA

The last thing papá said to me, the last word from his lips, was 'Kamchatka'.

We were on the forecourt of a petrol station, we had just had breakfast. Mamá went to get the Midget – a king of infinite space – who was still sleeping in the car. He wasn't simply asleep, he was unconscious: he didn't wake up when he was lifted up, or when mamá covered him with hugs and kisses, or when she put him in grandpa's arms. I remember that grandpa carried him to the truck and then it was my turn for hugs and kisses, mamá squeezed me hard and then put her hands on my shoulders, as though distancing herself, and said: 'Behave yourself'. She didn't say anything else – 'Behave yourself', that was all – in the same tone she always used if she was leaving us alone in the house. It was an attempt to impose limits on our flair for disaster, but also a way of letting us know what would happen if we didn't listen to her: mamá would come home and we would get what was coming to us; mamá would come home, that was guaranteed. I thought: the Rock, mamá never weakens, and if papá had been nearby I would have made the Rock sign and clenched my fist, but papá wasn't there, he'd gone back to the Citroën to fetch something.

Sometimes there are variations in what I remember. Sometimes mamá turns and walks back to the Citroën and, as she does, she

307

drops something small, something red, an empty packet of Jockeys she's scribbled on; I pick it up and read what's written on it; over and over she's scribbled my name – my real name – covering the whole cigarette packet, as though she's afraid I might forget, might end up believing I was Harry forever. Harry, the escape artist. I'm not Harry, at least not now. I don't perform escapes any more. I understand this as I read it, I'm sure of it; but now, as I remember that scene for the nth time, I understand it more than ever.

Time is weird. Sometimes I think it's like a book. Everything is inside, between the front and back covers, the whole story, from beginning to end. You could get a bunch of people together, give them all copies of the same edition and ask them to open the book at any page and start reading and *voilà*, everything is happening simultaneously, in a concert of voices, like listening to several radio stations at the same time. It would be hard to work out what anyone was saying, just as it's hard to pick up a book, turn to a page at random, read a paragraph and truly understand what it means. It's easy to assume you would understand better if you had read what comes before, but it's not always true; sometimes you pick up the Bible or the I Ching or Shakespeare, open it at random and it seems as though the sentence you have happened on is telling you exactly what you longed to know, what you needed, what is essential. It doesn't always work, I admit. I imagine that someone listening to me talking about the toads might assume that I'm a biologist or that I'm telling a children's story. But it could also happen that they hear me precisely when I say: love one another madly, the people you know, but more importantly the people who need love, because love is the only thing that is real, it is the light, everything else is darkness; and maybe whoever was listening would understand completely without needing to hear the beginning, without needing to question my moral authority, without needing to know whether I have any moral authority, without needing to know what I have lost – what we all lose.

For a long time I lived in the place I call Kamchatka, a place that looks a little like the real Kamchatka (because of the cold, the volcanoes, the remoteness) but it is a place that doesn't really exist, because some places cannot be found on any map. Now that I have learned the importance of goodbyes, I would like to say goodbye to it. I had spent all those years there before I found the empty packet of Jockeys again, but now that I have found it, now it has appeared as I told my story for the nth time, I don't need Kamchatka any more, I no longer need the security I once felt being far from everything, unreachable, amid the eternal snows. The time has come for me to be where I am again, to be truly here, all of me, to stop surviving and start living.

'Let's go home,' grandpa said, 'it's time.'

Papá has gone to the car to fetch the game of Risk. He brings it over to me, hands it to me with a smile: 'What an idiot, I almost forgot!' Then he kisses me and says I love you very much, his voice sounding like Narciso Ibañez Menta again: papá always gets kind of sombre when he has to say something important. Then I feel his stubble scrape my cheek and he whispers in my ear: he says a lot of things, but what I most remember is 'Kamchatka', because 'Kamchatka' is the last word from his lips; because it sums up all the others. Last words are important – Goethe's were 'Light! More light!' – you have to pay attention to them.

They get into the car and drive away. I run behind the green bubble until I can't run any more. They do not turn to wave; they don't want to turn into pillars of salt.

Since then, whenever the game turned ugly, I have holed up in Kamchatka and I survived. And although at first I thought that papá and I had left a game unfinished, I've since realized that we didn't. He told me his secret and in doing so made me his ally, and every time I've played since he has been there beside me, and when things turned ugly we'd hang on to Kamchatka and in the end everything would be fine. Because Kamchatka was where you needed to be. Because Kamchatka was the place from where you fought back.

ACKNOWLEDGEMENTS

In writing *Kamchatka*, I have relied on invaluable information from a number of writers to whom I would like to express my gratitude.

My adventures in biology I owe in large part to Fritjof Capra's *The Web of Life* (1997) and Ernst Mayr's *This is Biology* (1997). My journey through the heavens I owe to John North and *The Fontana History of Astronomy and Cosmology* (1994). I have also drawn on Stephen Hawking's *A Brief History of Time* (1988).

For the politics and history of the Argentina in which Harry and I grew up, I have relied on Volume II of Eduardo Anguita and Martín Caparrós' history, *La voluntad* (1998), and Miguel Bonasso's *Diario de un clandestino* (2000).

The translation of Herodotus I used is Robin Waterfield's: *The Histories* (Oxford University Press, 1998).

The quotation from *The Odyssey* is taken from Robert Fagles' translation, published by Penguin in 1996. The line of Margaret Atwood's appears in her novel *The Blind Assassin* (Bloomsbury, 2000). I found the Emerson quotation in a speech he gave at Harvard in 1837. The quotation from Sir Thomas Malory's *Le Morte d'Arthur* is from the Penguin English Library edition of 1981. And the Lawrence Durrell letters I quote were taken from Jorge Fondebrider's fascinating book, *La Buenos Aires ajena* (2000).

I am grateful, too, for the support of Amaya Elézcano and all of the team at Alfaguara España.

I dedicate this book to my children, Oriana, Agustina, Milena and Bruno, in the hope that this book forms part of that same, marvellous legacy.

Kamchatka

Marcelo Figueras

ABOUT THIS GUIDE

We hope that these discussion questions
will enhance your reading group's exploration of
Marcelo Figueras's *Kamchatka*. They are meant to
stimulate discussion, offer new viewpoints and
enrich your enjoyment of the book.

More reading group guides and additional
information, including summaries, author tours
and author sites for other fine Black Cat titles may
be found on our Web site, www.groveatlantic.com.

QUESTIONS FOR DISCUSSION

1. *Kamchatka* is about a family that goes into hiding when a military coup overthrows the government of Argentina. Do you think this is a political book?

2. The novel is narrated from the point of view of Harry, the oldest son of the Vincentes. What sort of a narrator is Harry? Is he reliable? How does his point of view shift throughout the novel?

3. Discuss the way that *Kamchatka* is organized—not just by chapters, but by sections. What do the section titles refer to? What are the lessons Harry thinks you can learn about life from biology, geology, language, astronomy, and history?

4. Early in the book, Harry says, "In the end, we always are what we once were" (p. 5). What does *Kamchatka* say about the possibilities for change in human lives, or in life in general? What does Harry think changes, and what stays the same?

5. Harry repeatedly mentions his theories of time ("Time is weird," he says often). In his first school, in Buenos Aires, Harry is taught that time and history are linear: "before our virgin eyes unfolded the history of humankind, the history of which, for better or worse, we were at that time the culmination" (p. 12). What does Harry think about how time works? What in his life would make him come up with these theories of time?

6. "My obsession with justice infuriated her," says Harry, about his mother (p. 37). What is a child's sense of justice? Why was Harry's mother infuriated? Do we get a sense of Harry's parents' ideas of justice?

7. On page 39, Harry describes how the experiences of childhood form our politics. Do you agree with him? Can you remember instances from your childhood that you feel formed your sense of politics?

8. When Harry discovers the book about Houdini, it provides not just a pseudonym but a mission. Harry is constantly reminding others that Houdini was not a magician, but an escape artist. What does Harry see as the difference?

9. Harry and the Midget entertain themselves for most of the time they are at the *quinta*. What roles do games and fantasy play in the boys' lives? Are their games different than those of other children?

10. How is Harry introduced to religion? What is his understanding of it? How is the Midget's relationship to religion different?

11. Discuss the presence of the toads in the backyard pool. Why do Harry and the Midget build their "reverse diving board"? What do they hope to achieve? Are they successful? What do you think the toads represent in the novel?

12. *Kamchatka* is mostly told from a child's point of view, but occasionally we get information from the narrator at a later time. Find one of these examples and explain what we learn and why the author has chosen to tell the story this way.

13. When we meet Harry's maternal grandmother, she's not a very likable figure. Later, though, he says, "My grandmother says that mamá saved her life" (p. 119). What does he mean?

14. What is Harry's first impression of Lucas? How does that impression change? How does their relationship build, and why is Lucas important to Harry? Why, when they are talking, will Lucas sometimes say, "Wrong question"?

15. Think about the different myths and stories that Harry has read, from *The Odyssey* to *King Arthur* to *Superman*. What does Harry learn from these stories? How do they affect how he sees himself and the world?

16. Do you think Harry sees his parents accurately, as real people? Does he understand them?

17. Who adjusts better to living in hiding, Harry or the Midget? At the end of the novel, Harry's mother says, "But if you build a wall to protect yourself from the world outside, you end up realizing you've shut yourself in. Don't shut yourself in, darling. It's better to suffer than to feel nothing at all" (p. 281-82). Where are some examples in the novel of Harry shutting himself in?

18. Discuss the father/son dynamics in the novel. What is Harry's relationship with his father like? What happens when they are on the boat at *abuelo*'s house? Why don't they tell anyone what really happened?

19. When Harry runs away for the day and returns to Buenos Aires to find Bertuccio, Bertuccio's mother lies and says he's not home. Why? What does Harry learn after this trip?

20. Kamchatka is both a real place and a region in the game Risk. It is also the last word Harry's father ever says to him. Discuss the role of Kamchatka in the book and what it symbolizes to Harry. Why do you think the author chose Kamchatka for the book's title?

Suggested Further Reading

The Ministry of Special Cases by Nathan Englander; *Eat the Document* by Dana Spiotta; *The Vagrants* by Yiyun Li; *The Last of Her Kind* by Sigrid Nunuz; *How the Soldier Repairs the Gramophone* by Saša Stanišić; *Something Red* by Jennifer Gilmore; *The Lotus Eaters* by Tatjana Soli; *Train to Trieste* by Domnica Radulescu; *The Appointment* by Herta Müller